Praise for Lisa She

"Fresh and exciting, humorous and action-packed... Urban fantasy at its best."
—*Ilona Andrews,* #1 New York Times *bestselling author of the Kate Daniels series*

"Makenna Fraser brings Southern sass, smarts, and charm to the mean streets of Manhattan as she battles monsters and other magical beings."
—*Jennifer Estep,* New York Times *bestselling author of the Elemental Assassin novels*

"Plenty more gasp- and laughter-inducing adventures... This is a thrilling series, so hang on tight, for things are going to get seriously bumpy!"
—*RT Book Reviews*

"A word of warning, don't start this book unless you have a solid block set aside as you simply will not be able to put it down."
—*A Book Obsession*

"Shearin has been on my auto-buy list for years. She is able to combine humor, mystery, suspense, slow burn romance, high stakes, and her own spin on the supernatural into a cohesive whole. I'm addicted to finding out what will happen next in the SPI Files."
—*Bookpushers*

"There is so much action that you can't put this book down... Fun and truly great adventure stories."
—*Night Owl Romance*

"There are twists, turns, danger, romance, action, but more importantly—lots of fun. Laugh out loud funny... A brilliantly addictive urban fantasy series."

—*Terror Tree*

Praise for Lisa Shearin's Raine Benares Novels

"Exceptional...Shearin has proven herself to be an expert storyteller with the enviable ability to provide both humor and jaw-dropping action."

—*RT Book Reviews*

"The kind of book you hope to find when you go to the bookstore. It takes you away to a world of danger, magic, and adventure, and it does so with dazzling wit and clever humor. It's gritty, funny, and sexy—a wonderful addition to the urban fantasy genre. I absolutely loved it. From now on Lisa Shearin is on my auto-buy list!"

—Ilona Andrews, #1 *New York Times* bestselling author of *Magic Shifts*

"A wonderful fantasy tale full of different races and myths and legends [that] are drawn so perfectly readers will believe they actually exist. Raine is a strong female, a leader who wants to do the right thing even when she isn't sure what that is...Lisa Shearin has the magic touch."

—*Midwest Book Review*

The Washington Monument had cracked, traffic had snarled, and people inside government buildings had thought we were having another 9/11. All in all, a big scare and a major pain for everyone involved. It'd been my first year in DC. Welcome to town.

"The runway is being checked for damage, and we've been asked to circle until ground crews confirm it's safe to land."

I settled back in my seat to wait it out.

It was a good thing the earthquake had waited a week. Last week had been the inauguration. I'd been happily out of the country, though part of me regretted missing the swearing in of our first woman president. What I didn't regret was missing the crowds that had descended on the city to witness it.

I stretched my legs out as far as they could go. Whenever it was available, I sprung for first class. It was worth it not to get caught in the aisle surge the instant the plane pulled up to the gate. It was worth even more to have a seat wide enough to keep from touching my neighbor.

It wasn't like I was a germophobe or afraid of crowds.

I was a psychometric, which went leaps and bounds beyond being sensitive or empathetic.

I received impressions and images from touching people or the objects they'd touched. However, direct contact wasn't always necessary. If the emotions involved were strong enough, proximity worked nearly as well. It was like having an additional sense I hadn't asked for and had never wanted. For most people, the worst part about being in a crowd was the noise. For me, it was emotions.

As long as I could get to where I needed to go without touching anyone, I was fine. Some people went through life calmly; nothing ruffled their feathers. I didn't have a problem

CHAPTER 1

Sleep was not overrated.

Whoever said otherwise never flew from Zurich to DC just long enough to repack a bag and catch a red-eye to Vegas for a poker tournament. Then for an added level of masochism, didn't see the sun for three days and caught another red-eye home.

Not only was sleep a distant memory, I think I'd forgotten how to get there. Sleeping on a plane wasn't an option. I'd never been able to do it.

Another half hour and we'd be landing at Dulles.

Home sweet home. Bed wonderful bed.

"This is your captain speaking. There's been an earthquake ninety miles southwest of—"

A collective groan went up from those of us who'd been in town for the 2011 5.8 quake centered near Mineral, Virginia. The distance the pilot cited indicated this one was a repeat.

ACKNOWLEDGMENTS

To Derek, thank you for supporting me in every way while I jumped genres to write this book. I love you so very much.

To Jill Smith, my book therapist, beta reader, and dear friend. Thank you for your encouragement and for assuring me that I could write anything I put my mind to.

To Laurence MacNaughton, fellow writer, agency brother, beta reader, and plotting lifeline. Your suggestions and keen insight were invaluable. Check out his books at laurencemacnaughton.com. You'll be glad you did.

To Kristin Nelson, my agent and much needed (and appreciated) dispenser of literary tough love. You taught me what makes a good book great, and always challenge me to do more.

To Betsy Mitchell, my editor and truly a partner in each and every project with your uncanny sense of what is needed to make a book the best it can be. I'm honored and blessed to call you my editor.

To Martha Trachtenberg, my incredible copyeditor. Your sharp eyes and attention to detail are truly awe-inspiring. (Any mistakes in this book are totally my fault.)

To Angie Hodapp, my amazing book designer. You're always there for me with your flawless design. You turn my words into beautiful books.

To James Egan at Bookfly Design. With a new series in a new genre comes a new cover artist. You took my simple suggestion, worked your magic, and spun it into a simply gorgeous cover. You're a design genius and an absolute joy to work with.

This book is a work of fiction. The characters, incidents, and dialogue are drawn from the author's imagination and are not to be construed as real. Any resemblance to actual events or persons, living or dead, is entirely coincidental.

THE ENTITY GAME © 2020 by Lisa Shearin
Published by Murwood Media, LLC

All rights reserved. Printed in the United States of America. No part of this book may be reproduced in any form or by any means without the prior written consent of the author, excepting brief quotes used in reviews. Address requests for information to Nelson Literary Agency, 1732 Wazee Street, Suite 207, Denver, CO 80202.

Writers spend years laboring over a single book. Please respect their work by buying their books from legitimate sources. The scanning, uploading, and/or distribution of this book via the Internet or any other means without the permission of the publisher is illegal and punishable by law. Please purchase only authorized electronic and/or print editions, and do not participate in or encourage piracy of copyrighted materials. Your support of the author's rights is appreciated.

Editor: Betsy Mitchell
Copyeditor: Martha Trachtenberg
Cover artist: James T. Egan of Bookfly Design
Book designer: Angie Hodapp

ISBN: 978-1-7327226-2-0 (print) 978-1-7327226-3-7 (ebook)

LISA SHEARIN

The Entity Game

An Aurora Donati Novel

"Tons of action and adventure but it also has a bit of romance and humor...All of the characters are excellent...The complexities of the world that Ms. Shearin has developed are fabulous."

—*Night Owl Reviews*

"If you're new to Shearin's work, and you enjoy fantasy interspersed with an enticing romance, a little bit of humor, and a whole lot of grade-A action, this is the series for you."

—*Lurv a la Mode*

"The book reads more like an urban fantasy with pirates and sharp wit and humor. I found the mix quite refreshing. Lisa Shearin's fun, action-packed writing style gives this world life and vibrancy."

—*Fresh Fiction*

"Lisa Shearin represents that much needed voice in fantasy that combines practiced craft and a wicked sense of humor."

—*Bitten by Books*

"The brisk pace and increasingly complex character development propel the story on a roller-coaster ride through demons, goblins, elves, and mages while maintaining a satisfying level of romantic attention...that will leave readers chomping at the bit for more."

—*Monsters and Critics*

with those people. They were like butterflies. If they brushed against me, their emotions were a light, tickling sensation.

However, most people were like bees, wasps, or super-mutant-ninja hornets. You never knew what kind of emotional baggage people were carrying on a day-to-day basis. It multiplied when they got on a plane. Emotional baggage built up over time, and nothing cranked up anxiety to absurd levels like air travel. Between parking, the stress of going through security, and getting to the gate on time, humans were pumped and primed for crazy by the time they set foot on their flights. Traveling first-class ensured that I was one of the first ones on and off—or the last to board, if I chose. I preferred the window seat and not because I enjoyed the view. It put as much space as possible between me and everyone who had to file by my seat to get to theirs.

Few people wanted to fly red-eyes.

That was why I loved them.

There was a reason why you didn't see YouTube videos of Red-Eye Passengers Gone Wild. There weren't any. The crazies flew during the day. The night was made for hard-core business travelers and people like me who didn't pick fights, act like obnoxious assholes, or make unrealistic demands; we just wanted to get home with the least amount of fuss. And for the ultimate benefit, terrorists ignored red-eyes. No one was lining up to fly a half-empty plane into a building in the middle of the night.

We'd had a brief layover in Chicago, where dejected gamblers and glassy-eyed conventioneers filed off and business people and political types headed back to DC filed on. Two men and one woman gave me a second look when they saw my gloved hands. I did what I usually did—I ignored them.

People wore surgical masks against infection. I wore gloves and long sleeves against connection. Mine only earned odd looks in the summer—or on a plane after midnight. Gloves couldn't completely block my psychometry, but it took the edge off.

People were curious about others to the point of rudeness, always ready to question or accuse. Carrying some extra weight? You must be pregnant. Darker skin than they had? Different accent? You must be a terrorist. Wear gloves inside or in the summer? People didn't know what to make of that, so they felt entitled to ask. I'd toyed with the idea of going with leprosy, but opted for severe burns instead—from the neck down. Once people heard that, they couldn't back off fast enough.

Very few people knew about my, shall we say, eccentricity. Those that knew called it a gift. They didn't have to go through life with it.

But since I had it, I put it to work.

I wasn't a professional gambler. I had a day job, but I'd used my ability to become highly successful in both. Poker was strictly for fun and profit, but only in amounts that didn't raise suspicions. Greed was not good.

I'd been wanting a 1941 Indian Sport Scout for a long time, and a friend of mine, who had a shop in Arlington and was a restoration wizard, had found one for me. I'd already paid for the bike and the work being done, but needed to replace the hole it'd put in my savings account.

Viva Las Vegas.

I needed just under twelve thousand. I'd won that much over the three days, plus a little extra to cover my expenses. When I traveled, I preferred to go first-class across the board, not only on my flights to and from.

It's said that eyes are the windows to the soul. That might be true, but the keys to a person's deepest, darkest secrets are found over their entire body. I'd studied kinesics, the interpretation of body movement, to supplement my psychometry. Nonverbal cues such as posture, facial expressions, and what people did with their hands told me when they were lying or not, when they were hiding something, and how good they thought they were at both. Words could lie and often did, but eyes, lips, facial muscles, hands, legs, feet, torso position and carriage— our entire bodies give away far more than most people would be comfortable with. Talented actors or professional gamblers are experts at modifying their expressions and body language, but few could keep up the deception for long.

I honed my skills by reading my poker tournament opponents. Between that and my psychometry, I could easily win far more than I did, but I enjoyed playing and the challenge of outmaneuvering my opponents.

Jack had made me work extra hard this time.

Not many on the amateur circuit wanted to see Jack Beckett sit down at their table—or me either, for that matter. Jack had sought me out this time. He knew me as Rory Mitchell, and I had the fake IDs and credit cards to back it up. It helped to have friends in federal places. My real name was Aurora Donati, but considering who and what I was, I protected my privacy and did what was necessary to keep it, though I did go by Rory in real life. According to my FBI buddies, when going undercover, it was best to keep the lies you had to remember to a minimum. Mitchell was my mother's maiden name.

Most poker players had at least one tell—that thing they did to hide what they were thinking or about to do. Players did their best to keep their expression perfectly neutral when they either had a great hand or were bluffing. That very neutrality or stillness could itself be a tell.

Jack had zero tells, though he was an expert at throwing out fake tells when at a table with less experienced players. At this tournament, we'd all been experienced. Jack had no facial tics, no change in his usual self-satisfied expression—which he wore regardless of how good or bad a hand he had—no change in his speed of play, the pulse in his neck didn't even alter its beat. In the final game, he'd sat one chair over from me, so I'd gotten an up close and personal view.

In the end, it'd been fatigue that'd cost him the game and had won it for me. It'd been a long tournament, we were all exhausted, and Jack slipped up before I could. He blinked. Twice. In as many seconds. I'd seen it on Jack once before and knew what it meant. Big bluff, bad hand. This time, Lady Luck had been with me and not him. To Jack's credit, he was a good sport about the loss. Whenever I'd beaten him, he'd always say "next time." He could be right. Next time he might win on his own, or I might let him—if there wasn't a big pot at stake. Like I said, when trying to fly under the radar, greed wasn't good.

Poker was my one and only game. I'd gambled with dice. Once.

Never again.

Those particular dice had held the emotions of the many people who had used them, and the strongest hadn't been the most recent. One man's despair had clung to my hand for days afterward.

Vegas attracted people looking for a weekend of fun. It also attracted the desperate and the addicted. Those who believed they would be one of the few to win big.

This man had gambled away his family's savings. Then his

child had sickened. Cancer. Final stages. No symptoms until it was too late.

He'd made one final roll of the dice. The money for his child's treatment was there for the winning. Except he didn't win. He lost.

I'd read later that while he was losing, his child had died.

He couldn't take the loss, of either his child or the last of his family's money. Distraught, the man had gone to the roof of his hotel and jumped to his death.

I'd read about the incident two days after it'd happened.

I'd made the mistake of not wearing gloves while playing, and by handling the dice he'd last used, I'd gotten the full impact of the desperation and heartbreak that'd led him to it.

It was more than enough for me—too much.

No more dice.

Poker tournaments were the way to go. Yes, the people who played wanted to win, but what most really enjoyed was the game and manipulating the competition.

I could read the cards they'd touched, but mostly, I could read them.

The man sitting across the plane's aisle from me had been staring out the window since we'd both boarded in Vegas. A single glance had told me that he wasn't a businessman coming home from a convention. At least four days of unruly stubble couldn't be called business casual by anyone's definition. His clothes were good quality, but the wrinkles told me they'd gone from his suitcase and back again over several days, never seeing a hanger or the inside of his hotel's closet. He'd gone there to gamble, and as with most who took their chances on the Strip, it hadn't gone well for him. He'd been drinking nothing but coffee the entire flight. Whether DC was home or a stopover to somewhere else, he wanted to be awake when he got there.

His repetitive motions told me who he wanted to be alert for.

His wife or husband.

Every time I'd glanced at him, he'd been holding or caressing the wedding band on his finger.

He'd screwed up. Badly. He knew it, and he was terrified of losing someone he loved dearly because of it.

"Ladies and gentlemen, this is your captain. We have been cleared to land. Please make sure your seat belt is securely fastened. Flight attendants, please prepare for landing."

The landing minutes later was smooth with no bumps that might mean a broken section of runway. Once the plane slowed to taxi to the gate, I loosened my grip on the armrests. I wasn't a big fan of landings, even the good ones.

A flight attendant stood and walked to the front of the coach section. "Welcome to Dulles International Airport," he said into a handset. "The local time is 12:45 a.m. and the temperature is twenty-eight degrees. Please remain seated with your seat belt fastened until the captain turns off the Fasten Seat Belt sign. This will indicate that we have parked at the gate and that it is safe for you to move about. At this time, you may use your cell phones. Please check around your seat for any personal belongings—"

I tuned the rest out and pulled out my phone. Five and a half hours was a long time for me to go without checking messages. My grandad, Ambrose Donati, was still in Zurich and wouldn't be flying back for another two days. In the interim, I was the Donati Detective Agency. We'd been at an international art crime conference. Afterward, I'd flown to

Vegas for the tournament while Grandad had stayed to visit with old friends and former colleagues.

He'd gotten into the work in Europe in the 1960s. The war had been over for about two decades, and there were still plenty of missing works of art and artifacts to recover that'd been stolen by the Nazis. Later, when he moved to the States, he'd made it his calling to continue that work and return those pieces to their rightful owners—or to any surviving relatives. When he started the Donati Detective Agency, he'd expanded that mission to include art stolen from museums and private collectors. When the FBI founded its Art Crime Team in 2004, they retained his services as a consultant, due to his contacts in the art world and his skills as an art authenticator.

I'd gone to work with Grandad after I'd graduated from UCLA with a degree in criminal psychology. He'd tried to teach me about art, but the finer details eluded me. We had the same psychometric skills, but with different goals. Grandad wanted to find and retrieve the art. I wanted to find and catch the thieves who'd stolen it. When people thought of art thieves, they saw Cary Grant or Pierce Brosnan. I've never run into an art thief who looked like either one.

Psychometry ran in the Donati family.

Grandad's mother had the ability, but she hadn't known of anyone further back. Either none of our Florentine ancestors had been psychometrics, or the ability wasn't spoken of for fear of being thought of as a witch or demon-possessed.

Now, it was just another tool we used to do our jobs. No one could spot a fake like Grandad. One touch could tell him how old a piece really was, and occasionally even the identity of the forger who'd painted it. Forgers with Old Master-level talent were few and far between. Grandad knew them all.

I relied more on the emotional residuals that thieves left at the scene of their crime. Whatever they'd touched, wherever they'd stood, I could pick up flashes of thought or images of what—or who—they'd seen. Few thieves worked alone. A thief's glance at a partner's face could give me a description. The mention or thought of a name or place could give me their identity or the stolen art's location. The big challenge for me was to convey what I found to police in a way that didn't out me as the psychometric I was.

I scanned my inbox. There wasn't anything that couldn't wait.

Then came the *ping* of an incoming text.

About time you landed.

My friend and frequent colleague, Berta Pike.

FBI Special Agent Alberta Pike, to be exact.

She'd known I was going to Vegas, but on the way back I'd changed flights for one that'd left two hours earlier than originally planned.

I grinned and started texting. *The FBI sees all, knows all.*

Damn straight. You got extra luggage?

Just carry-on.

Good. I'm waiting at the gate.

I didn't have to ask if anything was wrong. Berta Pike hadn't shown up at Dulles at nearly one o'clock in the morning to give me a hug and a ride home. She didn't have any active cases that I was involved in. It must be something new and urgent.

So much for sleep.

These days, in order to get to a gate, you have to be a federal agent on government business doing some serious badge-flashing, though it usually means someone is about to be arrested. We mere mortals used to be able to wait at the gate for friends and family to arrive. No arrests, just hugs. Terrorism put a stop to that.

Once the plane stopped, the man across the aisle stood to get his bag out of the overhead. I steeled myself, slid over to the aisle seat to do the same.

I wanted confirmation.

I reached for the overhead so my shoulder brushed his. The images flooded in.

"Sorry!" I gave him an apologetic smile. "Gotta get my land legs back."

He nodded once without looking at me.

He'd gone to Vegas for a friend's bachelor party. He thought he could resist the temptation. He was wrong. Three and a half years of progress gone. His wife loved him. He knew that, but how could she possibly love him now? He'd gambled. He'd lost. A lot. More than they could spare. She would hate him. He hated himself.

He was halfway up the jet bridge when I caught up to him.

"Tell your wife everything," I said. "You didn't mean for it to happen. It was too much for you to handle."

He stopped, his face gone pale. "Excuse me?"

I wasn't about to explain how I knew. That'd just open a can of weirdness neither one of us wanted.

"Talk to her," I told him. "She'll want you to. She'll understand. You know she will. Then promise her you'll get more help so you don't do it again."

I kept going up the jet bridge and didn't look back. I didn't need to. He'd still be standing there, stunned. I'd been there and induced that often enough to know.

Special Agent Berta Pike was waiting for me.

She was wearing a dark suit and an equally dark disposition that didn't scream Fed as much as it solemnly stated it. She wore her hair short and natural. I'd seen a couple of pre-FBI photos where she had shoulder-length braids that she'd artfully spun into a tight bun that accented her flawless cheekbones. When I'd first met her, I thought she'd gone short to prevent giving a hold to a suspect should an apprehension go south. I was wrong. No suspect or FBI workout partner regardless of size or speed had ever gotten close enough to Alberta Pike to get a good hold on anything. She was five inches taller than me, slender and solid, and in my opinion, was badassness personified. Before joining the FBI, she'd done two tours with the Army in Afghanistan.

Berta may have been here on business, but I still got that hug.

And I didn't try to read her when she did. A friend didn't read a friend's thoughts without permission. Though the tension she was feeling was obvious and in all caps.

"How'd the tournament go?" she asked.

I mustered a grin. "I won *just* enough for the bike, and a little extra for a suite and some room service. Laurence promised he'd get it finished and have it to me by next Wednesday."

Berta cracked a smile. "Amazing how it worked out like that."

"Isn't it though?" I pulled the strap of my messenger bag higher on my shoulder. "Now, how'd I warrant an FBI Uber at oh-dark-thirty?"

Berta's smile vanished. "Not here."

I'd have to be satisfied with small talk until we got to the car.

I saw the man again in the baggage claim area.

He was with his wife. Both had tears in their eyes, but they were the good kind. They kissed, then stopped, talking quickly, faces close together, their eyes seeing nothing but each other. Then the man tightly hugged his wife. She was his love and his lifeline.

He must have sensed me as Berta and I passed. His eyes opened and met mine.

I gave him a wink and a small smile.

His lips barely moved, forming two words, but I got the message.

I accepted his thanks with a single nod.

From time to time, what I did really was a gift.

CHAPTER 2

B erta didn't say a word until we got into the car.

It had to be bad.

It was.

"Senator Julian Pierce and his senior aide, Alan Coe, were found dead in the senator's office a couple hours ago."

I couldn't speak.

"I'm sorry," Berta said. "There's never an easy way to—"

I waved her off. "I know, it's just that…"

"When will your grandad be back home?" she asked quietly.

"A few days," I heard myself say. "I'll have to call him."

Julian Pierce was Grandad's best friend.

My grandfather didn't include politicians in his inner circle of friends, which was small by choice. Julian Pierce was the sole exception. Grandad wasn't a political animal, and neither was Julian Pierce—at least not around us. His passion for art and its recovery nearly matched Grandad's. I'd first met him at a National Gallery of Art fundraiser. It'd been July and the event had been casual. It would've looked odd for me to be wearing gloves. My smile that night as I had shaken hands when introduced to various people had been more like a gritting of teeth, but I'd gotten through it. With politicians, an entire conversation, albeit brief, could be contained in a single handshake. It invariably involved more than one hand. Hand on hand, hand on shoulder or upper arm. Or just bring the whole body into it and yank the opponent/constituent toward them. In a city full of alpha male—and often creepy—politicians, it was no wonder I hated shaking hands.

My initial impression of Julian Pierce had been that of a truly good man, sincere in his feelings, a man who cared deeply about the people he represented and was honest in his dealings—all of which was a rarity in Washington. He was the kind of man I didn't mind shaking hands with. As I'd gotten to know him better, I'd been struck by his wisdom, his humor, and his humility and compassion. Whenever I read or heard the term "elder statesman," I immediately thought of Julian Pierce.

I had only spoken with Alan Coe a few times at social gatherings at the senator's McLean, Virginia, home. He was young and earnest and fiercely devoted to Julian Pierce and the causes he championed. I remembered that Alan and Tina, his wife of only two years, ran marathons together.

Now both he and his boss were gone.

"How?" I managed.

"It looks like heart attacks, but the ME says she won't know for—"

"Both?"

"Uh-huh."

"That's impossible."

"Says you, me, Rees, and everyone else. We're treating this as if it were murder."

Special Agent Samuel Rees was Berta's partner, the Sherlock to her warrior Watson. Other agents considered Rees more of a Mulder. When a crime took a turn for the weird, the FBI turned to Samuel Rees.

And more often than I liked, Samuel Rees turned to me.

I'd met him ten months ago. The owner of an art gallery near Dupont Circle was suspected of having a side business trafficking stolen and fraudulent art. The owner turned up dead hours before a planned FBI raid, and the FBI called us. Grandad was in New York. I went to the gallery in his stead.

I knew most of the agents in the Art Crime unit. I didn't recognize the man crouched by the dead woman's body. I had an uneasy feeling. Not because of the dead body; I'd seen those before. It was the intensity of the agent's stare, as if he were willing the woman to open her eyes and tell him who had killed her. The other agents went about their business, giving the man plenty of space as he carried out his silent interrogation. I hadn't moved, and I didn't think he had seen me come in.

"Ms. Donati," he said without turning. "Please join me. I would like your opinion." He stood and walked to the back of the gallery.

I followed.

He introduced himself and opened the plastic evidence bag containing the dead woman's phone and held it out for me to take. "Please tell me what happened to her."

He knew about me.

There were a handful of people in the FBI whom Grandad trusted enough to let in on his secret.

Special Agent Samuel Rees was one of them, but Grandad hadn't told him about me; Rees had instinctively known what I was when I'd walked into that gallery. He had an ability of his own. He called it recognizing talent.

Rees was in a small department in the FBI that had only two official employees—himself and Special Agent Alberta Pike. I didn't want anyone in the intelligence community to know what I could do. Samuel Rees and Berta Pike had become the exceptions. The murdered gallery owner had been a friend of his late wife.

As I'd taken the phone, a mild electric current had run up my arm from fingertips to elbow. I'd learned to recognize that as the residual of strong emotion such as rage, betrayal, or terror. The gallery owner had experienced all of those. While the sensations were disturbing, I wasn't the one being killed. I'd learned to compartmentalize. It really cut down on the nightmares and kept me from getting PTSD from trauma that I hadn't experienced myself. Try explaining that to a therapist.

Unfortunately, even objects as personal as phones didn't give me a movie version of what had happened. Instead, I got flashes of images, impressions, and emotions. It was up to me to piece it together.

We eventually got to the truth. She had been killed by her business partner, who had been secretly moving stolen art and forgeries through the gallery.

A police car siren jarred me back to the present.

"Is Rees at the scene?" It felt surreal, calling Julian Pierce's office in the Russell Senate Office Building a crime scene.

Berta nodded. "Waiting on you. He won't let them take the

bodies until you've had a chance to…" She didn't need to say it, and I really didn't want her to.

I'd never worked a crime scene where I knew the victims.

I swallowed on a dry mouth. "I don't have my go-bag. Do you have some gloves I can doctor?"

"There's a pair of pre-cut gloves in the glove box. I did them myself."

"Did you—"

"I wore gloves while I did it, *and* when I put them in the zippy bag for you, so there's no Alberta Pike mojo for you to wade through this time."

To work a crime scene, I needed at least one pair of nitrile gloves with the pads of both index fingers cut out. Skin-to-skin contact with a corpse's pulse points—even though there was no longer a pulse—could give me impressions of their final moments. The less time that had passed since death the better. My job would be simpler if I could move through a crime scene, touching or picking up any object I needed to read. Crime-scene investigators frowned on that, hence the modified gloves.

Within the hour, I'd be touching Julian Pierce and Alan Coe. Hopefully at least one of them would be able to give me the help I needed to find their killer.

Elaine. Oh no.

Julian's granddaughter Elaine had been elected in November as one of the youngest members of the House of Representatives and had been sworn in a few short weeks ago. Grandad and I had attended the party in McLean that Julian had thrown for her.

"Has Elaine Pierce been notified?" I asked.

"By now she should have been."

I couldn't even begin to imagine what she was going through. Before running for the New York congressional seat, Elaine had served on the state level in Albany, and before that had put her law degree to work in the Manhattan DA's office. She was warm, funny, and scary smart. Julian had been so proud that his granddaughter would be serving on Capitol Hill with him.

Then there was Grandad. He had no idea what had just happened to the man he loved like a brother.

"You okay?" Berta asked.

I gave a tight nod. I was far from okay, but it didn't matter. I couldn't allow it.

I wasn't doing this for the FBI. I sure as hell wasn't doing it for me. What I was about to do was for Julian Pierce and Alan Coe. This hadn't been their time to die. If Berta and Rees thought they'd been murdered, that was what had happened. While nothing would bring them back, I could help find their killers, and give Elaine and Tina the small comfort of closure they'd need, and Julian and Alan the justice they deserved.

I stared out through the windshield as the rotunda of the US Capitol came into view. It was a Thursday in late January. Congress was in session, and next Tuesday would typically be the State of the Union address, but since Catherine Archer had only been sworn in as president for a little over a week, it would just be an address to Congress. Those who usually tried to go home on weekends were staying in town. The weather people were calling for snow on Sunday, which was yet another reason for them to stay put.

Berta was using the blue light on the dashboard and the siren to get through intersections. There was more traffic in predawn Washington than you'd think, though this morning, a lot of that traffic had flashing lights of their own, and signals were out at most intersections due to the earthquake. It was bad enough now; I didn't want to imagine what it'd be like in a couple of hours when the sun came up.

I tried to relax. Tension would cloud any impressions and images I'd be able to glean from Julian and Alan's bodies, and I couldn't afford to miss a thing. I had to be at the top of my game, and that meant calm and analytical. I couldn't let my emotions take control. As with any case I worked, I needed as much pertinent background on the victims as I could get. Most of what I knew about Julian Pierce was from his personal life. He and Alan had been killed in Julian's office. What I did know of his work in the Senate, I'd seen on the news or read online.

"Do you know if Senator Pierce made a habit of working this late?" I asked.

Berta shook her head. "According to the Capitol Police on duty downstairs, he told them he'd be working until at least ten o'clock every night this week."

"Who would have access to that information besides Julian's staff and the Capitol Police?"

"It was noted in their system for anyone on duty—or who could access it."

"In other words, more people could've known than were supposed to."

I'd heard that a surprising number of senators and congressmen slept in their Capitol Hill offices, but I didn't think Julian would have been one of them. The money-saving practice tended to be limited to the younger members, who could function the next day after spending the night on a cot or sleeper sofa.

"Who found them?"

"When the quake hit, one of the Capitol Police officers on duty started calling around to the senators known to be working late. Neither Pierce nor Coe answered. Two officers were dispatched to Pierce's office, where they found both men dead, bodies still warm."

"And the last time they were seen alive?" I asked.

"The custodian responsible for Senator Pierce's floor said he stopped by his office to empty the trash a little after eight. He said he stayed about five minutes, talking to the senator."

"Any security footage to back that up?"

Berta nodded. "The old guy's telling the truth. He was on the video at 8:22. But here's the kicker. The footage shows him coming back at 9:15. Nate Baxter, that's the custodian, denies being there a second time."

"Any witnesses that he was somewhere else?"

"No. He claimed he was in the breakroom, and left just before ten o'clock. Our people picked him up at his home and brought him in for questioning."

"Was anyone in the breakroom with him?"

"No. He says he was the only one there. If the guy that went to Pierce's office the second time wasn't Baxter, it was his twin."

"Has he been arrested?"

"He's in custody, but hasn't been charged. They're waiting on the autopsies."

"You said it looked like heart attacks. Is there another theory?"

"They checked for an airborne toxin first thing," Berta said. "Nothing happened to the Capitol Police who found them, but no one else was allowed inside until the check was done. All tests were negative. You have to admit, the hearts of two otherwise healthy men failing at the same time…"

"Yeah. Not very likely."

"The security camera shows only three times someone entered or left that office. At 7:17, Alan Coe went downstairs to pick up a Thai food delivery. At 8:22, Nate Baxter emptied the garbage and stayed for five minutes to talk. Then Baxter, or his twin, was there again at 9:15."

"How long did he stay that time?"

"According to the time stamp on the video, he was in there less than a minute."

"Who's in charge of the investigation?" I asked.

"Hudson." Berta paused. "For now. Considering who the victims are, the director and deputy assistant director will probably be calling all the shots by the time the sun comes up. They might let me and Rees stay on the case. They might not."

Roger Hudson was one of four special agents in charge in the FBI's Washington Field Office. Rees reported directly to SAC Hudson. Unlike others in the DC office's upper ranks, Hudson was secure enough in his abilities and position that he didn't feel threatened by Samuel Rees's well-earned reputation for solving the unsolvable. I could see Capitol Hill being disputed territory between the DC Field Office and headquarters. In addition, the crime involved the death and possible murder of one of the most loved and respected senators in the US. There was going to be a fight over who got this one. I was grateful that Hudson jumped on it and brought in Rees while he had the chance, otherwise I wouldn't be on my way there right now.

We'd be working against the clock. Even more reason why I had to get it right the first time.

"Do you know what the senator was working on so late?" I asked.

"Rees said he was drafting a pharmaceutical bill."

"I'm not exactly a political junkie. Is that a bill worth killing for?"

"From what Rees told me, it sounded like it'd close the loopholes that let drug companies jack up prices for no good reason."

"And the senator writing the bill suddenly dies of a heart attack, along with his senior aide." I hesitated. "I know that Julian served in the Marines in Vietnam and was ex-CIA, but I don't know what committees he served on."

"Finance, Armed Services, and Intelligence," Berta said.

"A pharmaceutical bill is under finance?" I asked.

"It is."

All high-profile committees, and all providing endless possibilities why someone would want Senator Julian Pierce dead.

Berta turned onto Constitution Avenue, and with our arrival at the Russell Building, she stopped talking, and I knew I'd gotten all the information I was going to get until I saw the bodies.

CHAPTER 3

I'd been in the Russell Building before, though it'd been during the workweek. The rotunda amplified the sound of the voices of the people inside, and on that particular day, with TV cameras and crews, the interior had reminded me of a gigantic human hornet's nest. I treated it as one. Move carefully and I wouldn't get stung.

Washington was chock-full of high-strung, stressed-out overachievers whose chances for professional survival could change with the next tweet. Needless to say, I steered clear of Capitol Hill watering holes in the evenings and DC nightclubs anytime. Accidental contact could register as anything from a sting to what you'd get by dropping a hairdryer in a bathtub. On-purpose and unwanted contact would result in blunt force trauma—to the asshole who thought it'd be fun to put his hands on me.

I didn't need to worry about being touched, brushed, or

groped in the Russell. At least not right now. Every man and woman there was focused on two highly suspicious deaths that had occurred upstairs.

Berta was watching me take it all in. "They're searching the entire building."

"Good. Though that's a lot of nooks and crannies."

Even with Berta and my FBI consultant's ID, I was concerned about being allowed past the security checkpoint. On the other hand, Samuel Rees was the proverbial eight-hundred-pound gorilla. When we'd first started working together, Rees had seen to it that I had the clearance necessary to go where I needed to go. No one knew exactly what I did, but word had gotten around the FBI that any case Rees brought me in on had been quickly solved.

I'd gone to a lot of trouble to go as unnoticed as possible. I didn't want anyone questioning who and what I was now. I certainly didn't want anyone to know what I did.

An FBI agent was standing at the checkpoint with a tablet. He checked our IDs, consulted his tablet, and we were in.

I was average height and build, so that didn't stand out in a crowd, but my hair did. On humid days—and right now—it nearly had its own zip code. My tan had everything to do with my Italian heritage, and nothing to do with spending time in the California sun.

Berta and I threaded our way through the crowd, my coat taking the brunt of any contact.

Suddenly and without warning, I felt the pressing weight of someone's attention on me: not merely watching, but studying. Intently and with full knowledge of who I was and what I had come here to do. It wasn't Samuel Rees or Roger Hudson, or anyone else I knew.

I dimly heard Berta ask if I was okay.

I looked around me, then scanned the second-floor balcony that ran around the entire rotunda.

The presence had vanished as quickly as it'd appeared.

"Fine," I told her. "I'm fine." I headed toward the stairs. "Let's do this."

We took the stairs to the second floor, where a familiar figure awaited us at the top.

Special Agent Samuel Rees was tall and thin in his trademark dark suit. Even when perfectly still, there was an intensity to him that was vaguely unnerving, like he knew every remotely illegal thing you'd ever done and was adding them up to see if the total was enough to warrant jail time. Nearly everyone else looked like they'd rolled out of bed to come here. Not Rees. He was as meticulously dressed and groomed as always, regardless of the hour, location, or circumstances. His carefully trimmed hair was black shot through with silver, and his eyes a vivid blue that missed nothing.

"I'm sorry I had to call you here under these circumstances," he said.

"No apology needed. I want the same thing you do, to catch whoever did this. I just hope I can help." I hesitated. "I'm glad Grandad isn't here to see this."

"How much longer will he be in Zurich?"

"He'd planned to stay another couple of days and then stop off in London on his way home, but once he finds out about Julian…I'll call him when we're finished here."

Rees nodded. "The senator's office will be issuing a statement to the media within the hour." He started up the next flight of stairs to the third floor. "How was the conference—and the tournament?"

He was interested in my answer, but his intent was to distract me for a few minutes. He knew I did my best work with a clear and calm mind. "Zurich was cold and wet," I told him. "Vegas was warm—in comparison—and dry. The tournament went as planned."

One corner of Rees's lips curled up in a brief smile. "I'm glad to hear it. I know you'll enjoy that motorcycle."

"The conference session on antiquities looting and global terrorism funding was worth the trip," I continued. "As always, there was a lot of networking." Rees knew how I felt about networking. Talking was great, but Europeans were entirely too touchy for my comfort. Well, except for the Germans.

He led the way down a wide corridor, though even without him, I could've found Julian's office. All I had to do was follow the trail of people in dark suits and blue FBI windbreakers. As we got closer, the number of people increased, and the noise level decreased. Voices were kept low, whether out of respect for the dead men, or shock at where the men had been killed, I didn't know. Talk stopped as we approached, and whispers started once we'd passed. Rees's reputation both preceded and followed him. The Sherlock comparison applied to his uncanny ability to solve the seemingly unsolvable, as well as his disregard and disdain for anything that got in his way, be it interagency protocol, politics, or the toes of his FBI colleagues.

Julian Pierce was considered an elder statesman by his peers on both sides of the aisle. He was known for reaching across those aisles, brokering deals when the possibility of agreement had seemed long past. Such a man was sure to have made enemies, but revenge on Capitol Hill consisted of figurative backstabbing. Senators and congressmen would gleefully murder reputations without a second thought, but to kill a colleague, even a hated one, in cold blood? They might want to do it, entertain themselves with the thought while their rival held forth on the Senate or House floor, but to actually commit murder or even hire it out? No. In Washington, it might take years for the truths of scandals and crimes to become known, but if you had a big enough shovel and were willing to dig deep, they would be found. That was the kind of publicity—and potential prison time—no elected official wanted.

A senator killed in his office would tighten what had to already be stringent security measures. Not only were the FBI looking for a killer, they would uncover the lapse in security that had allowed a senator and his aide to be killed. When they found that lapse, heads would roll down Capitol Hill, and then get kicked down the mall. Whether the individuals were actually to blame or merely had the bad luck to be on duty in the right place at the wrong time didn't matter. In DC, blame must be laid at someone's feet, preferably a person or persons associated with the opposite party of the one who ended up in the position to cast the blame.

The activity only increased the closer we got to Julian's office.

I hadn't been in any offices in the Russell Building, but I would imagine that after serving in the Senate since the mid-eighties, Julian would have the seniority to warrant one of the larger ones. What probably would seem quite spacious under normal conditions was nearly claustrophobic now. Maybe it was just me.

"I'll wait in the hall," Berta told us.

Every man and woman in that room knew that what had happened here would soon be a Breaking News banner on every news channel and site in the country, if not the world. My earlier comparison to a hive was right on target. Buzzing, not of contented worker bees, but angry hornets. An improbable thing had just happened in an impossible place, and those here knew from experience how this would likely play out. The press would descend, higher-ups would start looking for the killer—or in the absence of a killer, a convenient scapegoat they could feed to the press. Everyone here would do their job at two hundred percent, no paperweight would be left unturned, no question left unasked. The spotlight was on them, though right now that spotlight probably felt like a magnifying glass on a hot summer sidewalk. If they took too long to find an answer, they'd burst into flames.

I stopped in the doorway to the office suite. There were two side chairs and a sofa, all facing an oval coffee table. The walls of the outer office were full of framed photos of Julian smiling or shaking hands with celebrities or famous constituents. Scattered among these were photos of the senator with at least seven presidents. Whether Republican or Democrat, all of them would have wanted to stay on the good side of one of the Senate's most powerful men.

Alan Coe's desk was near the door to Julian's inner office. I pressed myself against the wall so I wouldn't be in anyone's way while I came to terms with what I was seeing. Alan was slumped over the top of his desk as if he'd merely fallen asleep over the papers he'd been working on. His laptop was on the floor in front of the desk. The handset of his desk phone was off the hook. I wondered if he'd tried to call for help. From where I stood, I couldn't see his face, and I was grateful.

The outer office was a hub of activity. Across from Alan's desk was a small table that served as the office's coffee station.

The coffee machine's glass carafe was about half a cup from full. No one drank half a cup of coffee. That meant samples had been taken for testing. Nitrile-gloved techs were also taking the grounds, filter and all. The sugar and creamer had already been bagged and tagged. Alan had made a fresh pot and neither man had lived long enough to drink it. Who had died first? Alan or Julian?

I moved around the desk, careful to stay out of the way. Alan still held a pen in his hand. I leaned in for a closer look, careful not to disturb anything on his desk. A Lamy AL-Star fountain pen, not expensive, but a dependable German pen. A workhorse. I had two. The line was relatively new, so Alan was probably its first owner. Old pens retained residue from their previous owners. Many people didn't like vintage pens with the owner's name or initials engraved on them. For me, it made the connection to its past all the more tangible.

I needed to get my hands on that pen, but there were too many eyes on me now. It could wait.

I saw the flash of a camera from Julian's office.

I leaned toward Rees. "Are the techs finished with Alan?" I asked quietly.

"They are."

I pulled on my altered nitrile gloves.

There were five agents and investigators still in the outer office with Alan's body. One of the techs bagged the pen. I quickly glanced from the pen to Rees, letting him know I wanted it. He'd be able to get the pen for me later. I then gave him the barest of nods.

We'd done this dance before.

As I moved around behind Alan's office chair, Rees stepped between Alan's body and the agent and tech closest to me, blocking their view.

"Did the ME check for a pinprick in the neck area?" he asked the tech. "Of a size that would have been made by a needle-sized dart?"

That was my cue.

Alan's head was turned to the side, his carotid artery helpfully exposed just above his shirt collar. I quickly steeled myself and touched it with the exposed tip of my index finger for one second, two, then three.

In those three seconds, I was flooded with pain so intense I had to clench my teeth to keep from gasping. Alan hadn't even been able to do that. The pain and tightness in his chest kept him from breathing. Fear. He hadn't known what was happening to him. The pain intensified, squeezing, constricting. Panic. He knew he was dying. His mouth opened, but no sound came out. He fell forward, the wood of his desk cool and smooth against his cheek. Alan dimly heard a voice call his name as his vision darkened…his heart slowed…and he was gone.

CHAPTER 4

I stepped back from Alan's body. No one had seen what I'd done.

I slowly inhaled and exhaled through my nose, calming myself. Yes, it was possible for a healthy, active man to suddenly die from a heart attack with no warning, but Julian had died in the next room at the same time and in the same way. This was no macabre coincidence.

"Yes, we checked," the tech was telling Rees. "Though the ME won't know for sure until she gets him on the table."

Rees nodded his thanks and went to the door leading to Julian's office, waiting for me to join him. He wouldn't expect me to tell him anything until we'd left the office suite and were well away from any overly attentive ears. To get in we had to pass several agents who would have questioned my right to be here if I hadn't been following in Rees's wake. Though with Rees, it was more like gravitational pull.

I paused at the two empty trash cans sitting together beside the door. I was still wearing my gloves. I'd touched Alan with my right index finger. I quickly bent and touched the rim of the trash can with my left.

Nothing out of the ordinary. There was a jumble of many people who had touched it. None of them stood out to me. I needed to see the security video for myself.

I entered Julian's inner office.

I avoided looking at the body on the floor beside the desk, instead beginning my study of the scene with the room itself. I knew Julian the man; I had next to no knowledge of Julian Pierce the senator.

The only photos in his inner office were those of his family and close friends. One of them was of him and Grandad. Julian had been a father, grandfather, and had recently become a great-grandfather. There were almost as many photos here as in the outer office, and many of them included a smiling Julian Pierce. It wasn't the business smile he'd had in the outer office photos. These smiles lit up the face of a man who obviously loved and was proud of his large family.

On his desk was a silver-framed photo of his wife, Beryl Hoffmann Pierce. She had died of cancer three years ago. Grandad and I had gone to the funeral. Next to her photo was a more recent addition: Elaine's swearing-in ceremony with Julian as a proud grandfather holding the family Bible for his granddaughter.

The art in the office was limited to two paintings and one bronze sculpture—all by Frederic Remington. Grandad had introduced Julian to an art dealer friend of his who'd given him a good deal on them.

Work lights had been set up by the medical examiner on

the other side of Julian's desk. Aside from the body, absolutely nothing seemed to be out of place, no sign of any kind of struggle or of the office having been searched. The position of the body suggested that he had been sitting when he'd been stricken. He'd stood, possibly to confront his killer, been overcome, and then died.

I followed Rees to where he stood close to the body, but with enough distance not to trigger the medical examiner's territorial instincts.

Julian Pierce had not died peacefully.

I didn't know whether his facial contortion had been due to pain from the heart attack or fear. Julian was a man who wasn't afraid of much, if anything. So, if what he'd seen tonight had scared him, it must have been something worth fearing.

I looked at his body, pushing my emotions aside in favor of clinical detachment.

From his position on the floor, it appeared that he had stumbled forward and gone down on one or both knees, and from there had fallen on his side. I moved to get a better look and was rewarded with a glimpse of a metal watchband. It'd been an anniversary present from his wife. He'd been wearing it every time I'd seen him. Watches touched the wrist pulse point, imbuing them with the emotions of their wearers. Julian had been dead only a few hours. I should be able to pick up more than mere traces of his final moments, and hopefully what had immediately preceded them.

Unfortunately, Julian's body was the center of attention of nearly everyone in the room. There was no way I'd be able to get close enough to touch either him or his watch.

But what I had just noticed was potentially even more telling.

Between Julian's body and the door was an area of carpet in front of a wall that every agent in the office was unconsciously avoiding. They seemed to be more comfortable standing near a corpse than they did that wall.

Intuition was a powerful thing. Some called it a gut feeling; others thought of it as instinct. All of those went back to how our primitive ancestors had survived from one day to the next. Fight or flight. Those who listened to their instincts survived. Those who didn't became dinner for the sabre-toothed tiger stalking them, or the victim of a club-wielding rival. Either way, they were just as dead.

Law enforcement professionals and soldiers often had a more highly tuned sense of danger than the general population. There'd even been military programs to attempt to magnify this ability in soldiers. The FBI agents in Julian Pierce's office were avoiding that spot.

I left Rees and went to stand directly in front of the wall.

Occasionally, if a crime had been particularly violent, I could get a sense of what had happened from opening myself up to the crime scene itself. If that was fear frozen on Julian's face, perhaps a trace of what he had seen or sensed remained.

I emptied myself of everything I had seen so far, shutting out voices around me until they were as white noise, and waited for whatever may have remained to seep into my consciousness.

I sensed an intense focus from whoever had stood here, along with a complete absence of emotion. There was no hate, anger, or desire for revenge. None of the usual emotions of a killer for their victim were present.

A crash came from the outer office, breaking my connection to whatever I'd found.

The coffeemaker had been knocked off the table, and judging from the language, the contents had still been hot, and now those contents were all over the floor, compromising the hell out of the outer office crime scene.

I stepped back from the wall, caught my heel on a fold in the rug, and stumbled.

The next instant, Rees was there, his hand supporting my elbow. "Are you alright?"

"I'm—"

"Let's get you out of here," he said before I could tell him that I was fine.

"Excuse us," he said, smoothly steering me out of the office suite and farther down the hall, away from the direction in which we'd come. "There's a conference room around the corner where you can sit down." He gestured to Berta to follow us.

Rees had seen me at worse crime scenes, and knew I was perfectly all right. His words expressed concern, but his eyes remained neutral. One did not go with the other. Something else was going on here, so I played along.

CHAPTER 5

"Guard the door, please," Rees told Berta.

"From inside or out?"

"Inside."

That told me Rees didn't want anyone to even suspect we were here, and if someone did get curious, Berta would deal with it.

The agent crossed her arms and leaned back against the closed door. Privacy ensured.

"There are no security cameras," Rees told me. "You may speak freely."

"Good. Now what was that back there?"

"You gathered information from Alan Coe, and it was apparent that you had an unexpected encounter in Senator Pierce's office."

"Yes, to both."

"I reasoned that you would appreciate being able to share your findings undisturbed and in private."

"Again correct."

Rees spread his hands. "I did my best to ensure an environment to your liking."

"Nice try. I mean, what was your hurry in getting me out of Julian's office? I don't appreciate getting the fainting-female treatment."

"I am aware of that, but the situation left me with little recourse. You have my sincere apologies. I required a distraction, and you and whoever caused the coffee mishap most thoughtfully provided one."

I gave him a look. "What did you do?"

Rees leaned back in his chair and steepled his fingers in front of his lips. Lips that twitched in the briefest of smiles. "In a moment. I would prefer to know your findings first."

I told him what I'd felt when I'd touched Alan Coe. The confusion at the source of his pain, then a spike of fear, which escalated into panic when he knew he was going to die.

"At no time did he sense anyone in the office with him?" Rees asked.

"No. I didn't get any indication he knew anyone was there. There's only one door into or out of the senator's suite, right?"

"Correct."

"His desk faces the outer door, and anyone going into the senator's office would have to pass right next to him. He did hear someone call his name. I wondered if that might have been Julian, checking to see what was wrong."

The knob on the conference room door turned as someone tried to open it from the other side.

"In use," Berta growled.

Footsteps quickly retreated down the hall.

Rees inclined his head. "Please continue, Ms. Donati."

"That was all I learned from Alan. I'd thought I'd need his fountain pen, since he died with it in his hand, but I touched Alan himself, so I won't be needing it."

Rees slowly leaned back in the chair. The leather creaking was the only sound. "What did you learn from the floor in front of the wall?"

I should have known Rees would notice everyone avoiding that patch of carpet.

I answered his question with one of my own. "Did you stand there?"

"I did earlier, and I experienced a distinct sense of unease when I did so."

"My creepy meter was tapping the red zone, too. I felt an intense focus but no emotion at all."

"So, no one was there?"

"I didn't say that. It's just unusual that I wouldn't pick up any emotions, especially if this person was there to kill two men. There was no anger, no hate, no need for revenge. Even a psychopath would feel the satisfaction of a job well done. Just intensity. That's all I got. The air was nearly vibrating with it."

Rees sat forward. "Can you be more specific as to the time?"

"Time?"

"How long ago was this person standing there? Might that be an explanation for the lack of emotion? Could it have been an imprint left from earlier in the day?"

"It's...possible."

"You don't sound convinced."

"Because I'm not. My gut says no more than three hours."

Rees gave me an enigmatic smile. "This might help your viscera clarify matters." He reached into his jacket pocket and pulled out a silver-banded wristwatch.

A watch I had last seen on Julian's wrist.

Personally, I was horrified. Professionally, I was impressed. "You stole a watch off a dead man?"

"I consider it an acquisition of critical evidence in a murder."

Berta snorted.

"Nice way to say 'stole,'" I said.

Rees slid it across the table to me. "If you can use it to find his killer, do you believe Senator Pierce would have minded?"

I didn't touch the watch. Not yet. "He would've wholeheartedly approved. So that's why you needed to get out of Dodge."

"I beg your pardon?"

"Never mind."

"I'll have it returned when you're finished with it."

I was sure he would. I was even more certain I didn't want to know the details.

I picked up the watchband between my thumb and forefinger, handling it like the hot merchandise it was.

The connection was instant.

Recognition. Doubt. Confusion. Then the same agonizing pain Alan had experienced, only it was worse for Julian. Beneath the pain was fear, then denial. This couldn't be happening. It wasn't possible.

David tried to warn me.

Then nothing. Darkness.

I dropped the watch on the table and pushed it away from me. I sat back and took a couple of good, deep breaths. Rees didn't speak. Berta was a silent sentinel. They knew I'd talk when I had sorted through what I'd sensed.

I closed my eyes and tried to rerun what I'd gotten in my mind while I tried to explain.

"Julian may have recognized his killer…or thought he did. I sensed confusion. That's when the pain started. It was worse than what I felt with Alan. Maybe it was his age. Then I got denial. It could have been denial that he was dying, fear that this was happening to him, that it wasn't possible. Then I actually got a name. David. 'David tried to warn me.' I heard that very clearly."

"Curiouser and curiouser," Rees murmured.

"That's one way to describe it." The inside of my mouth felt like sandpaper, so I fumbled around in my messenger bag for a bottle of water. While I was in there, I snagged a granola bar.

"Do you have any idea who David might be?" Rees asked.

"None."

"As soon as the autopsies are complete, I'll have more information for you," he said. "In the meantime, your assistance has been invaluable, as always."

We both looked at Julian's watch on the conference table between us.

Rees spoke. "Would you be willing to—"

"Take it with me and try again later?"

Rees nodded.

I slid the watch into one of my messenger bag's zippered compartments. I didn't want an unpleasant surprise when I got home and reached in my bag for my house keys. "Hopefully I won't get arrested for theft on my way out." I was only half joking. "Though if I could keep the watch for a few days, I think it'd be good to have Grandad have a go at it. There's a possibility he might know who David is. I can ask when I call him."

"I agree. Good idea. And I'll inquire among the senator's staff."

"Do you know if the cleaning crews here wear gloves?"

"They do," Rees told me. "Nate Baxter was wearing them when he emptied the garbage at 8:22, as was the man at 9:15."

"You don't believe the second man was Baxter?"

"I do not. The similarities were remarkable, but there were more than enough lapses to make one doubt his performance. The way he walked, for instance. Though the imposter is to be admired for his most thorough preparation—at least in his physical appearance."

"Would you be able to send me the security footage showing Nate Baxter and whoever it was the second time?" I was sure the FBI had been over the video pixel by pixel, but I needed to see it.

"Not a problem. I'll also send the video of Mr. Baxter's questioning." Rees glanced at his watch. "It's 3:35. Hopefully, you can get some sleep. May I call you in a few hours, if urgency warrants it?"

"Please do." I seriously doubted I'd be able to sleep, but I owed it to myself to try, even though what I'd experienced here had created more questions and provided no answers.

CHAPTER 6

Berta dropped me off in the alley that ran behind my carriage house apartment. Sunrise was still a few hours away. I opened the door, quickly stepped inside, and keyed in the alarm code.

The Donati Detective Agency was based out of Grandad's Georgetown town house. His 1971 Mercedes 280SE occupied the former carriage portion of the carriage house. My 1957 Harley XL Sportster occupied one of the two former horse stalls. My soon-to-be-restored Scout would be right at home in the other. I lived in the apartment upstairs.

There was a small light on in my bedroom and a few in the town house. We had selected lights on timers to mimic us being at home. For example, they would turn on the kitchen lights in the main house during the night as if Grandad were getting up for a late snack, turning them off ten minutes later. The kitchen light was on now.

I needed to call Grandad, and I wanted to check the town house and his cat Pablo, but first I needed to take care of myself. One of our neighbors, Mrs. Hughes, had been feeding Pablo while we were gone. She was one of the few people outside the family he would tolerate. The cat was well fed. I wasn't.

A couple of years ago, the massive orange tomcat had presented himself for adoption on the town house's doorstep. He'd been missing part of his left ear, so Grandad had dubbed him Pablo, as in Picasso, and had invited him in to join the family. The big tom appointed himself the protector of his new home and attacker of anything or anyone that didn't belong. When we met with clients in the office, Gerald had to make sure Pablo stayed in the kitchen. Gerald was Grandad's butler and cook and had been with the family for as long as I could remember. While we'd been in Zurich, Gerald was in Boston visiting family.

I dropped my bags next to the door and went straight to the fridge. I'd thrown out most of the perishables before I'd left for Zurich, but I'd made sure to stock some things I could fix fast and with minimal consciousness. Bagels. Cream cheese. Smoked salmon. Blessed carbs and protein. Just toast and slather. I could handle that. I put on the kettle for a cup of tea. I went with chamomile and lavender.

I called Grandad, but it rolled over to voice mail. I asked him to call me. There was no way I was about to leave a message that his best friend had been murdered.

I took a shower and changed into yoga pants and a T-shirt. When I checked my phone, there was a message waiting.

Samuel Rees, not Grandad.

I listened. Rees had emailed Nate Baxter's interrogation video, as well as the pertinent sections of the security footage for my review. He also said that Julian's office had sent out a statement to the media. Alan's family had agreed to hold off on announcing his death for at least the next few hours.

I knew why.

An older senator dying of a heart attack at his desk would cause a brief but sizeable ripple in the national news. "Julian Pierce" would trend for maybe a day on Twitter, but it wouldn't go far beyond that. But an older senator *and* his young and healthy aide dying of heart attacks at the same time in the same place? It would be a media feeding frenzy, and it'd only get worse the longer the FBI went without an explanation that could calm the conspiracy theories. From what little we knew, a satisfactory explanation wouldn't be coming in the immediate future.

Rees closed by saying he'd call if anything else turned up.

I got my laptop and second cup of tea and made myself comfortable on the couch.

Occasionally, Rees asked me to be onsite for an interrogation. I'd watch from another room and afterward, I would go into the room and sit in the chair the subject had just vacated. Solving crime by the seat of my pants, so to speak.

Rees would often leave a pen or two on the table where the suspect would be sitting. Being questioned by the FBI made most people nervous, whether they were guilty or not. Few people could resist picking up the pen and holding, fidgeting, or playing with it. Playing with a pen gave the nervous an object with which to soothe themselves—and gave us details about the person without them saying a word. The more the suspect played with the pen, or the way they held it, signaled fear, anger, impatience, nervousness, or concern. In the absence of a pen or other pacifying object, they would touch necks, face, arms, hands, or hair, depending on the emotion involved. All were self-calming behaviors.

Later, I would hold the pen to see if I could pick up any additional impressions. A lot could be learned by how the person interacted with the pen as they answered specific questions.

I sipped my tea and opened the first attachment.

An FBI agent was on one side of a small table with the custodian Nate Baxter on the other.

Mr. Baxter appeared to be in his late sixties to early seventies, and he looked tired, not merely of body, but of spirit.

He was sitting straight in a chair with metal arms but kept his hands flat on his thighs. As the questioning started, he alternated between rubbing his hands on his pant legs and clasping them together in his lap, the thumb on top rubbing against the other. When he became aware of it, he would stop, or cross his arms with his hands clasping his upper arms in an attempt to calm himself. His eyes appeared red and he would sniff, occasionally reaching in his pocket for a handkerchief to wipe his eyes. Tears were easy to fake. It didn't take much to squeeze out a few drops and run a handkerchief over eyes to redden them. It was an obvious way to convey sadness, but on Baxter I believed it was genuine.

Gifted actors or guilty killers could fake both and more, but Nate Baxter wasn't an actor, and my first impression was that he hadn't killed anyone, nor did he know who did. He recognized the seriousness of his situation and was trying to maintain what composure he had left. He'd lost someone he considered a friend, a man he respected and admired.

The agent asked Mr. Baxter to detail for him when he had last seen the two men. Unfortunately, even the FBI sometimes tended to focus more on what was said, not how it was being said—or what was left unspoken. Facial tics and body movements didn't qualify as admissible evidence.

Micro-expressions were like a piece of a puzzle. The more pieces you had, the better the chance of getting an accurate picture of what the suspect was truly thinking. *Relaxed* didn't necessarily mean *innocent,* very often quite the opposite.

"I stopped by on my rounds to empty the trash," Baxter was saying. "Any cans that need emptying are left outside the office doors. Senator Pierce's staff hadn't left anything, so I took that to mean he was working late again. I knocked and Mr. Coe answered the door. He handed me two cans and thanked me for stopping by. That's when the senator called out from his office, 'Is that you, Nate?' I said it was, and Senator Pierce invited me in." He paused, his lips pressed together against a surge of emotion. "He asked about my new great-grandbaby. He'd recently become a great-granddaddy himself, and we shared pictures from time to time."

"How did Senator Pierce appear to you?" the agent asked. "Any unusual paleness, signs of a tremor—"

"No, sir. Senator Pierce may have been up in years, but he was in good shape. Once a Marine, always a Marine. He stood as smooth as could be and came around his desk to shake my hand, same as he always did." Baxter paused and stared down at his clenched hands. "The senator had a strong grip. There was nothing wrong with him.

"If he had looked sickly," Baxter continued, "I would have noticed and asked him about it. Two years ago, in November, the senator came down with the flu and he was out for five whole days. In my opinion he came back too early and I told him so." He sat straighter and looked the agent right in the eye.

"But that was the senator. Nothing was gonna keep him from serving the people who put him in that office. He didn't care how much money a man had, or what kind of work he did to make a living and support his family. Honest work was good work and worthy of admiration and respect. Not like some of the others who get the honor to walk these halls. They either came from money or would do anything to get it. That and power. If you can't help them get or keep either one, then you might as well not exist. That or they treat you with as much consideration as these chairs we're sitting in. Men and women like that don't serve the people who voted for them. They serve themselves and those who gave them the money to keep them in their fancy offices. Senator Pierce wasn't like that. I've been here going on forty years. I've seen 'em come in here all puffed with pride. And I've seen them go with their tails between their legs. Good riddance. The folks of Senator Pierce's state knew a good one when they found him, and they've kept him here. His granddaughter's just come into the House. This is her first year in office." Baxter sadly shook his head. "The senator was so proud of his girl. Smart as a whip, she is, and tough, just like her granddaddy. I hope to get a chance to extend my condolences."

"How did Alan Coe look?" the agent asked.

"Just fine. Mr. Coe ran those marathon races. In fact, he'd run one just two weeks ago. He didn't mention winning, but he seemed pleased when he came in that Monday morning. Said he'd beaten his personal best."

"Did Mr. Coe lock the door after you when you left?"

"No, sir. Not that I heard. Senator Pierce liked to keep his door unlocked. Most of the senators do. They feel safe here, or at least they used to. During the day, Senator Pierce kept it open whenever he could. I guess Mr. Coe could have locked it after I left, I just didn't hear it."

The agent referred to a tablet on the table in front of him. "And you said that you didn't see anyone else in the area?"

"No, sir. It was just me. There are three others besides myself who work here at night, but James Knox called in sick tonight and I offered to take care of his floor. That's why I was earlier than usual stopping by Senator Pierce's office. I wanted to finish my work first, then take care of Jimmy's."

"And your usual time to reach Senator Pierce's office is…?"

"A little before or after eight. At least as of last week. That's when I got approval to change my hours to come in earlier. This is my night job. I work on Tuesday, Wednesday, and Thursday."

"Why did you change your schedule?"

"It's five blocks from my place to the closest Metro station. My neighbor drives a cab at night. If I started my rounds an hour earlier, he could drop me off at the station." Baxter smiled a little. "At my age, the less I have to walk, the better."

"Who knew about your schedule change?"

Baxter thought for a moment. "My neighbor and my supervisor, of course. And I'd told Jimmy…I can't really think of anyone else."

"And you didn't come back to the senator's office at 9:15?"

"No, sir. I had no need to."

"Where were you at that time?"

"Down in our break room."

"Was anyone else there with you?"

"No, sir. I wish there had been, or we wouldn't be having this conversation."

The video continued for a few more minutes, but I didn't think Nate Baxter had killed Julian and Alan. He was a sweet, old guy who'd probably regret having to kill a roach in the basement. I didn't know if the FBI had confronted him about his doppelgänger, or if they'd actually shown him the security video. I doubted it. There would have been a protestation of innocence, and even more shock than I was seeing now.

If I'd been in the room with him and could have laid a comforting hand on his arm or my hand on top of his in consolation, I don't think I would have sensed anything different than I did now. I'd be able to say so with certainty after talking to him for a few seconds. For me, as in the business world, a handshake would seal the deal.

I closed the video and opened the two security footage attachments side by side, so I could compare them.

Rees was right.

Since he specifically pointed out the way the second man walked, I initially focused on that. I watched the real Nate Baxter in the first video. His head was up and his features as clear as they could be given the quality of the footage. The cameras in the Russell Building really needed to be upgraded. Baxter moved with purpose, going from one side of the hall to the other, emptying trash cans. At one point, when he was close to the camera's location, I could see that he was whistling. He knocked on Senator Pierce's door and Alan Coe answered, smiling when he saw Baxter. Coe handed him two trash cans and Baxter emptied them in the container on his cart. Then he and Coe went into the office and closed the door behind them. Baxter was inside for nearly five minutes, according to the time running in the corner of the screen. When he came out, he was pulling on his right glove. Presumably he'd removed it to shake Senator Pierce's hand. He resumed his rounds, vanishing out of the range of that particular camera.

The video that started at 9:14 p.m. showed the person who appeared to be Nate Baxter repeating his rounds. Whoever this was knew Baxter's old schedule, but not the one he'd changed to this week. He rolled his cart past the trash cans lining the hall, not even looking to see if they were full.

That was Nate Baxter's job, not his.

If his job was to kill Julian and Alan, I could see where he wouldn't want to stick around any longer than he had to. The disguise was amazing in its detail, movie quality.

At 9:15, he didn't knock on the door, instead pulling out a key and quickly opening it to slip inside, closing it behind him. The timer in the corner of the screen said he was inside for less than a minute. Thirty-seven seconds, to be exact. He then came out, closed the door behind him, locked it, and smoothly turned away from the camera and rolled his cart back the way he had come.

Two men, dead of apparent heart attacks in thirty-seven seconds.

I agreed with Samuel Rees.

Curiouser and curiouser.

CHAPTER 7

Soon after I'd finished watching the video, the bagel, tea, and the blanket I was curled under did their collective work. I woke up nearly two hours later in a warm and happy little ball. Yes, I had a lot on my mind, but exhaustion would not be denied indefinitely.

I checked my phone. Grandad still hadn't returned my call.

I glanced over at my messenger bag on the coffee table. Julian's watch was still inside. I'd promised myself that I wasn't going to touch it until I'd at least tried to sleep. Sleep and sinister didn't go together very well.

Now that the impressions I'd gotten standing in front of that wall had had a chance to sink in, "sinister" was the best description for what I'd felt.

Since I'd slept, I really had no reason to put it off any longer. Just get it over with.

I put on a glove and took the watch out of my bag.

In the conference room, I'd picked up the watch while wearing my altered nitrile gloves, but to get all that it could tell me, I needed to put it on with the clasp and the band on either side touching the pulse point on my wrist, as it had on Julian's just before his heart had stopped. His wrist was larger than mine, and even if I adjusted the band, it still wouldn't fit me. However, I could slide the watch over my hand, and use my gloved right hand to pull the band tight against the underside of my wrist. Sounded like a plan. I slid it on and pulled it tight.

Startled. Julian hadn't heard the man come into his office, and initially hadn't seen him very well. I wasn't seeing through Julian's eyes, rather I sensed his confusion at who he expected to be there versus who he actually saw. Then came the doubt I had sensed before, followed by confusion and pain. Interspersed with the pain were the same fear and the denial that this wasn't possible, and *David tried to warn me.* Then darkness.

I slid the watch off my wrist onto the sofa cushion beside me.

I leaned back to let what I'd experienced settle in, waiting for the inconsistencies to surface along with the questions.

The first one was something I hadn't considered.

There had been no struggle or even physical contact between Julian and whoever had been in the office with him. He hadn't been attacked. The autopsy could confirm whether there were any defensive bruises or abrasions on his body, but from what I sensed just now, the killer never laid a hand on him.

Nate Baxter had been in his office just an hour before and Julian had welcomed him in. However, he had heard Baxter's voice in the outer office first and had recognized him that way. So, had he not seen the intruder clearly, or did he think he initially recognized him as Nate Baxter, then realized he couldn't be Baxter, hence the confusion? Julian wore glasses. I didn't notice them either on his desk or on the floor by his body.

Who had he seen? And who was David, and what—or who—had he warned Julian about?

I reached for the watch again. I preferred to do at least three links with an object if I could. I wanted to learn everything I could from it and get her grandfather's watch into Elaine Pierce's hands as soon as possible.

I pulled the band tight.

Startled, doubt, confusion, pain, fear, denial, then darkness. Nothing new.

I put the watch back in my messenger bag and went to the kitchen, taking my phone with me. I rummaged through the fridge and found some yogurt. It was a little after five o'clock. The city would be waking up soon and checking the news. I suspected my two-hour nap would have to last me for a while. Time for some caffeine. I was going to need all the help staying awake I could get.

I glanced out the kitchen window as I filled the tank on my Keurig. The sky would begin to lighten in about an hour, but for now the only illumination between my apartment and the town house were the path lights leading from the garage to the town house's kitchen door.

They should be the only lights, but they weren't.

Grandad's desk lamp was on in his study, which I also used as the office for the Donati Detective Agency. The desk lamp was touch-activated and wasn't attached to the timer system. Pablo could've turned it on, but the office door was closed, as were other rooms Grandad didn't want Pablo visiting while we were gone. However, Mrs. Hogan might have left it open if she'd had to go looking for him. Pablo liked to rub up against the lamp and turn it on and off. It was a game with him.

A shadow passed between the light and window that sure as hell wasn't a cat. Almost immediately, the light went out and stayed out.

I put the pot down. I was awake now, no caffeine needed.

CHAPTER 8

Ambrose Donati wasn't a silent-alarm kind of guy. If one of his Old Masters or Picassos so much as shifted on the wall, he wanted to know about it. Grandad had a lot of art. Some he had bought for himself. The rest had been payment from incredibly grateful clients. He treasured each and every piece.

If someone was trying to steal his art, he wanted to make it impossible for them to stay in the house long enough to finish the job. He didn't mind the noise. He called it the "clarion call of avenging angels." I called it screaming demons.

Someone was in the house and the demons weren't screaming.

A quick check of the security system's phone app told me why. The intruder hadn't bypassed the system, they'd used the freaking password. The new one. The one Grandad had implemented the day we'd left for Zurich. I'd been in the office with him when he'd called the security company to change it to Rembrandt's birthday. Gerald had the new password, as did the security company. That was it. We'd provided Mrs. Hughes with a guest password and had notified the security company that she would be in the house twice a day.

The intruder had used the new owner password.

I pulled on my boots, quickly laced them over my yoga pants, and grabbed a jacket I wore while running. It was close-fitting and wouldn't impede any movements I needed to make, either offensive or defensive. I hoped I wouldn't need either one, but my gut told me Gerald hadn't come home early from Boston.

I wasn't going to do anything stupid. I had an idea, and the more I thought about it, the more I liked it.

But before I called the security company, I wanted a better idea of who we were dealing with. To get an impression of someone's thoughts, I needed direct contact with them or an object they'd recently touched. I could sense strong emotions from a distance, such as fear or anger, but I was too far away for that. I needed to get closer. Right now, all I could tell was that the intruder was still in the office. According to the app, the system hadn't been rearmed. I could get next to the window without being seen or setting off the alarm.

There was no moon and the backyard was dark. Still, I clung to the even darker shadows next to the house. I stopped a few feet to the right of the window, tried to tell myself I wasn't freezing, stilled my mind, and reached out to learn whatever I could.

It didn't take long, because it was the same presence I'd felt in the Russell Building's rotunda only a few hours ago.

Now that I was closer, I could tell it was a man.

I didn't sense any strong emotions coming from him. He was cool and calm, cocky even, as he searched the office, but I couldn't get any sense of what he was looking for—only that it had nothing to do with Grandad's Rembrandts and Renoirs.

That was all I needed for now.

I backtracked, slipped into the garage, and called the security company. It was run by former NSA operatives. They were fast and they were good, if good meant being a little heavy-handed with anyone they found inside one of their clients' properties. I had no problem with that. Julian and Alan were dead, and this guy was somehow involved.

"This is Aurora Donati, 2613 Thirty-fifth Street. The account holder is my grandfather, Ambrose Donati. We've had a break-in. One man, and he used the new owner password to get in." I kept my voice down, but my tone said loud and clear that the leak wasn't our doing, and I wasn't happy.

There was an uncomfortable silence on the other end. "May I have your identification word, please?"

"Caravaggio." Grandad loved the bad boys of art. "My grandfather's out of the country at a conference. I came back early and saw a lamp on in the office that's not connected to the network. I saw the guy when he moved between the lamp and the window." They didn't need to know that I'd recognized him and how.

"Ms. Donati, we've dispatched a team to your location."

I flashed a cold, little smile in the shadows as I imagined the unpleasant surprise our intruder was about to get. "Thank you. I appreciate it."

"Please do not attempt to enter the house until our representatives have secured the premises."

"I wouldn't dream of it. Oh, by the way, he didn't rearm the system once he was inside. Would you change the password for me, lock down the house, and turn the alarms back on until your people arrive?"

"It would be our pleasure, Ms. Donati. What password would you like to use?"

"Pablo, as in Picasso."

I heard keys clicking. "Done. Though if the intruder attempts to leave, it will get noisy."

"That's what I wanted. I don't mind, though the neighbors might. I'll just consider it the clarion call of avenging angels."

I settled down to wait for the show to start.

It didn't take long.

If I had blinked, I would have missed their arrival. Our security company called them representatives. Any of our neighbors who were awake and sharp-eyed enough to spot them in the shadows would've described them as commandos.

I thought of them as Grandad getting his money's worth— and the intruder about to get what he deserved. Once they caught him, I was going to get some answers.

The guards turned off the alarm to enter the house, and must have armed it again, because about ten seconds after they went in, the intruder ran out to the accompaniment of Grandad's avenging angels.

The man was all in black and wearing a balaclava, so I couldn't see his face or hair color. He was fast, Olympic-sprinter fast, his long legs taking him across the yard to the brick wall in record time. There was no sign of the guards.

He was going to get away.

Oh, hell no.

I did some sprinting of my own.

The wall was an eight-footer, but he grabbed the top with both gloved hands and easily hoisted himself to the top.

All I could get was an ankle, but I held on for all I was worth, and my words blistered the air blue.

I expected a kick from his other combat-booted foot.

What I got felt like I was picked up and thrown, but the man's hands never left the wall.

He smoothly vaulted to the other side as I lay flat on my back trying to remember how to breathe.

CHAPTER 9

"He kicked me."

That was the story I was going with, at least to the security company and police. I grabbed his ankle, and he kicked me with his other boot. It wasn't the truth, but the truth would make me sound crazy, so I kept it to myself, at least until Rees and Berta arrived.

I knew what he'd done, and it was scary as hell.

My parents were psychiatrists who ran a private clinic in Sedona where they specialized in helping people cope with any unique abilities they had, meaning they convinced those with psychic abilities that they weren't insane. My parents had a network of contacts at psychiatric hospitals and clinics across the country who let them know if they had any new patients who they suspected had an ability and not a problem.

Some of their patients had both.

Whenever I'd visited the clinic as a child, I'd been restricted to Mom and Dad's offices and the administrative section. But I was a curious kid, and more than once I went exploring. I was ten years old on the day I encountered way more than I was prepared to deal with.

Eleanor Franklin was an elderly lady with dementia. She was also psychokinetic, meaning she could move things with her mind. On the day when I was where I wasn't supposed to be, Miss Eleanor was letting everyone in the solarium know that the things she could move included people.

Treating dementia was difficult enough in normal patients. Those with psychic abilities at Eleanor Franklin's level increased the factor of difficulty to nearly impossible. Psychics—and their abilities—responded differently to drugs. My parents had to start from square one when she'd first arrived at their clinic.

Miss Eleanor was allowed to go for walks outside only under the watchful eye of a senior staff doctor and two orderlies—and when no other patients were on the grounds. She wasn't usually violent, she simply wanted what she wanted when she wanted it. On that particular day, she wanted to go outside, and there wasn't a senior staff doctor available to go with her.

When she was told she'd have to wait, the situation deteriorated rapidly.

I arrived in the solarium just in time to see an orderly the size of a linebacker go flying across the room. Fortunately, he landed on a sofa. The orderly was fine. The sofa and the end tables on either side, not so much. Mom arrived soon after and calmly explained to Miss Eleanor that throwing people was rude. I never knew how she did it, but Mom had a way with Eleanor Franklin.

Miss Eleanor apologized to the orderly and asked Mom when she might expect an escort to go on a walk with her. Mom replied that she would be able to go with her in less than an hour, and that she should go back to her room to wait. In the meantime, Mom promised to send tea.

My presence did not go unnoticed. Mom had a way with me, too.

I never wandered around the clinic alone again.

Tonight, the intruder had taken a page from Miss Eleanor's book. He'd wanted to leave, and I was preventing him from doing so.

That earned me a tossing.

Believe me, watching someone go flying through the air is entirely different when that someone is you.

A suit-wearing representative of the security company arrived soon after three of the guards returned from trying to track the intruder. No luck. It was as if he'd never been here, though my bruised backside knew different. I wasn't happy, but the commandos were pissed. It'd been one man against six, and he'd gotten away after incapacitating two of them. One was still unconscious. The other said the man never pulled a weapon, and he didn't remember being struck, just regaining consciousness.

It sounded like I wasn't the only one to experience the intruder's hands-off style of self-defense.

The police arrived once the alarm had alerted everyone within two miles that all was not well in our little slice of Georgetown. I answered their questions for the report, but had no description other than tall, cocky, and annoyingly limber.

"Looks like none of us have gotten any sleep tonight," Berta said from the foyer. Samuel Rees was talking to the security-company suit, who'd introduced himself to me as Edward Simmons. "You okay?" she asked.

"Just bruises—ass and ego," I told her. "Other than that, I'm good." I caught Rees's attention and gestured for him to join us. "Let's go in the kitchen. The forensics people are still in the office."

I went to the side of the kitchen farthest from the door. I didn't want anyone else to hear what I was about to say.

I told them about the presence I'd sensed in the Russell Building rotunda, and that the intruder was the same man.

Rees was not happy with my omission. "You didn't tell us."

"I had a lot on my mind then. I'm telling you now."

He settled against the fridge. "Go on."

"He had to be on the second-floor balcony, though I never spotted him. He knew who and what I was, and most importantly, why I was there. A couple hours later, he breaks into the house to steal something from our office. The security company people are still in there, so I haven't had a chance to go over the room the way I want to."

A raspy meow came from the corner of the kitchen.

"Is that Pablo?" Berta asked.

"Yep, that's him. Totally stoned."

Pablo the Attack Cat was happily rolling in a small pile of catnip that'd been dumped in his bed. Soaking wet, he closed in on thirty pounds, though God help anyone who tried to introduce Pablo to water, either falling from the sky or out of a faucet.

"Our intruder came bearing gifts." I said. "In addition to our password, he apparently knew Pablo doesn't like strangers." I knelt and ruffled the cat's big belly, my hand instantly engulfed in four paws like a furry Venus flytrap. All gentle, of course. Pablo was a mellow stoner. "He was worthless. Though I'm glad he didn't go after the guy and get himself hurt. I'll be giving Grandad enough bad news as it is."

Simmons tapped twice on the kitchen door, then opened it enough to stick his head inside. "We're finished, Ms. Donati."

"What did you find?"

He held the door open for us. "No fingerprints. He was wearing gloves. They were thin, the kind you wear when you don't want to leave prints, but need dexterity. We don't think he was here to steal art. We've done an inventory of your grandfather's entire collection. Every piece is accounted for."

"He'll be glad to hear that."

"However, there are scratches on the locks of both your desk and Mr. Donati's, and we believe the safe was opened as well. I'll need you to confirm if anything was taken."

"If he did get anything, it'd have to have been small enough to fit in a pocket. He didn't have any kind of backpack with him."

From the frustration I'd sensed when I'd grabbed him, I knew he didn't get what he came for, but that didn't mean he hadn't taken anything.

Simmons paused outside the office. "We discovered how he got the new password."

"The landline was tapped?"

"No, but we found four bugs, tiny and well hidden. NSA-quality stuff. I'd say your visitor has intelligence-agency connections. We'll take them back to the lab to see if we can get any identifying marks that'll help us trace their source." He motioned us inside. "I'll show you what we found, and where."

Our office looked like a Victorian gentleman's study. Grandad had an antique oak desk, and I had a smaller version to the side. The arrangement was kind of like Nero Wolfe and

Archie Goodwin, except Grandad was tall and lean and had absolutely zero interest in growing orchids. Like Archie, I did a lot of Grandad's legwork. As he liked to say, he wasn't as nimble as he used to be back in the day.

Rees glanced around. "Tidy, wasn't he?"

Simmons nodded. "The only outward indication he was here are the bootprints he left in the carpet."

"They were big," I said. "I got up close and personal with them."

"Size twelve," Simmons confirmed. "From the depth of the depression in the carpet, we think he's around two hundred pounds. And from your description in relation to the height of the back wall, we estimate he's about six two."

"We can thank Gerald for the ease of spotting the footprints," I told him. "He said he was going to clean the house after we left. When he vacuums, he always begins in the farthest corner of a room and works his way to the door, so he doesn't leave prints. This guy had some unusual tricks up his sleeve, but thankfully levitation wasn't one of them. I'm almost glad he took on two of your guys on his way out, otherwise I'd have had trouble convincing the police we'd even had a break-in."

Simmons went to the big oak desk that Grandad had cleared before we left. The company's two forensics techs were using it as their worktable. He picked up what looked like a square petri dish. "Step over to the light. These are hard to see."

Inside were what looked like four computer chips. All four of them would've fit on top of a pencil eraser without overlapping.

"So, he's been listening to us?" I asked.

"Someone has, and they've been able to access information on any device used in this room."

"Phones and computers."

Simmons nodded. "Both compromised. You'll want to change all your passwords, and alert your credit card—"

I waved him off. This intruder didn't want to hack my Ikea account, and I couldn't think of anyone else we'd dealt with recently who would've gained anything from bugging our office. "Noted. How about the rest of the house? Is it secure?"

"Unknown. We're scanning it now."

"Thank you. I'd like you to check my apartment over the carriage house as well."

"Consider it done."

"And you should probably go over Grandad's car, too. Let's cover all the bases while you're here."

"Agreed."

An hour later, Simmons and his people had found three more bugs in the town house and two in my apartment. There was also one in the car, which in addition to listening, allowed whoever planted it to track where we went. Surprisingly, they'd left my Harley alone. Simmons installed jamming devices in the town house, my apartment, and the car that would prevent any future bugs from transmitting, plus gave me a portable version to use in whatever room I happened to be in when I didn't want to be listened to or followed. Simmons changed the password for my apartment directly on the control panel and did the same in the town house. *Pablo* had been the password for less than an hour. Yes, it was paranoid, but I felt more than entitled. Someone had come into our home, planted bugs, and had been listening to us, day and night. Violated was only the beginning of what I felt.

I locked the apartment, armed the alarm, and returned to the town house, where Berta and Rees were waiting in the office.

The security-company reps had finished their work and gone. For the next few days, our house would be under constant surveillance. Now it was my turn to investigate. They hadn't found much, but I wasn't looking for the same things.

Berta started to speak, and I quickly put a finger to my lips.

Yep, paranoia and I were going to be besties until further notice.

The intruder had left plenty of other footprints in the room, so I didn't feel bad messing up two of them. I stood next to the prints and removed my boots and socks. I put a glove on my left hand, leaving my right bare. A wood panel that blended with the rest of the wall concealed the safe. I pushed aside the panel with my gloved hand. I wanted my first contact to be with the safe's keypad and the bootprints. I knew the safe's seven-digit code. I stilled my mind, stepped into the prints and placed two of my fingertips on the keys that were repeated, since the intruder would've touched them more than once.

The impressions were fresh and immediate.

He'd known I was in the carriage house and was unconcerned about being caught. On the contrary, he hoped I'd sense he was there and come looking for him. I didn't get a sense of what he was looking for. It was almost as if he wouldn't allow himself to think of it. I felt his frustration here as I had when I'd grabbed his ankle outside. He knew time was running out. He was being forced to react rather than being the one in control. This was a game to them, and it had turned deadly. I didn't know who the intruder was referring to by "them," but I knew that "turned deadly" had to mean Julian and Alan.

I stepped out of the prints, cleared my mind, then stepped back into them for a second try. I didn't get anything new. The same visceral emotions, frustration and anger at an unknown person or persons.

Berta and Rees were waiting patiently for my findings.

I gave them a grim thumbs-up, then moved on to Grandad's desk. I pulled out his chair and sat.

Damn. One of the techs from the security company had been the last to sit here. The intruder hadn't used it at all. The tech had been impressed by the sophistication of the devices that'd been planted here and wondered what Grandad and I really did for a living. I had news for him: it wasn't anything that would attract the kind of man who'd been here tonight. The intruder hadn't needed to sit to go through our desks. If I'd been breaking into an office, I wouldn't have made myself at home while I ransacked the place. Get in, get what I came for, and get out.

I pushed the chair back and scanned the floor. There were more bootprints that matched the ones in front of the safe. I stood and put my bare feet in them, getting nothing more than what I already knew, just a sense of searching for something; but again, no indication of what.

I went from drawer to drawer in Grandad's desk, running my hand just above the contents.

Nothing.

I moved to my desk and did the same, sliding out the big drawer under the top of the desk. I didn't touch anything at first. I simply let my eyes roam over the contents, remembering what should be there, versus what might be missing now. Everything appeared to be in order, but then neither Grandad nor I kept neat desk drawers, so it wasn't exactly easy to tell.

I stood where the intruder had stood and held my right hand just above the desk contents, moving it from right to left, working my way through the drawer, trying to get a feel for whether anything had been—

My flash drives.

I kept them in a box in the front left corner. He'd stood here and picked up each and every one—and he'd put them back in the box. He hadn't been in the office long enough to have opened the files, and Grandad and I had both taken our laptops with us. He could've copied the contents onto a phone. He'd bugged us with the latest spy tech. Quickly copying the contents of my flash drives would've been a piece of cake. He was going to be disappointed. I hadn't used any of them in years.

I finished scanning the top drawer and moved to the other three.

He'd only been interested in the flash drives.

Data. Files. Of course, I had absolutely no clue what was on the files he was looking for, but I was all but certain he'd been barking up the wrong tree. If he'd been the one who had planted those bugs, he'd already had access to our laptops and probably our cloud accounts. When he hadn't found what he was looking for there, that would be when he'd decided to come here. At least I had the satisfaction of knowing he'd struck out again.

Perhaps that had been the cause of his frustration and anger.

I smiled. I hadn't been able to pull him down from that wall, but I'd take what I could get. For now.

I glanced at Rees and Berta, then pointed toward the door behind my desk. The narrow hallway would take us to the kitchen. Simmons hadn't found any bugs in that room, so I felt relatively safe talking there while using the portable jammer.

Time for that coffee I still hadn't had.

It was going to be a long day.

CHAPTER 10

Gerald kept emergency muffins in the freezer. Grandad and I defined any time Gerald wasn't home as a gastronomic emergency. The events of the past few hours had broadened that definition considerably, so I felt entirely justified thawing three of them.

While the microwave worked its magic and Pablo snored happily from his corner bed, I started a pot of coffee and told Rees and Berta what I'd sensed in the office.

"He wouldn't even let himself *think* of what he was looking for," I said. "That's tough to do, so I can add 'extreme mental discipline' to 'annoyingly limber,' and he had to know I'd be literally following in his footsteps. This guy's a professional who can get his hands on intelligence-agency tech, plus he was in the Russell Building and recognized me."

"In all likelihood, if he's not with an agency, he's got contacts with one," Rees told me.

"Not the kind of person I want to know about me," I said. "I'm not accusing you, but who else in the FBI, other than Roger Hudson, knows what I do?"

"No one. And Hudson knows how vital it is that your secret stays that way."

"I know you're careful," Berta said, "but it wouldn't really take that much to do the math. Where you go, cases get solved quickly, and most of the time there's not any kind of physical evidence trail to go on. Bear in mind that the 'intelligence' in 'intelligence community' also means smart. There's a lot of scary-smart IC people in this town."

I held up both hands. "Well aware. No reminder needed."

The microwave beeped, and I plated and served the muffins. I knew scary-smart people were out there. And if some of those people found a man like our intruder with a high level of psychokinetic skill, they'd latch on to him with every hand they had and never let go. That was the main reason Grandad and I were very careful of what we did in public and in front of whom. He'd made it clear to me that there were dark depths to the intelligence community that were best left unexplored. Grandad had been in government work since his early twenties, skirting the edges of its occasional forays into psychic research without revealing himself to have any talents of his own. He'd discovered that true PK skills were incredibly rare, and of those who held them, less than one percent had any ability past the spoon-bending level. Rolling a pencil across a desk was the limit for most, much to our government's disappointment. Party tricks wouldn't give you a leg up on the latest terrorist threat.

As a result, any work I did with Rees and Berta involved me keeping my head down and trying to blend in with the drapes. I thought I'd been successful. Apparently, I'd thought wrong.

I took a bite of muffin and glanced at the coffeemaker. Still brewing. Grandad had found it on his last trip to Florence. I'd had to watch a video to learn how to use it. I liked my Keurig just fine, but Grandad considered them barbaric and coffee a ritual to be savored. What was barbaric was having to wait more than a minute for a cup of coffee, though I had to agree with Grandad on this one. That machine didn't make coffee; it brewed elixir.

"Coffee's almost done," I said. "While I was waiting for the rent-a-commandos to arrive, I got close enough to the house to sense that he *wanted* me to walk in on him."

Rees put his fork down. "For what purpose?"

"He didn't elaborate. But when I tried to pull him off the wall, I got a big wave of frustration and anger. He was thinking that time is running out. He's used to being in control, and now he's being forced to react. He doesn't like it one bit. This is a game to them—whoever they are—and it's turned deadly, which I feel safe in assuming refers to Julian and Alan."

"Julian Pierce was the chairman of the Senate's intelligence committee," Rees said. "This man recognizes who and what you are in the Russell Building, then breaks into your house three hours later. There's a connection. We merely need to find out what it is."

"There's more than a connection," I told him. "There's a problem. He didn't kick me. That's just what I told the police. He picked me up and threw me—without using his hands."

Berta went still. "Like Miss Eleanor?"

"Exactly like Miss Eleanor. Two of Simmons's guys got the same treatment. The one that wasn't knocked out said his attacker didn't use a weapon, and he didn't remember being hit. He just thought the guy was that fast." I snorted. "At least the intruder's secret is still safe."

Berta and Rees knew about my encounter with Eleanor Franklin, and that she was the only psychokinetic my parents had ever treated or heard of with enough power to toss a human being like a sack of potatoes.

I waited for Rees's reaction. I already knew how I felt about it. I was creeped the hell out. Especially with this guy working for or in some way connected to the intelligence community. I'd always heeded Grandad's warning and had taken extra precautions to fly under the radar.

Tonight, I'd been detected by a man in the top one percent of PK talents. Then the bastard had broken into our family home, searched our office, drugged our cat (if only recreationally), and set off the alarm before vanishing into the night.

None of that was good.

My phone rang. I glanced at the screen. Grandad. I snatched it up. "There you are! I was—"

"I just heard that Julian—"

"I know. I'm so sorry." I paused. "I need you to call me back on Berta's phone."

Silence.

"Berta? Do I need to call from a landline?" His voice was calm and measured. He knew something was wrong.

"I think that would be best. Is that a problem?"

"No. I'll call her phone in no more than ten minutes."

While I waited, I fixed the coffee, pouring mine into a travel mug. I'd be taking this call outside. The sun was up. Yes, it was cold, but I needed to move.

Grandad called less than five minutes later. Rees was taking a call from Roger Hudson. Berta stayed inside to listen, but kept an eye on me through the kitchen window as I talked and paced. I was outside and on a phone that wasn't mine, but I still kept my voice down.

"Berta picked me up at the airport and we went straight to the Russell Building," I was saying.

"CNN claims it was a heart attack," Grandad said. "So do the *Post* and the *Times*. That's impossible. Julian's heart was—"

"Agreed. Especially since Alan Coe was at the office with him and died the same way at the same time."

Silence. "That wasn't mentioned."

"Good, though I'm not counting on it lasting much longer. Alan's family has agreed to keep his death under wraps for now. They just *looked* like heart attacks. It was something else."

That was as much as I could say about what I'd sensed from Julian and Alan. Grandad knew this. We never discussed our work over the phone. It was always face-to-face in a secure location. Until now, the town house had been a secure location. We'd been broken into at least twice—tonight and whenever those bugs had originally been planted.

"I'll get an earlier flight," Grandad said.

I heard a woman speaking flawless Parisian French in the background.

"One moment, darling," he told me. He put his hand over the phone, but I could just hear his reply to the woman, also in French.

I smiled. When he came back on the line, I said, "Tell Madame Montfort I said hello."

Collette Montfort was one of Grandad's former colleagues and a close friend. What had begun in the '60s hunting stolen art from World War II had ended after a long career with INTERPOL's Works of Art Unit. She'd been at the Zurich conference, and she and Grandad had spent much of it together catching up on old times.

"I'll do that. As soon as I have my flight information, I'll text you. *Ti voglio bene.*"

"I love you, too."

I ended the call. I didn't tell him about the break-in. He'd worry, and I chose not to put that on his mind in addition to the death of his best friend. It was bad enough that he'd be stuck for nearly ten hours on a plane with that running through his head, I wasn't about to add another source of stress he couldn't do anything about.

I looked at the back wall where the intruder had gone over.

I was going to put that ten hours to good use.

CHAPTER 11

Berta and Rees had to leave. They had work to do.

So did I.

I assured them I was fine and that I'd be at their disposal when any new details surfaced. After they left, I armed the alarm, told Simmons's two guards I was going for a run, and went to my apartment to gear up.

I didn't lie. I was going for a run.

In the intruder's footsteps.

They weren't easy to find, but I did find them.

On the other side of the brick wall was the alley that ran behind the row of town houses. The entrance to the carriage house was less than twenty feet from where he'd landed. We'd had a light dusting of snow at some point last night. The sky was clear and the sun bright. Another hour and those tracks would've been gone. They'd have been easy to miss last night, especially since Simmons's guys had been looking for a man, not his prints in the dark. I knew the man was long gone; I was searching for emotional traces.

I estimated that after he'd thrown me, I'd been flat on my back for a good thirty seconds. He'd taken down the two guards who'd intercepted him in the house, crossed the yard and gone up and over the wall in two seconds after he laid me out, and he would've been halfway down the block by the time anyone else had made it outside. The breath had been knocked out of me, but I'd pointed to where he'd gone over the wall to the first guard who'd run out of the house.

They hadn't found him.

Now it was my turn.

He'd hit the ground running. Literally.

The estimate of his height at six two sounded about right from the spacing of the bootprints. The man could move, I'd give him that. The prints had turned right at the wall and gone down the alley to the end where he'd taken a left. The next block was commercial, with restaurants and boutiques.

And traffic cameras.

It'd be worth having Berta or Rees get hold of the footage from an hour before and after my unwanted guest had made his appearance and escape.

The prints were less clear the closer I got to the corner of the next block. There'd been more foot traffic this morning since he'd been here. That was fine. I no longer needed to use my eyes to see where his feet had been, I could sense him now. That few seconds of physical contact at the wall had let me pick up his psychic spoor. Certain personality traits revealed themselves to my psychic senses better than others. One of the most clarion-clear was arrogance. This guy had it in spades, though he probably thought of it as confidence. Yes, he was frustrated and angry, but he was good at his job, and his job had most recently been to break into and escape a home with the best security money could buy. The unexpected arrival of our own rented commando squad had shot a dose of adrenaline into his system. Arrogance and adrenaline. A potent combination that was leading me to his getaway vehicle. Yes, he could've had someone waiting for him, but this guy didn't like giving up control. Men like that wouldn't want to depend on a partner being there to pick them up. He'd have his own transportation.

A narrow alley ran behind the businesses from the corner to halfway down the block where it intersected with a short side street. That was where I started my search.

It didn't take long.

He'd tucked it on the back side of a dumpster.

A motorcycle.

There was more than a dusting of snow here. The sun didn't get back here, or if it did, it wasn't for long. I took photos of where it'd been parked, taking note of the tread width and distance from front to back. Judging from the tread, the bike wasn't a crotch-rocket, but it was close. I should be able to get the make, if not the model, from the tread photos. The footage from those traffic cameras could seal the deal. I was betting there wouldn't be many six-foot-two men wearing all black on any of the surrounding streets in the hours before dawn. I could also call Laurence once I knew the make and model. He knew the local owners of American bikes, but he was linked in to the fast and foreign crowd. I had a feeling this bike would be in that category. I loved my Harley, but it and the soon-to-be-mine Indian weren't built for crime-scene-getaway speeds.

I stood in in his tracks and let them and the surrounding air speak to me. He'd been relieved to find his bike safe and sound. He hadn't wanted to leave it here, but he'd had no choice.

I found and followed the tread and footprints beside them to the end of the alley. He'd pushed the bike to the side street before starting it. Once there, he'd taken a left onto M Street.

I texted Rees and Berta to get the ball rolling on that traffic footage.

When the intruder was in our office, he'd wanted me to find him. I smiled and tucked my phone back into my jacket pocket. I was going to do everything I could to make his wish come true.

CHAPTER 12

Grandad was always easy to spot.

Ambrose Donati was from the generation that dressed up to travel, and that included a full suit and a hat. He was tall and distinguished, and when I wasn't traveling with him, he usually had a flight attendant help him up the jet bridge. Being on a plane for nearly ten hours didn't do good things for his circulation, and while he could disembark on his own, he nearly always found a pretty flight attendant to assist him, usually one he'd chatted with during the flight. She didn't mind helping a charming, old-world gentleman, and Grandad certainly didn't mind having a beautiful woman on his arm. Everyone was happy. And he wasn't too proud to accept the electric cart waiting for him at the gate. At least not anymore. Airports were huge, and a drain on the endurance of much younger men. A couple of years ago, I'd started insisting that we request a cart to be waiting at the gate. When he'd originally balked at the idea, I told him to think of it as saving his strength for something worthwhile. That'd done the trick.

Grandad arrived in style at the Dulles baggage claim. The cart driver was female, young, and pixie cute. I should've known. I wondered if that'd been happenstance, or if Grandad had reserved her along with the cart. He was movie-star handsome and attracted plenty of attention wherever he went. I'd always thought he resembled Douglas Fairbanks, Jr., in his silver fox days. Grandad's suit, topped by a long cashmere coat and a hat tipped at a rakish angle, only emphasized his aged swashbuckler look.

I suddenly regretted this afternoon's wardrobe choices. I'd dressed for warmth and comfort, not New York Fashion Week.

It was too late now.

Grandad spotted me and his face lit up. *"Ciao, bella!"*

Instantly, everyone looked for the gorgeous creature that had to be the object of such a greeting. What they found was me. A few people glanced back and forth between the two of us in confusion.

I'll have you know I clean up very well. Just not this afternoon.

I was wearing jeans and a sweater, topped by a fun and funky car coat I'd found in a vintage clothing store. I was wearing my favorite combat boots in deference to the slushy patches left from the last snow—and present circumstances. Grandad was Hollywood's Golden Age. I was shabby chic—and proud of it.

Grandad used his cane to disembark. He didn't really need it; he just liked the look of it. Like me, Grandad was fond of his accessories. He'd had his sword cane with him in Zurich, but he would've had to check it with his baggage.

I gave him a longer than usual hug, then slipped my arm through his.

"Ms. Harper, this is my granddaughter, Aurora. Aurora, this is Claire Harper."

"Nice to meet you." I reached in the back to get Grandad's carry-on satchel. "Did he behave himself?" I asked with a smile.

"The perfect gentleman," she assured me. "And so interesting to talk to."

"Oh, he's a talker all right." Grandad found stolen and lost art for a living. For fun, he could meet someone and know their entire life history in less than ten minutes. Everybody in the art crime world knew him, and he knew them—everything about them. He was a networking master.

He gave her a dazzling smile and tipped his hat. "Never have I had such an entertaining and enjoyable journey from the gate. My thanks, Ms. Harper."

Grandad waved and his smile faded as she drove away. "What an abysmal flight."

I slid an arm around his waist in a hug. "I'm sorry. That's a tough flight under the best of circumstances."

"That you couldn't tell me anything made it worse."

"I know. And again, I'm sorry. I'll tell you now. Turn off your phone."

We walked close, our heads together, and our voices down. I told him everything I knew and had sensed, including at the crime scene, the town house, and the block beyond. To say he was angry that his home had been broken into was an understatement, but he didn't blow up. Grandad wasn't a blow-up kind of guy. He merely added it to the rage he had simmering at the murder of his best friend. Someone, or multiple someones, would pay in due time.

The ground crew was slow in unloading the luggage on Grandad's flight, and for once I was grateful for the delay. We found seats away from any potentially prying eyes and ears where we could see any luggage arrive while I finished my report.

Grandad was leaning forward, elbows on his knees, his hat between his hands, hands that worried at the brim. "Julian called me less than an hour before we left the house to fly to Zurich. He said he needed to see me."

"Did he give any indication what it was about?"

"None. When I told him we were on our way out the door, he said it would keep until I got back. I didn't believe him. I tried to get him to tell me over the phone, but he insisted it would keep. I accepted him at his word. If our conversations were being monitored, perhaps that was why this man was in our office last night."

"So you don't know anyone named David in relation to Julian?"

"No. But Julian kept his personal life strictly separate from his government work." He sighed and sat back. "I should have pushed. I could have asked him to meet me here or gone to meet him and taken a later flight."

"You couldn't have known what was going to happen."

"Julian's dead, and Alan, too. I can't believe it. Did you bring Julian's watch with you?"

"In my bag. I wasn't about to leave it at home."

"I can take a look at it during the drive."

"No way. After ten hours on a plane, you're exhausted. That watch packs a punch. I'm not about to have you pass out while I'm behind the wheel in rush-hour traffic. It can wait."

"That's what Julian said."

The conveyor belt started and seconds later, luggage began moving into the claim area.

Grandad stood, leaning more than usual on his cane. "When did *you* last sleep?"

I got up and gathered my coat and Grandad's carry-on. "Other than a two-hour nap just before sunup, I've been trying to remember, and I'm not really sure."

"That's what I thought."

"Once you're home and rested, I'll give you Julian's watch. Then I might take another try with it." I put my arm through his. "We can pass out together. Then it'll be Gerald's problem."

CHAPTER 13

I'd driven Grandad's vintage Mercedes to pick him up.
Like Grandad, it had all its original parts, no restoration, just classic elegance and grace. A real head-turner. He'd owned it since it was almost new. He'd only driven it around town and on the occasional trip up to New York, so the mileage was low for its age, which Grandad preferred to think of as life experience.

I knew that with his flight getting in around 4:00, we'd be right in the middle of Washington's notorious rush-hour traffic going home, so I'd packed us a snack. Grandad thought airline food was intrinsically wrong. We Donatis lived life with our hearts and stomachs. I'd made prosciutto paninis with melted burrata cheese and cut them into bite sizes because Grandad was picky about eating in his car. I'd also included plenty of napkins to stave off any potential protests. I figured that the sandwiches and two bottles of Pellegrino would be enough to keep either one of us from getting peckish. Whether or not I experienced flashes of homicidal road rage was up to the other drivers. Too bad they didn't make signs to put in your back window warning others of a sleep-deprived and irritated driver. But if there were such a thing, every car inside the Beltway would be sporting one.

Grandad didn't complain about me turning his treasured car into a rolling restaurant, and actually ate half his sandwich before resuming his questioning. "What is Simmons doing to keep the sanctity of our home from being violated again?"

I grinned. "He left two guards that are at this very moment making the neighbors either feel safer or confirming that we're as much trouble as they've always believed we were."

"They have no sense of adventure."

"Their loss," I agreed.

Grandad saluted me with his Pellegrino.

"Simmons also left gifts." I nodded toward the device nestled in the car's console storage slot. "If someone slipped a tracker on us while I was in the airport, this little beauty will block its signals. We have one in our office and my apartment as well."

Grandad nodded in approval. "Nice to know my investment in home security hasn't been a complete waste."

"Talk to me about the reason we've turned the house into an armed camp," I said.

"Pardon?"

"The guy who pulled a Miss Eleanor in our backyard," I clarified.

"An outlier."

Now it was my turn to be confused. "Excuse—"

"It sounds better than freak or mutant, does it not?"

"Is that what we're dealing with?"

"Talent at that level isn't an impossibility, merely rare. *Extremely* rare. Miss Franklin spent most of her life locked away in her own home or institutionalized. Marcus and Anne's clinic was a heaven on Earth for her. Asylums in the early part of the last century were barbaric storage facilities where humans were treated like animals, and what they called cures were little more than medically sanctioned torture. It's no wonder Miss Franklin came into your parents' care a shell of a human being who would strike out at the slightest provocation, and it's a testament to their talent and compassion that her last years were probably the happiest and most peaceful she had ever experienced."

Mom was an empath and Dad was a psychometric like me and Grandad, except Dad's gift was with people rather than objects. My parents made an amazing team. What better way to treat those with mental illness than to be able to diagnose them with a touch, knowing precisely what their patients were feeling and the reasons behind those emotions. I could never do what they did. They were my heroes.

"The man in our office last night had nothing wrong or off about his mind," I said. "He was the consummate professional."

"Which makes him all the more dangerous. He controls his PK; it does not control him. Does Samuel have any idea of who he may be?"

"None. Though Rees does suspect that he's connected to the intelligence community either officially or unofficially."

"Not a surprise, really," Grandad said. "Such an individual

would go to extreme lengths to keep themselves hidden. That he used his PK last night indicates not sloppiness, but a need to escape with the least possibility of identification or capture. The most efficient means to an end."

I slowed down for yet another traffic backup on the GW Parkway. "But he wanted me to find him."

"I believe he wants something from you. When you sensed him in the Russell Building, he knew who and what you were. That and the care he took in our office says that not only does he know about you, he's aware of the high level of your ability. He's dangerous, and as far as I'm concerned, he has now extended that danger to you. We need to discover who he is and neutralize his threat to you."

"Neutralize? Now you sound like the intelligence people we try to avoid."

"To successfully engage a lion, one must not think like a gazelle."

I smiled. "Okay, Mufasa, what's our next move?"

"I will make a few discreet inquiries among those I know in the government's psychic research community whom I trust not to broadcast my interest. And yes, there are a few. Regardless of whether those inquiries bear fruit or not, we will continue to investigate Julian and Alan's deaths under our FBI cover. If our PK intruder does not find the answers he seeks elsewhere, I believe he will contact you."

"Why doesn't that fill me with the warm and fuzzies?"

"It shouldn't. You know him now and will be able to recognize him when he crosses your path. I don't suppose you would agree to Simmons assigning a guard to you for the duration?"

"You suppose right. I'll be careful."

Grandad sighed. "Why does that not fill me with the 'warm and fuzzies'?"

When we got to the town house, Gerald met us at the door. Grandad had alerted him that he was returning early, so Gerald had caught the morning shuttle back from Boston.

While Gerald put the finishing touches on dinner, Grandad went upstairs to unpack, and at my insistence, take a nap. I told him there was no way I was letting him get his hands on Julian's watch until he rested and ate.

My phone rang.

Samuel Rees.

"Anything new?" I asked, dispensing with a greeting.

"Yes, but not nearly enough. The autopsies are complete. Cause of death for both men is cardiac arrest, not heart attack. Their hearts were healthy for men of their ages and there were no blockages, and there were no burn marks or indications that any type of device had been used."

"Any drugs or poisons?"

"Not in the first pass. Final toxicology reports will take more time. In addition to the air being tested for inhalants, the ductwork was searched for any canisters. All negative." Rees paused. "The time of death for both men was nearly identical."

"And Nate Baxter's doppelgänger was in Julian's office for less than a minute."

"Doppelgänger. A ghostly double who haunts its living counterpart. An appropriate analogy."

"And equally spooky since it's looking like he killed two men. The big question is how. Does anyone have any ideas?"

"The ME hasn't given up. We've also brought in two specialists from the CDC and an expert on exotic poisons. Some elements are undetectable in an autopsy."

"Working all the angles."

"Until we run out of angles to work."

"What then?"

Silence.

"Yeah, I thought so." I changed the subject. "I connected two more times with the watch. I picked up that there wasn't any physical contact between Julian and his killer. If there had been, I would've sensed it, and I didn't."

"That would corroborate what the ME found, or didn't find. No bruising or injuries from a struggle with an attacker."

"I just picked up Grandad from the airport. He wants to have a go with Julian's watch after dinner. I'll let you know what he finds."

"Good."

"Did you turn up anything from Julian's staff?"

"We're still interviewing and following up on potential leads. The senator's appointments as well as Alan Coe's have been checked going back six months. There are five Davids on the list. Elaine Pierce doesn't know of any man named David who was in her grandfather's social or professional circles. Also, we can't assume that the senator was the primary target. We're looking into Coe's background and personal associations as well."

"What about Nate Baxter?" I asked.

"He's being held temporarily, more in protective custody than anything."

"You think he could be guilty?"

"I don't believe so, but someone went to a lot of trouble to impersonate him. We checked his financials, and a hundred thousand dollars was deposited into his savings account late yesterday."

I whistled. "That doesn't look good."

"Mr. Baxter was most astounded and dismayed." I could hear the smile in Rees's voice.

"I'll bet he was. Though for what he's being put through, he deserves to keep the money."

"I think Mr. Baxter is very fortunate to be alive, and we're determined to keep him that way. By the way, we got a hit on the M Street traffic cams."

"You got him?"

"Somewhat."

"That doesn't sound promising."

"He knew there were cameras, so he ran without lights and covered his license plate. We've identified the motorcycle as a BMW K1300S."

"Nice bike."

"We're running down registrations in the area—or reports of stolen."

"It was his. He loves that bike. I felt it."

"Then it shouldn't take long."

"Did you get any good stills?"

"A few."

"Could you send me the best one? I want to see him."

CHAPTER 14

There was a surprise waiting for me in the dining room. Grandad was already up and sitting at his usual spot at the head of the table, a glass of red wine at his elbow, reading the latest *Washington Post*.

A lot of people got their news on their phones or tablets, but in DC, there was still a thriving business in newsprint. Grandad subscribed to the print version of the *Post* and the *Times*—both the New York and UK versions.

"Anything about Julian?" I asked.

"On the front page, but beneath the fold. They probably had to pull a similar-sized story this morning to fit it in."

"What are they calling it?"

"Heart attack. Most of what's here is the obituary they had on file."

"You couldn't pay me enough to be famous," I said. "Knowing your obit's already written and whenever you screw up, they go back in your file and add a couple more sentences. By the way, Rees just called." I recapped our brief conversation.

Grandad was looking straight ahead, brow furrowed in concentration. He slowly shook his head. "Has Rees spoken with Elaine? She must be devastated."

"He has. She doesn't know of anyone named David in Julian's personal or professional circles. Have you been able to think of anyone who would want Julian dead?"

"Just all of the opposition. Julian was one of the most powerful senators on Capitol Hill. Openly, they'll mourn the death of a true patriot and great American who was taken from us too soon. Behind closed doors? I imagine there will be more than a few celebratory toasts from the bottom-drawer bottle of Scotch. The maneuvering will have already begun to take advantage of the other side having suffered a loss to its ranks."

"Washington's vultures don't have wings," I said.

"No, they don't. Julian was in the Senate for nearly forty years. He was a good, decent, and kind man. A straight shooter. Incorruptible."

"And that's probably what got him killed."

Grandad nodded. "Directly or indirectly. Unfortunately, the list of those who tried to get Julian to push his principles to the side is long. I don't believe any of his political rivals would have done it or paid to have it done. The manner of death only raises more questions."

I sat in the chair next to Grandad's, Julian's watch in my gloved hand.

"I never asked how you got it," he said.

"I didn't. Rees did. He took advantage of a distraction and stole it right off Julian's wrist."

Grandad nearly choked on his wine. Though it was hard to tell how much was choking and how much was laughter.

"That Rees is a rascal," he finally managed.

"And then some," I agreed.

"Julian wouldn't have minded."

"That's what Rees said."

"If Julian had been drawing his last breath and knew that watch would help catch the bastard who'd killed him, he'd have sat up and given it to Rees himself." He set his wineglass far enough away from him that he wouldn't accidentally knock it over if the visions got too intense. He knew only too well how this could go.

"I'm ready," he told me.

"At the dinner table?"

Also like Nero Wolfe, Grandad adamantly refused to do business at the breakfast, lunch, or dinner table. Brunch, he refused to acknowledge as a meal at all. Too nouveau.

"Julian was my best friend. For him, I'm willing to make an exception."

I placed the watch on the table in front of him.

"After dinner, I'll call Elaine and arrange for a visit tomorrow morning," Grandad said. "That is, if it's convenient for her. Julian knew about my abilities. It's possible he told Elaine. I hope he did. If not, I intend to tell her and ask if we can have access to his home office. Desperate times call for desperate measures."

"You know her well enough to trust her?"

"Yes. I've known her since she was a little girl."

I'd met Elaine during a Christmas party at Julian's McLean, Virginia, home. The handshake had revealed that she was cut from the same cloth as her grandfather. Grandad knew her better, and I trusted his instincts about people without hesitation.

Grandad quickly picked up the watch and slid it over his hand and onto his wrist. It was a perfect fit.

Grandad leaned back in his chair and closed his eyes, preparing himself to sense what his friend had experienced in his final moments. He could block images from an object until he was ready to receive them. He was teaching me how, but it still wasn't easy for me.

His breathing remained steady, his chest slowly rising and falling. The only sign anything unusual was happening was behind his closed eyes. They were darting back and forth as in REM sleep as he "watched" Julian's thoughts. Unfortunately, he wasn't actually seeing anything; if he had been, he would've seen the man in the office with Julian and that would've solved all our problems.

Seconds later, he opened his eyes and removed the watch. I detected a mild tremor as he did so. He had just witnessed his best friend's death and had been unable to do anything to prevent it.

Grandad gazed down at the watch for a few moments. As I had when I'd linked with the watch, he was processing what he had sensed and comparing it to the facts we knew so far.

"Julian was in full command of his faculties," he said. "There were no drugs, nothing that disoriented him in any way. His mind was as I remembered." He paused, his blue eyes glistening with unshed tears. Then he cleared his throat, all business. "I don't believe he was in denial about having a heart attack. He knew very well that it was possible for a man of his age regardless of how healthy he was. He used to joke about it, saying that was how he wanted to go, quickly, at his desk, working—or better yet, on the Senate floor to the inconvenience of his opposition. Admittedly, there's never a good time to die, but the denial I sensed that 'it wasn't possible' doesn't fit with what I knew about him. He meant something else."

"I hadn't considered that," I said. "You knew him, I didn't." Grandad's hands were flat on the table on either side of his friend's watch. I put my hand over one of his with a quick rub and light squeeze. I didn't want to disrupt, but at the same time, I needed to offer some comfort for what he was having to do.

"I also believe we can eliminate any individual or event in his personal life," Grandad continued. "Julian compartmentalized like no one I'd ever met. With all that he'd done during his life, he had to. This had to do with his job. I'm almost certain."

"Being a senator covers a lot of ground, and in his case, a lot of years."

"The warning he received from whoever David is was recent and had been weighing heavily on his mind."

"So, he may have talked to someone about it."

Grandad sighed. "Or tried to, the day we left for Zurich."

"That wasn't your fault," I said. "Julian could have told you. He chose not to."

Grandad waved a dismissive hand. He knew I was right, but that did nothing to lessen his pain and guilt. "Julian believed in keeping his own counsel, especially if it was of a sensitive nature involving his committee work. Also, he'd been out of the CIA for many years, but he still had contacts there."

"Berta said he was on the Intelligence, Armed Services, and Finance committees. I knew he'd served in the Marines and was ex-CIA."

"It was in his younger days, but neither organization believes in being an 'ex.' Once a Marine or a spook, always a Marine or a spook. Julian always said he left the CIA for politics because at least politicians had some morals."

I snorted.

"Exactly. Much of his work on the Intelligence and Armed Services committees was classified, and he wouldn't have been able to discuss it with anyone outside of the committee. Alan Coe would have been a goldmine of information. He's been Julian's senior aide for nearly ten years. Every phone call, email, meeting, appointment—Alan kept him on schedule. Julian told me that Alan was part gatekeeper, part attack dog. If anything pertaining to Julian's committee work could be shared, he would have shared it with Alan."

"And now Alan's dead, too. I'd thought he simply was in the wrong place at the wrong time. Maybe he wasn't collateral damage after all."

CHAPTER 15

Julian Pierce's house in McLean was walled and gated, much to the media's disappointment.

Berta was driving an FBI SUV with blacked-out windows. Grandad and I were on the bench seat in the back, out of the line of sight. We'd known better than to drive the Mercedes. The last thing we needed was for an enterprising reporter to run the plates, and then we'd have a three-ring media circus of our very own outside the town house.

After Grandad had linked with Julian's watch, I'd called Rees back and told him what Grandad had discovered, and about his idea to pay a condolence call on Elaine first thing in this morning. The plan was that if she didn't already know about Grandad's abilities, he would give her a demonstration and make a quick believer out of her. He was betting she was open-minded enough to accept it.

Rees approved and asked Berta to see us there and back

unseen by the media. He'd tell the agents guarding the house to expect us. He said Elaine had already been interviewed, but between Grandad's abilities and his being a good friend of her grandfather, he'd probably learn more than they had, which hadn't been nearly enough.

Two FBI agents met the three of us at the door.

Julian's granddaughter was standing motionless in the hall a few feet behind them.

Elaine Pierce was slender, poised, and confident. Only the slightest hint of red around her eyes betrayed the emotion she had allowed herself to release. As one of the youngest congresswomen ever elected, and the granddaughter of the country's most beloved senator, she had attracted more attention than she'd probably ever wanted, especially from those who still refused to believe she had been elected on her own merits and platform, instead seeing her as having used her grandfather's name and influence to get elected. Now that her grandfather was dead, that attention would be magnified tenfold.

The hotshot freshman congresswoman, a lawyer, top of her class at Harvard. The pundits were saying that the only reason she ran for Congress was that her grandfather was already the senator from their state. Once he retired, look out.

But Julian hadn't retired. He'd been murdered.

My heart went out to her, but Elaine didn't want my pity or even sympathy. Her alert eyes met mine, her gaze strong and direct, her jaw set. This was a woman who wanted answers. Now.

Grandad broke the ice. He stepped forward, his arms open. "Elaine."

She pressed her lips together against the tears that threatened to come. In three strides, she was in Grandad's arms. I knew from experience that when you needed some serious comforting, that was the best place to be in the whole wide world.

After a few moments, she pulled back a little, and Grandad slipped one arm around her shoulders as he steered her toward the back of the house. He'd been here before and knew where he was going.

I followed. Berta stayed with the two FBI agents.

Grandad had guided Elaine to a small sitting room. Adjacent, with the door mostly open, was a classic English gentleman's study.

Julian's office.

Leave it to Grandad to be comforting and calculating at the same time. I was in the presence of a master.

"Elaine, do you remember my granddaughter and agency partner, Aurora?"

Elaine turned and dabbed the underside of each eye with a Kleenex. She might have been wearing a little makeup, but not anything on her eyes. Smart move, and practical. She knew she'd be crying, that mascara would run, and screw anyone who'd see her without TV-camera-ready makeup.

Good for her.

I extended my hand. "Please call me Rory."

She took it in a firm clasp. "Elaine."

I instantly got strong impressions, albeit contradictory. Elaine Pierce was having some strong emotions, but on the surface, she'd quickly regained her composure. As a politician, she'd mastered the art of maintaining a calm and cool exterior when she was angry, frustrated, impatient, exhausted, any and all of the emotions she'd experienced during the race for her New York congressional seat. It'd been a brutal one.

The incumbent had gone after her with everything he could find. Then he started digging for dirt on her grandad to see if he could find anything that could rub off on her. Elaine had hung tough, refusing to stoop to her opponent's level—at least not publicly. The media got wind of two particularly juicy scandals involving her opponent from a mysterious source. I'd wondered if that source had been one of Elaine's staffers acting on her instructions. At that point, Elaine had simply stepped back, taken the high road, and let the media do their worst. She'd had made her first cuts count, putting blood in the water. The media smelled it, and soon it was a piranha feeding frenzy. If he hadn't deserved every last bit of it, I'd have almost felt sorry for him. He'd lost in a landslide.

"Please, make yourselves comfortable," Elaine told us. "Could I get you some tea or coffee?"

"Thank you, dear," Grandad said, "but no. We're here to extend our condolences, but we've also come to—"

Elaine held up a hand, stopping him. "I was so glad to get your call last night. If you hadn't called, I was going to call you. My grandfather had told me of your unique talent, and I believe you can help find his killer. Is that why you're here?"

So much for Grandad having to put on a dog and pony show.

His smile lit up his blue eyes. "Yes. You just saved us a lot of effort."

Elaine quickly glanced at me. "Us?"

I gave her a little shrug. "It runs in the family."

"I was in Zurich until late yesterday," Grandad said. "I came home as soon as I heard." He gave me a fond smile. "But Aurora had already been called in within an hour of Julian and Alan's deaths. We have several contacts in the FBI who are aware of and appreciate our 'unique talent,' as you expressed it."

Now I had Elaine's full, undivided attention. "You saw my grandfather's body in his office?"

"Yes."

"They tell me the autopsy results indicate a cardiac arrest. Is that true?"

"That's what the report says."

"But you don't believe it."

"It was a cardiac arrest," I told her, "but considering his exceptional health, the FBI is looking into what may have induced it—and who was responsible for it."

Elaine nodded, as if I'd confirmed her own suspicions.

"He just had a physical," she said. "There was absolutely nothing wrong with his heart. I asked that he allow me to speak with his doctor. He would've said everything was fine even if it wasn't. He wouldn't have wanted me to worry. But after Grandmother's death, if there was anything wrong with him that could be fixed or treated, or if a change in diet would—" Her voice broke. "I wanted to know about it so I could help him."

"And he gave permission."

Elaine nodded, crushing the tissue in her hand. "Dr. Hare said my grandfather was in amazing condition for his age, and that his heart and everything else was perfectly healthy. And to hear that Alan died of cardiac arrest at the same time…That's impossible. He and his wife ran marathons."

I didn't know what Rees or anyone else from the FBI had told her, so I kept the search for undetectable poisons to myself.

"I would ask who would want to kill my grandfather," Elaine continued, "but being in politics myself now, I realize that question would be rather naïve. I know that my grandfather had been threatened before, many times over the years. That was one of the reasons for having a house here with a wall and gate. He wanted to make sure his family was safe. Any threatening communication he ever received was immediately sent to the FBI. He didn't take any chances."

"Are you still living here?" I asked.

"Yes and no. I have an apartment in Albany, but during the election madness, I moved back here when I wasn't on the road to have some semblance of privacy. I'm living here temporarily until I can find an apartment in DC. Grandfather thought it was ridiculous for me to even look for another place, but I knew he understood." She hesitated. "Why kill him in his office? I'd always thought the least safe place he ever went was the golf course. All that open area surrounded by woods." She gave Grandad a smile. "I know you don't play golf, Mr. Donati. My grandfather used to tease him about it," she said to me as an aside.

Grandad thought golf was an absurd and pointless game. First, he would have to wear clothes he wouldn't be caught dead in. He would have to hit a little white ball until it landed in a hole. Then he would be forced to stroll around a ridiculously manicured lawn and repeat the first step another seventeen times. He said it was no wonder men drank while playing golf. How else could they deal with the mind-numbing tedium?

Grandad preferred fencing and chess. Fencing was known as physical chess, so they went together well. Grandad had insisted to my parents that I take fencing. I'd been taking ballet, and while I liked it okay, I dropped it in a hot minute to take fencing. Grandad had been thrilled. He'd had a fencing strip installed in the town house's basement gym. I had yet to win a match against him—either fencing or chess.

"Did you notice whether Julian seemed worried or preoccupied during the past few days?" Grandad asked.

Elaine tried to smile. "How would that be different from his normal? There was no limit to the number of irons he had in various fires."

"Had he received any warnings or threats in the past few days?"

"No, not that I'm aware of. But my grandfather was extremely high-profile and never turned from a fight. He made a lot of enemies over the years: on the Senate floor, in Washington, in corporate boardrooms."

All were the kind of people who had the power, influence, and money to kill Julian Pierce in one of the most public ways possible to stop his interference.

I glanced at Grandad, who gave me the barest nod.

"I'd like to tell you what I sensed while in your grandfather's office," I said to Elaine.

"I want to hear it."

I told her what I'd felt from touching Alan, what I sensed from the area of carpet in Julian's office, and lastly, the impressions I received from holding his watch.

Then Grandad told her what he had learned.

Tears were running down Elaine's face when we finished.

"We're so sorry," I told her. "I didn't think how much that would—"

Elaine waved my apology away, her voice breaking. "No, no. I'm grateful to know his last moments. He died in pain, but at least it…It was quick." She then broke down sobbing.

Since I hardly knew her, I let Grandad do what he did best. I just kept handing her Kleenex.

One of the FBI agents opened the door and stuck his head

in. I told him it was okay. He probably should have stayed to have heard it from Elaine herself, but he was obviously uncomfortable with a crying woman and grateful to be able to close the door.

It didn't take long for Elaine to regain control of herself. I really didn't want to do what I had planned to do next, but it was time to return Julian's watch. Grandad and I had gotten everything we could from it.

I took the watch out of my messenger bag, steeling myself against the contact—and held it out to Elaine.

She took one look at my face and knew. "It's still speaking to you, isn't it?"

I stopped trying to hide the wince. "Yes. But it's the same each time."

"Each time?"

"I've connected with it three times," I smiled tightly. "And now is number four."

Elaine quickly took it from me. "Thank you. Especially for this. I had no idea what an ordeal it must be for you, for both of you."

I resisted rubbing my hands on my legs to negate the sensations they'd picked up. "It's what we do. I wanted to be sure I'd gotten everything I could from your grandfather's watch before returning it to you. I didn't want to miss any clues. Repetition is important, to confirm and to hopefully sense something new."

Grandad got to the real reason we were here. "Elaine, may we search Julian's office?"

CHAPTER 16

Julian Pierce obviously spent a lot of time in his study.

There were hundreds of books, a desk that was used for work and not just for show with every inch of surface covered with papers, and an impressive collection of art and trophy fish. In between various stuffed fish on the walls were antique fly-fishing rods.

The sensations coming off each object and every surface came close to being overpowering. We had our work cut out for us to find any relevant clues when the room was saturated with the man's presence.

One presence I didn't feel was the man who had broken into our house and searched our office. Odd that he hadn't at least attempted to do the same here.

Grandad shrugged out of his suit jacket, popped off his cuff links, and rolled up his sleeves.

"Looks like you're up for the challenge," I noted.

"It's not like we have a choice," he said grimly. He turned to Elaine. "Have you opened your grandfather's safe behind the Remington?"

"Yes. It was insurance and legal papers, and a copy of his will."

"May I examine them, please?"

"Of course."

I went to the bookshelves. Three walls of the office were lined with them from floor to high ceiling. When Grandad didn't find anything in Julian's papers, he started on the top of his friend's desk, working his way down to the drawer contents.

Unfortunately, we didn't know what we were looking for, but we knew the sensation we were hoping to get from one of the thousands of objects in the room.

The psychic zap of strong emotions.

Julian had died while wearing his watch. He'd received a warning from a man named David within days of his death. This office had been his inner sanctum. Maybe, just maybe, there was a clue to David's identity or what he had warned Julian about.

Julian had a little bit of everything in his library. A lot of military and political history, biographies, art, literary classics, and political thrillers. I also found the complete collections of Sherlock Holmes and Nero Wolfe.

I wholeheartedly approved of Julian's literary taste.

I ran my hand just above the spines of each and every book. I could tell the ones he'd read most recently, but none radiated the strong emotion we were looking for.

I had to stand on tiptoe on the ladder to reach the last, topmost shelf, home to what I could only call esoteric funkiness, much of which could be described as government conspiracies. As he came from a CIA background, I could see where Julian would find some of it entertaining or perhaps hitting close to home. Maybe they'd been gag gifts from his CIA days. Most of the books had a fine coating of dust.

One did not.

It was also out of place. It belonged down with the classics. The rest of Julian's collection was shelved according to genre, then author. This book had a single fingerprint in the dust on top of the spine, right where you would tip a book to remove it from a high shelf.

Or to put it there.

Julian, or someone, had climbed this ladder and touched this book very recently.

There, among the government-conspiracy books, was *Frankenstein* by Mary Shelley.

I put my hand just above the spine, having to lean out to do so.

I quickly drew my hand back. FBI techs would have to confirm that it was Julian's fingerprint, but I didn't need any tests to know that Julian had held this book within the past few days, and that he'd felt concern bordering on fear when he'd done so.

"I think I've got something," I said. "Grandad, could you get my leather gloves out of my bag?"

He did and passed them up the ladder to me.

I slid on the gloves and gently removed the book, careful not to touch the single fingerprint. Once I had a good grip, I went down the ladder. I didn't want to touch the book with my bare hands until I had both feet solidly on the floor.

"Did *Frankenstein* mean anything in particular to your grandfather?" I asked Elaine.

"Not that I know of."

Odd that he would've chosen this book at random. Equally odd was the book's weight. It felt a little off. I carefully opened it.

Oh boy.

Grandad peered at what was nestled in the small cutout section of pages. "What's that?"

"My guess is a burner phone."

Elaine was appalled and didn't try to hide it. "Why would my grandfather have a burner phone?"

"Movies and TV have given burners a bad rap," I assured her. "Yes, criminals use them, but so do people who don't want others to have their primary phone number. Like if you're selling something online or going on a date with someone you just met. They can contact you, but only on the number assigned to the burner phone. There are even apps now that let you use your regular phone with a temporary number. Your grandfather may have been protecting his contact's identity. There's nothing wrong with it."

Or there could be everything wrong with it, but I didn't tell Elaine that.

I wasn't about to touch that burner phone. I knew what it was and whose it was. This was not my area of expertise, and this little phone was the first real break we'd had.

That being said, I could put my hand above the cutout section that was just large enough to accommodate the flip phone. I'd be almost touching it, but not quite.

We called Berta in to the room and showed her what we'd found. She immediately called Rees.

"He'll be here within the hour with a tech who'll make that phone sing," she told us after ending the call.

I concentrated on getting my bare hand as close to the phone as I could without making actual contact. "I'm going to have a chat with it right now. And no, I'm not touching it," I added.

I sensed anger and worry directed at whoever Julian had used the phone to call.

Too close…foolish risk…we're not ready…go fish.

"We?" I muttered. "Who's 'we' and what's 'go fish'?"

"Like the kids' card game?" Berta asked.

"That's all I can think of. Elaine, does that mean anything to you?"

She shook her head. "My grandfather used to fish with some of his friends—as you can see from the walls. Mainly trout, but occasionally bass."

"Where did they go?"

"The Adirondacks. There were a couple of rivers and lakes they liked."

"Could you get us a list? Of the places he went and who he went with?"

"I could try. He liked photography and took a lot of photos of those trips. I'll see if I can find them. Though when my grandmother got sick, he stopped going, so it's been at least six years since he last went."

Elaine went in search of photos or anything related to her grandfather's fishing trips. Rees and two techs arrived a few minutes later—only thirty minutes after Berta had called him—no doubt breaking many traffic laws on the way.

I showed him the book.

"Isn't that clever?" he murmured. "And such an interesting choice of title."

"Yeah, I got the feeling it wasn't a random choice. I don't know what it means, but I don't think he just pulled a book off the shelf."

"Gentlemen," Rees said to the two young agents, "work your magic."

One tech dusted the phone and the spine of the book for prints, finding that all of them belonged to Julian Pierce.

"How do you guys have his prints?" I asked.

"They took them in the morgue," Rees said.

"What all can you get from the phone?" I asked the other tech.

He glanced at Rees, who nodded.

"I'll access any deleted voice mails or texts and get all the numbers from incoming and outgoing calls." He glanced down at the phone and pushed a few keys. "The last texts that were sent and received weren't deleted. They were sent Wednesday afternoon at 12:44. The outgoing text says, 'Go fish.' It's signed J. The response of 'Done' came at 12:46. It was signed D."

Could D be our elusive David?

Grandad indicated the burner phone. "May I?" he asked Rees.

"Pete, may we borrow the phone for a few minutes before you get started?"

"Yes, sir."

Rees gave it to Grandad who went back into the sitting room out of sight of the two agents. I followed him, and Rees followed me. Grandad and I operated on a "need to know basis." Those two young agents didn't need to know, but Rees did.

"By the way," he said, "the registration on that BMW bike came back to an Adam Granger."

"Where does he live?" I asked.

"He doesn't."

"He's dead?"

"He doesn't exist. Neither does the address. It's a vacant lot in Alexandria."

"What does that mean?"

"If he's with an agency, we have no way of finding out which one." He paused. "Or he could be a foreign agent."

"Crap."

"Agreed."

"The few words I got from him were in English," I said. "It doesn't mean he's a native speaker, but generally a person's thoughts are in their primary language."

Grandad told Rees about Julian's call.

"And he gave you no indication of why he wanted to meet?" Rees asked.

"None. Though I think we can safely conclude Aurora's visitor would know the reason." Grandad sat and pressed the phone between his palms, head bowed, eyes closed. He remained that way for about ten seconds. Then he opened his eyes and leaned back, sorting and pondering what he'd sensed. He was still holding the phone.

"Three things," he said quietly. "*The project was successful months ago. The failures were a diversion. It wasn't supposed to happen this fast.* I got the feeling that 'it was successful months ago' was unwelcome news for Julian. The 'failures were a diversion' was Julian's own conclusion, as was 'it wasn't supposed to happen this fast.'" Grandad held out the phone to me.

I took it. "Can I open it to hold?" I asked Rees.

"Please do."

I opened the flip phone and held it as Grandad had.

They're too close...you took a foolish risk...we're not ready to move...go fish.

I told them what I'd gotten, which was only a little more than I had before.

"And judging from that text," I added, "I think that 'go fish' may have been some kind of prearranged signal. I think Julian was telling David to run."

CHAPTER 17

Minutes later, Rees got a call from his boss, SAC Roger Hudson. We had a new problem, a big one.

The media had found out about Alan Coe's death. Not only that he was dead, but when, where, and how.

Within the hour, the news channels were filled with conspiracy theories and the "experts" who peddled them. Some were speculating about the "sound attacks" at the Cuban, Russian, and Chinese embassies in recent years, and that perhaps heart attacks could be brought on this way as well.

It now seemed that everyone in Washington knew Julian Pierce or Alan Coe. The media was interviewing their colleagues or anyone who even remotely knew them or could get away with claiming to know them or had an opinion about how they really died. Since the FBI was keeping its collective mouth shut and only issuing official statements, the rest of Washington was leaking like the sieve it was. It was the nature of the political beast. The men and women filling the slots on CNN, MSNBC, and Fox were looking for any excuse to get their faces on TV. It didn't matter that they were essentially stepping on dead men to reach those cameras.

The media outside Julian's home had thinned a little because they now had more people to cover. Rees said that the FBI had dispatched agents to the homes of Julian's other two aides. They had also moved Nate Baxter to a safe house. It'd be only a matter of time until the media found out about a suspected assassin and the attempt to frame Baxter for the murders. The money that had been deposited into his account had come from a bank in the Cayman Islands by way of a bank in Cyprus.

"This particular bank is known for handling Russian and Middle Eastern money that comes from less than savory sources," Rees was saying. "I believe the money trail was too easily detected."

"It was hidden, but not too well hidden," I said. "Kind of like hiding Easter eggs for toddlers."

"An apt analogy. Someone wanted us to find it."

While Elaine was looking for any photos from her grandfather's fishing trips or any documentation such as fishing licenses or cabin rental agreements that would tell us where Julian and his fishing buddies had stayed, Grandad and I continued searching Julian's office. Just because I'd found a burner phone he'd used to communicate with a person who was probably David didn't mean there weren't more clues to be found.

Rees's phone chirped with an incoming text. He glanced down and chuckled. "On occasion, the media is most helpful."

I paused while inspecting the gullet of yet another

mounted large-mouth bass for a hidden object like a flash drive. "What happened?"

"Hudson had Brandon Trevor brought in for questioning, and the media caught wind of it and was waiting for him when he left."

"Who's he?" I asked.

"The smarmy weasel everyone in America wants to punch," Berta said.

"He's the CEO of Ripton Pharmaceuticals," Rees replied. "The bill Senator Pierce was working on the night he was killed was to rein in arbitrary drug pricing. In recent weeks, Trevor has been threatening the government with a lawsuit for defamation of character and damage to his company's reputation. Last month, Trevor testified before the Senate committee investigating drug price increases. Trevor made the tactical error of losing his temper with Senator Pierce on national TV."

"And now it's come back to bite him," Berta said nodding in approval. "Nice. He and his company have essentially extorted billions from the elderly, the last people who can afford it. Trevor said that no one was forcing them to buy his drug." She snorted in derision. "Yeah, they have a choice all right. They don't buy the drug and die of a heart attack, or buy it and die of starvation while homeless."

Rees put his phone away. "Ripton's top-selling drug significantly reduces the chances of a heart attack in at-risk patients."

"And the senator who grilled the guy on TV and was writing the bill to take a big bite out of his profits dies of cardiac arrest along with his aide." I nodded. "I can see how the media came up with this."

"A most convenient diversion for us," Rees said. "After his company's latest price increase, Brandon Trevor found himself the object of derision and disgust, not the kind of attention he wanted. Hence his threat of lawsuits."

"Like the media could be controlled once they'd sunk their teeth into Ripton's collective ass." Berta gave us all a rare smile. "And it couldn't have happened to a more deserving guy."

Since moving to Washington, I'd learned that it didn't matter what the truth was. No one wanted to hear the truth. They wanted scandal, and big pharma was one of the favorite and most used punching bags. Everyone hated big pharma and loved a juicy scandal. It was two things most Americans, regardless of political party, could agree on. The politicians and pundits were always eager to pounce. If the past was any indication, a few of the pundits and guests on various news shows would take it further before too long. They would appoint themselves judge, jury, and reputation-executioner in the court of public opinion. A network or pundit's beef with their chosen target might be personal, political, business, or all of the above. The truth—or their version of it—might be stretched to the snapping point, but that didn't stop them or even slow them down. Their like-minded viewers or readers lapped it up like mother's milk.

They were all happy.

And the majority of the time, they were all wrong.

Berta had pulled up the lead article on CNN. I took a look. The video snippet was a shot of Brandon Trevor coming out of the Hoover Building after he'd been questioned. He appeared to be in his late forties, was pale, had a starter gut, and was wearing a smirk that had probably earned him more than one ass-kicking as a kid. He was also too old to have a name like Brandon.

"You're right," I told him. "I've never seen the guy before and I want to haul off and punch him."

"I'd punch him twice," Berta said.

"I don't think he'd be upright for number two."

"Bending down would be worth the effort."

I had to agree.

Elaine came back into the room carrying an open photo album.

"I think I may have something." She set the album on her grandfather's desk, peeled back the clear sheet on one of the pages, and removed a photo.

Five men were standing in a stream wearing hip waders and geared up for trout fishing. They were smiling at the camera.

"These are Grandfather's fishing buddies." Elaine turned over the photo. Julian had written the date: July 27, 2011.

Under that was a list of names.

One of them was David Barrington.

"My grandfather called him Barry," she said. "I only ever knew him as Uncle Barry. I had no idea his name was David."

"Do you have any more recent photos of him?" Rees asked.

"This one was taken just a couple of months ago." Elaine indicated a framed photo on the wall directly behind the desk of two men, both smiling—Julian Pierce and David Barrington. It was set among the senator's family photos. "There must be a reason Grandfather called him Barry. I just don't know what it was."

Rees had made a call and had the phone to his ear waiting for whoever he was calling to answer. "We'll simply find Mr. Barrington and ask him."

"Doctor," Elaine said. "It's Doctor Barrington."

"Medical doctor or PhD?" Rees asked.

"Medical. I don't know his specialty. He worked with Grandfather at the CIA."

CHAPTER 18

Dr. David Barrington had been married twice and divorced twice, most recently three years ago.

A quick dive into his medical career told us that Barrington was a neurosurgeon with a PhD in electrical engineering and computer science from MIT. He wanted to help those who were paralyzed to be able to walk, move, and live as close to a normal life as possible through chip implants in the brain that could trigger muscle movement. Rees said Barrington had disappeared into the black hole that was the CIA's science branch about five years ago.

The condo complex was named The Battery and resembled the gracious houses along Charleston's waterfront, that is if there was absolutely zero space between them. Each condo was a narrow, three-story town house backing up to the Potomac and looking across the river to Arlington. David Barrington's condo was on the end.

"Nice," I noted. "Either Barrington had a great lawyer for both divorces, or the CIA pays him enough that he can still afford this and two ex-wives."

Rees's digging had determined that one ex lived in Seattle, the other in Los Angeles. Both women had originally been from the East Coast, yet they'd seen the need to put an entire continent between them and their former dearly beloved. Rees was also working on what Barrington was doing for the CIA. His initial query had run into a brick wall. Samuel Rees had never let brick, whether actual or metaphorical, stand in his way. If he couldn't get through, he'd go around, above, or beneath. It was merely a matter of time before he had what he was looking for.

Grandad had stayed to finish his search of Julian's office, and Rees promised to see him home after they'd finished.

"This is probably naïve of me," I said, "but why don't intelligence agencies work together and share information?"

"Supposedly it's gotten better since 9/11," Berta said, "but we all have secrets that we'd rather keep in-house, especially the embarrassing kind. We're kind of like estranged siblings that way. Screw up badly enough and your brothers and sisters will never let you live it down."

"Aren't we all on the same side?"

That earned me a laugh. "Every agency in this town has two sides—ours and theirs. I expect Rees will have to call in more than a few favors to get what he wants on David Barrington."

We didn't expect to find the CIA doctor at home. You didn't use burner phones to leave cryptic messages and then hang out in the den in front of the TV.

Rees was getting a warrant for us, and would dispatch an agent with it, but we didn't need one to knock on the door and do a little discreet snooping.

There was a pair of windows on the front of the town house, but I'd have had to stand on tiptoes in the bushes to see inside, if the wooden shutters inside hadn't been closed tight.

We rang the doorbell and waited. We knocked and waited some more.

No answer.

"Judging from the amount of mail piled up, I don't think the good doctor has been home for some time." Berta had bent down and pushed open the brass mail flap on the front door. "He didn't stop the mail. He left quickly; whether it was his idea or someone else's remains to be seen. Let's take a look around back."

Floor-to-ceiling windows took up the second- and third-floor balconies. A brick patio and small yard were secured behind a six-foot brick wall and gate.

Berta tried the knob on the gate. It was locked. She took a lockpick out of her badge wallet and had the gate open in two seconds flat. "Oh look, it's unlocked."

"You're way too good at that," I told her.

"If you have a God-given talent, you should use it. Dr. Barrington is a missing person. He could be in there needing our help."

"Or dead, and past anyone's help."

"Then we owe it to his next-door neighbors to get the body out of there. I'm not breaking into the house; I'm just going to look inside."

The first-floor shutters were closed, but the slats on one were raised just enough to give us a peek.

We peered into David Barrington's living room.

Or what was left of it.

The doctor may not have been in, but someone had been,

and they hadn't cleaned up when they left. Berta had her phone out, calling Rees. When she slipped her phone back in her jacket pocket, she had her pick out again.

"We're going in without that warrant, aren't we?"

"Oh, we're still getting a warrant. We're just not waiting for it or the forensics team Rees is now sending along with it. And since we're clearly not the first people here, we probably don't need to worry about setting off an alarm." Berta quickly worked her magic on the back door, put the pick away, and drew her gun. "Stay put. I'll make sure it's clear."

I was already in. "How about I just stay behind you. You might need backup."

Berta snorted.

"Then I'll keep you company."

The furniture was overturned, the cushions slashed open, and the stuffing strewn everywhere. The books on the two built-in shelves on either side of the fireplace had been taken off the shelves, opened and tossed in a corner.

The condition of the kitchen was even worse. Every bottle, package, and container—in the refrigerator, pantry, and cabinets—had been opened. The dishes weren't broken, but they had been taken out and the cabinets searched.

Barrington's office was also on the main floor. More care had been taken in here. File drawers had been pried open and searched, but the contents had been left inside. The bookshelves had been emptied, the books searched and thrown into a pile along one wall.

I sat in David Barrington's office chair. It stood to reason that he would have spent a lot of time in his office. I needed to get a baseline sense of the man, so I could recognize his presence later.

None of the people who had ransacked the house had sat in this chair. I'd go with the assumption that the serious, inquisitive, brilliant mind I sensed from sitting in the chair was David Barrington, though I had the feeling he hadn't sat here in quite some time.

There was no phone on Barrington's desk. No landline anywhere in the house. A lot of people had ditched their landlines in favor of cell phones. Grandad still had landlines in the town house. Over in the carriage house, I did not.

I pointed out my observation to Berta.

She took out her phone and started texting. "Letting Rees know. Maybe he can track his cell." When she finished, she scanned the destroyed office. "Do you get the feeling they found what they were looking for?"

My eyes went from file cabinet, to desk, to book pile. "Same as our office. They were looking for data storage devices: flash drives, hard drives, CDs. They were only hired to find and retrieve. They didn't know what was on what they took with them, nor did they care. That wasn't their job, and they were being paid enough not to ask. They took everything they found. Unlike the guy in our office, they weren't frustrated, had no emotional attachment to what they were doing. Search everywhere, find anything that could contain data, and get out."

I sat absolutely still.

There was something else, or more to the point *someone* else. Running under the chaos of the people who had been in this office—and yes, there had been two, possibly three individuals—was a strong presence. Exceptionally strong, but faded with time. He'd been here first. Several days ago.

Before he'd paid our office a visit.

"Bingo," I murmured.

"Bingo?"

I gave Berta a slow smile. "He was here. Three, maybe four days ago."

"Mr. Tall, Cocky, and Annoyingly Limber?"

"In person."

"Before Pierce and Coe's deaths—and before he tossed your office."

I nodded.

"Everybody's looking for flash drives."

"Perhaps." I closed my eyes, letting the faded presence and his intentions wash over me. "Mostly he wanted to find David Barrington."

We went upstairs to search the rest of the condo. The two bedrooms and bathrooms had been given the same treatment. Closets had been emptied, shoe boxes opened and dumped, the mattress slashed and searched, and the art taken off the walls. Behind one was a safe. It stood open, empty. Every bottle and container in the bathrooms had been opened and emptied.

Our mystery man had come upstairs as well, but he hadn't spent as much time here as he had downstairs.

There was no blood, at least not that we'd seen, and no sign or sense of a struggle. They hadn't found David Barrington here, just his worldly goods.

The front door opened and closed.

"Excuse me, Agent Pike," a smooth male voice called from downstairs. "Perhaps I could assist."

Berta rolled her eyes and spat a silent curse. She pointed at me, then emphatically at the patch of carpet I was standing on. "Stay," she mouthed.

I didn't like it, but I couldn't object without speaking, so for once I kept my mouth shut and did as told.

For now.

Berta drew her gun, though she kept her arm down, the gun against her thigh. I'd been to the shooting range with her. She could have it up and leveled between the newcomer's eyes in an instant. "Did you make this mess, Marshall?"

"You wound me, Agent Pike. I would never be so untidy. If I'd searched this house, you'd have never known I'd been here."

The sense of the man reached me at the top of the stairs, flowing over me.

I froze.

I knew he'd been here—and in our office.

I steadied my breathing, pulling air in and out as quietly as possible. Berta and the intruder continued their banter. He didn't know I was here. Good.

I heard pieces of mail landing on the dining room table. "There ought to be a law about this much junk mail," the man was saying. "It's a wonder there are any trees left." He was moving around the table to get a better view up the stairs. He knew someone was with Berta, but he didn't know who. He had seen me in the Russell Building's rotunda. He hadn't seen me here. Yet.

I smiled in the shadows. I knew what I wanted to do. I could resist the urge, but I wasn't even going to try.

I came down the stairs. "Well, hello there, Adam Granger. We meet again."

Silence.

I'd gotten him. I could tell. Outwardly not one twitch

betrayed his surprise, but the psychic shockwave that met me said otherwise. I stopped on the small landing. It let me keep my head above his. Yes, it was petty, but I wanted to maintain as much dominance as I could.

The man was tall, dark, lean, and thirty-something. Any other man who met him on the street would consider him to be unfairly good-looking. He was wearing a suit he clearly hadn't bought off any rack. Thanks to Grandad's sartorial choices, I knew a bespoke suit when I saw one.

Berta was confused. "Adam Granger? That's not—"

"I know. It's the alias he used to register his BMW getaway bike." I kept my eyes on his pale gray ones. "Other than that, I only know him by my description to the police: tall, cocky, and annoyingly limber."

Instantly, Berta had her gun leveled on him.

The man had enough sense to raise his hands. Slowly. Then he smiled at me in a flash of white teeth. "You didn't call me any of those at the wall."

"I was exercising my vocabulary," I told him.

"I can attest that it's in fine shape." His attention went to Berta. "I assure you this is hardly necessary."

"Oh, it's necessary, and it's also my pleasure. In fact, I can't remember the last time I've enjoyed holding a gun on a man this much."

"You know my name," I told him, "but I don't know yours."

"Gabriel Marshall, CIA."

"Hmm, CIA. That explains a few things, but not nearly enough. Why were you in my grandfather's home last night?"

"Working."

"On what?"

"Classified."

"Of course."

"If it will put your mind at ease, I will not be back. Last night was a one-time visit."

"What about your other visit, when you bugged the town house, my apartment, and my grandfather's car?"

"That wasn't me."

He had no reaction that our homes and car had been bugged, not even a twitch. Yet he hadn't hesitated to deny responsibility.

Gabriel Marshall hadn't planted the bugs, but he had a good idea who had.

"Do you know who did?"

"Not at this time."

"I don't believe you."

"I didn't expect you to."

The elephant in the room was his psychokinesis. I wasn't ready to let on that I knew about his PK. He knew my secret. I'd let him think I didn't know his, and that he'd fooled me like he had Simmons's men. For now.

"Agent Pike, may I put my hands down?" Marshall asked. "As much as you would like to shoot me, you won't, at least not now, if for no other reason than all the paperwork you'd have to do."

Berta lowered her gun, but she didn't put it away. She didn't trust him, probably for good reason. It was obvious this wasn't the first time the two of them had butted heads. Right now, she had a physical advantage over Gabriel Marshall, CIA, and she wasn't about to give it up.

Marshall lowered his hands, but wisely kept them in sight. "You didn't wait for your warrant, Agent Pike. How naughty. I'm so proud. There may be hope for you yet."

I had no problem understanding why Berta didn't like this guy.

"Naturally, you don't have one," Berta said.

"I don't need one. I've been asked by Dr. Barrington's superiors to find him. He's missing, and his CIA family is concerned for his well-being."

Again, he was telling the truth. Though there was a deep undercurrent of what Gabriel Marshall wasn't saying.

"What has your family told you to do with Barrington if you find him?" Berta asked.

"You know I rarely do as told."

"True. Not unless it suits you. What does it suit you to do with Barrington?"

"Ask him a few questions, then keep him safe."

"Safe implies unharmed."

"I have no reason or need to harm Dr. Barrington." He glanced around the room. "Others do." His movement was casual, the interest negligent. The reality was that those gray eyes were making a detailed inventory of the room, its contents, their condition, and based on the damage, compiling a list of items the intruders could have been looking for.

"What do you think they wanted?" I asked him.

"Dr. Barrington could hardly have concealed himself in a sofa cushion. What these men may or may not have found here does not matter to me. My only concern is the safety of Dr. Barrington."

"So, you're staking this place out."

"Officer Marshall is a busy man," Berta said. "I'd say he's installed at least one video camera here. Who else did you see paying Dr. Barrington a visit?"

"Unfortunately, no cameras this time. If I knew where Barrington was, I would be where he is and not here."

Berta's phone rang. She answered it, never taking her eyes off the CIA officer. "Guess who's here? Our friend Gabriel Marshall."

It had to be Rees.

Her mouth twitched in a fierce smile, and I wondered if Rees's word choice had been similar to hers. "Yes, sir. I'll take care of it." Berta ended the call. "Hate to search and run, but you'll have plenty of company soon. An FBI forensics team is on the way—with a warrant."

Gabriel Marshall held out his card to me.

"Don't bother," Berta said. "I've got his number."

Marshall smiled. "In more ways than one."

CHAPTER 19

Most of the FBI hated the CIA or at least distrusted them—and the feeling was mutual.

Boy Scouts versus spooks.

By-the-book versus "Rules? What rules?"

Marshall had implied that the CIA was one big, happy family. Big families like that were seldom happy. They could put on a good act, but behind closed doors, the knives came out.

I'd taken to carrying the device Simmons had given me for Grandad's car in my purse.

I took it out and looked at it.

The little red light was on. We had a bug.

Berta saw and didn't say a word. She didn't need to. I could read her lips just fine.

I pushed a button, and the red light flashed and then turned green. Simmons had explained that if it's green, the car/house/apartment is clean. Well, not clean, but no signals would be going out.

It didn't matter if the bug was Marshall's doing or that of the same people who'd done a number on my apartment and Grandad's town house and car. Someone wanted to know where we went, and possibly what we said while we went there.

Berta pulled out her phone and sent a text, then she showed me the screen. She'd told Rees we had a bug and that we needed another car. She was in no mood to take any chances of being followed to where we were going next.

We drove in silence to the McDonald's on Wisconsin Avenue, where Rees had a replacement car waiting for us. We traded off and went to our next destination. The agent in our bugged car proceeded to lead Gabriel Marshall or whoever had planted the tracker on a scenic tour of Pentagon City.

Berta and I were heading out to Dulles.

Pete had tracked one of the calls made to Julian Pierce's burner phone to an extended-stay hotel near the airport.

"So, how did Gabriel Marshall know about me?" I asked Berta.

"We didn't tell him."

"I know you didn't, but someone did."

"You work with me and Rees. We're the Odd Couple, emphasis on odd. If a case smells like woo-woo, we're there, and you're right alongside. It wouldn't take much to figure it out." She glanced at me and then back to the road. "Impressive back there, IDing Marshall as your intruder. I thought you had to touch someone to get that kind of information."

"Most of the time I do. Occasionally, a person has a strong enough presence that I can place them in a room they were just in. Gabriel Marshall's not the kind of guy who enters a room unnoticed. People would either do the moth-to-flame thing or prey-to-predator. Flirt or flee."

Berta nodded. "I could see that." She huffed a laugh. "I'm glad you didn't tell him he had a strong presence. We'd never hear the end of it."

I grinned. "How often does he cross your path?"

"Not that often. Though he manages to show up when he's least wanted, or you say his name three times and he appears, like a combination of Beetlejuice and Voldemort."

"So, is he entertainingly crazy or completely psycho?"

"Washington's full of psychos and sociopaths. I'd put Gabriel Marshall in the high-functioning sociopath basket. I think."

"What do you mean, 'think'?"

"He's what he needs to be, depending on the situation. I don't believe I've ever met the real Gabriel Marshall. I'm not even sure there is one."

"How about him wanting to keep Barrington safe?" I asked. "Is that on the up-and-up?"

"There's all kinds of safe. What did you get from him?"

"The condo being trashed was news to him. He knows what they were looking for, and it's the same thing he broke into Grandad's town house to find."

"How about the bugs in your office, apartment, and car? Do you think he planted them?"

"No, and I wish he had. That just means somebody else did, and I don't know who or why. But Gabriel Marshall does."

Berta scowled. "I'm not surprised. You didn't get a sense of someone having been in your office who didn't belong—aside from Marshall?"

"None. And I'm tuned to that sort of thing. I know if someone has been in my home who doesn't belong."

"Maybe it was someone who *did* belong. Have those security people been in your apartment?"

"Yes, but other than last night, it's been at least six months."

"Had any repairs done?"

"None. Believe me, I've been wracking my brain trying to think of who it could be. Tell me everything you know about Gabriel Marshall."

"Apparently I don't know everything. I didn't know he was psychokinetic."

I grinned. "Is that why you kept your gun on him?"

"That and he just pisses me off."

"I can see how he'd do that. Neither you nor Rees likes him. May I ask what he did to earn it?"

"Marshall works for the CIA, but they've been known to greenlight his 'cooperation' with other agencies if the CIA wants to be owed a big favor."

"He lets himself be used as currency? That's surprising."

"No one uses Gabriel Marshall, and he doesn't take orders. He's a wild card, but he's good at what he does, so the CIA lets him call the shots." She paused. "Literally."

"He's an assassin?"

"He was, and probably still is. He's more of a fixer. When there's a big mess, Marshall cleans it up—and if it can't be cleaned, he makes it go away."

"Including people."

"Last year, we were close to busting a human trafficking ring that was operating out of Baltimore. Locals were running the ring, but the strings were being pulled further up. Russian mafia. We had a lead on the boss, Dimitri Arkolev, a Russian-American who split his time between New York and Moscow. His lieutenant was running the Baltimore operation on the side for himself. We got the lieutenant, but we wanted Arkolev. So did the CIA. He was an arms dealer. Not a big player, but getting there. We wanted him alive to prosecute and give us more names. The CIA wanted him as a bargaining chip. Arkolev was a weasel who'd made a lot of enemies, powerful enemies who had information the CIA wanted—for a price. That price was Arkolev dead. Enter Gabriel Marshall. I don't know if he pulled the trigger himself, or just made the arrangements. That hit bought us information to prevent an attack on two US Army bases in Turkey and Syria."

"Human lives used as currency, and Gabriel Marshall is the collection agent."

"Pretty much. Though that operation resulted in one bad guy gone, and hundreds of American lives saved. I can't fault the math. But that wasn't the only time Gabriel Marshall has forced his way into one of our investigations and scooped up our perp. The CIA will only cooperate with other agencies if there's something in it for them, but they sure as hell don't share their catches."

"I didn't think they could operate on US soil."

"That's where the 'cooperation' with other agencies comes into play. Marshall always has whatever credentials he needs when he needs them."

"Wonder who he's cooperating with now? A senator and his aide are dead, killed in their Capitol Hill office. Marshall was there—and knew why I was there. Julian said that David warned him, so Barrington is involved in some way. He's in the wind, and Marshall is looking for him. I think it's safe to say we're all looking for Julian and Alan's killer."

Berta flashed a fierce grin. "We'll get him. Gabriel Marshall's not gonna steal this one. Are you sure the man you sensed in Pierce's office wasn't Marshall?"

"Positive."

"That means we have two assassins to tangle with."

"Lucky us," I muttered.

CHAPTER 20

We had a copy of the photo of David Barrington from Julian's office. It was more recent than any that'd been found online, and definitely better than his CIA ID, which looked more like a mug shot.

Barrington wasn't CIA in the sense that Gabriel Marshall was CIA. He was a doctor, a scientist, presumably not used to moving around undercover. However, he had been a Marine in an infantry unit in Vietnam.

Barrington had made a phone call from one of the extended-stay hotels that had sprung up like a ring of mushrooms around the Beltway.

"These are great places for hiding and blending in," Berta said as she pulled into the parking lot. "You get all kinds of people, and no one pays much attention to anyone else. It's Joe Q. Government Contractor's home away from home. There always seem to be plenty of bars nearby. Makes coming back at the end of the day to glorified cheap-ass furniture bearable."

"I take it you've stayed in one before."

Berta nodded. "It's about all you can afford on an FBI expense account. Though the free breakfast bars are good."

Grandad called extended-stay hotels storage units for people. They often had a leading hotel chain's name attached to the words "home," "extended stay," "suites," or the like. They tried to make the logo or the outside of the building look like something other than what it was—a place to put your stuff, nuke a Hot Pocket, and sleep while you were in town doing what you wanted to get done so you could go back home to your family and/or dog.

The Japanese had dispensed with trying to make their version look homey and had taken it to its ultimate conclusion with those sleep pods for business travelers.

We walked into the lobby. Berta was right. If you came in and out wearing business casual or the cheap suit and tie that was the uniform of government contractors everywhere, you wouldn't be seen and only barely noticed. And if you were trying to hide, you'd want to go where you could blend in with the local flora and fauna.

David Barrington had come here to hide.

Thanks to Elaine Pierce, we had his name. Thanks to Pete, we were where he'd called Julian from. I didn't know if it would be enough, but at least it was more than we had a few hours ago.

Berta went to the front desk. She was the one with the badge. I was just the two-legged psychic bloodhound.

I took a tour of the lobby and elevator area. It was small, so it didn't take long.

The man working at the front desk was shaking his head at the photo. "I'm sorry, ma'am. He doesn't look familiar, but then I don't work during the first half of the week. Let me see if he was registered." After a few computer key clicks, he shook his head again. "We haven't had anyone by the name of David Barrington registered here this week or last."

Elaine had known him as Uncle Barry.

"How about anyone with the first name Barry?" I asked.

More clicking. "Yes, we had a Barry Davis here for one night. He checked out Thursday morning at 6:05."

Close enough to be probable. And David Barrington, aka Barry Davis, had checked out the morning after Julian and Alan had been murdered, probably after seeing it on the morning news.

"Heck of a morning what with the earthquake and all," the clerk said.

"Yes, it was," Berta readily agreed. "Has anyone stayed in his room since he checked out?"

The clerk looked at the screen and shook his head. "No, ma'am. It was cleaned a few hours after he left, but no one's stayed there since then."

"We'd like to see it, please."

"Let me get someone to cover the desk for me, and I'll take you up."

What I hoped to find, no amount of cleaning and vacuuming could remove.

Berta deftly got rid of the desk clerk, requesting the make, model, and tag number of the car Barry Davis had been driving when he'd checked in and whether there were any security cameras that had captured his image while he was checking in or out. The clerk dutifully went to look, leaving us alone.

As Berta quietly searched for any remaining physical evidence, I stood for a few moments in the middle of the room to see if I could pick up any emotional remnants David Barrington might have left behind.

There wasn't anything, but that didn't mean that direct contact with, say, the bed wouldn't get me the information we were looking for.

The room had a kitchenette. Other than that, the furnishings were what you'd find in any other hotel room: bed, bathroom, desk, phone and clock radio on a bedside table, and a table and two chairs in front of the window. Considering that David Barrington had stayed for only one night, only three of those things had probably been used.

Bathroom, bed, and phone.

I started with the phone and just as quickly eliminated it. The phone hadn't been used by anyone in quite some time, which made sense considering that most people carried their own. Not to mention, David Barrington had a burner phone that he used to communicate primarily via text. Rees was trying to locate Barrington's cell phone and trace any calls that had been made on it. Or better yet, track his location. But since he'd been using a burner and was on the run, in his entirely justified paranoia, it was highly unlikely he'd have left his cell phone powered up.

I moved from the phone to the bed, hopeful that Barrington had used it so that I wouldn't need to resort to sitting on the toilet. But if it was necessary, I'd take one for the team. I'd done it before.

If Barrington was on the run, he would have at least tried to rest.

There was only one double bed. Generally, regardless of what side of the bed a person slept on at home, while in a hotel, they slept on the side closest to the bedside table and phone.

I lay down on the side nearest the phone, closed my eyes, and tried to relax.

David Barrington had lain precisely where I was now, and on top of the bedspread as I was doing. He'd known he wouldn't be able to sleep and hadn't bothered getting under the covers or removing any of his clothes.

He'd also wanted to be able to move at a moment's notice.

David Barrington was being hunted.

He'd been betrayed and was terrified. He couldn't trust anyone except Julian. He was wracked with guilt about involving his friend more than he already had. They didn't want him dead, at least not yet. If caught, he'd vanish, never to be seen again.

He'd created a monster. Now he was paying the price.

The room was completely silent. I could sense Berta watching me.

I opened my eyes.

Berta was standing by the window. "Anything?"

"Well, I can confirm that Barry Davis is David Barrington. And if he hadn't been an absolute nervous wreck, he could've gotten some sleep on this bed. This mattress isn't half bad. I've slept on much worse."

I swung my legs over the side of the bed, sat up, and told her what I'd sensed.

"Sounds like the monster he created has gone on the rampage," Berta noted.

"And Julian hid his burner in a copy of *Frankenstein,* a story where the creation turns on the creator."

"They didn't want him dead…yet. It would've been nice if he'd told you who 'they' are."

"Tell me about it." I rubbed my hand over my face. Closing my eyes and stretching out on a bed for just for those few minutes had made me realize just how tired I was. "He's worried about being caught because they'd make him vanish and he'd never be seen again. Does that sound like a certain CIA officer?"

"Yeah, but from what I know, Gabriel Marshall only kills people who deserve it."

"And David Barrington doesn't strike me as the needs-to-stop-breathing-our-air type, meaning Julian and Alan's killer is probably after Barrington as well."

Berta gestured at the brightly patterned bedspread, which most people would refuse to have in their home. "Do you need to take that designer bedspread with you?"

"I've gotten all I'm gonna get from it." I stood up. "Though let me go sit on the toilet before we go back downstairs. Some people do their serious thinking in the bathroom."

Less than five minutes later, we were back at the front desk.

I hadn't gotten anything helpful from the toilet in Room 312.

The desk clerk had called the manager with our request. They came up with a surprisingly good photo of David Barrington at the front desk checking in, and a side view of him leaving.

He wasn't exactly dressed for Washington's present weather.

They were calling for snow on Sunday, but Barrington had

been dressed for snow on Thursday morning in jeans, a down jacket, and snow boots, and had been carrying a medium-sized duffel bag. The doctor was traveling light. There wasn't enough snow in DC to warrant that kind of gear, but there'd be plenty in the Adirondacks where Julian Pierce and David Barrington used to go fishing with their friends. Berta reported to Rees, who said he'd touch base with Elaine Pierce to see if she'd made any progress on getting those fish camp locations.

Barrington normally drove a 2019 BMW 7 Series M760i. He'd arrived at the hotel in a white 2019 Range Rover. Berta called it in to run the tags and found that he'd rented it at Dulles. Rees would have the long-term airport parking checked for Barrington's Beemer. I didn't think I'd get anything from the car that I hadn't gotten from the bed, but a forensics team would go over it.

We'd just gotten back in the car when Berta's phone rang. "Pike."

Then she listened, and as she did, her jaw tightened, and eyes narrowed.

"We'll be there as fast as we can." She ended the call.

"Where?" I asked.

"The Hart Senate Office Building. There's been another death."

CHAPTER 21

"Mark Dalton was the most hated man in the US Senate," Berta said. "Republican or Democrat, it didn't matter. Everybody hated this guy."

Now he was dead.

Cause of death was unknown, but it'd been sudden, and Dalton had been relatively young and healthy, pointing to a third cardiac arrest.

The Russell may have had classic architecture with a fireplace in every senator's office, but I preferred the Hart Senate Office Building. It'd been built around a center atrium capped by massive skylights that allowed sunlight in for the trees planted below. Each floor of the nine-story building alternated walkways with windowed offices looking out over the atrium. There was the prestige of having an office in the Russell Building, but if I were a senator, I'd rather work here.

Senator Mark Dalton may have felt differently.

He'd died on one of the building's toilets with his pants around his ankles.

What a way to go.

Berta was speaking. "Rees said Dalton had just spoken to the media about the 'tragic death of a noble opponent and fine American,' stopped by the head on his way back to his office and—"

"Did an Elvis," I said before I could stop myself.

"Not exactly," Berta pointed out. "Elvis fell off the toilet. The stall broke Dalton's fall."

We both paused to push down any morbid giggles.

"We're horrible," I said. "Though maybe we're punchy from lack of sleep."

"I vote for horrible."

"And you're not in the least bit sorry."

"Hey, I didn't like the guy, either."

It was Friday afternoon. Between the call for snow on Sunday and the president's address coming up on Tuesday, senators and representatives staying in town, and the halls were packed with people who didn't look like FBI. Outside Julian's office, the FBI agents had spoken in hushed tones. There was nothing quiet or reverential going on outside the Hart Building's third-floor men's room. Some people were at least making an effort to show respect for the dead. They were in the minority. I caught snatches of conversation as we made our way through the crowd to the cordoned-off men's room.

"Good riddance."

"Karma's a bitch."

"Served him right."

"Appropriate way for the bastard to die."

"Probably dragged to Hell kicking and screaming."

"See? There is a God."

"And he answers prayers," another voice added, followed by a few muffled laughs.

I also heard a couple of Elvis references, though the King was getting more respect than Senator Dalton, as was the Almighty for his dual senses of humor and irony.

I could see the Capitol Hill area bars being more festive than normal tonight.

We got to the men's room and the Capitol Police manning the tape were scrutinizing Berta's badge and my FBI consultant's ID when Rees's voice cut through the noise.

"They're with me."

And we were in.

Not that I was looking forward to this particular scene, whether it turned out to be a crime scene, or was just what Dalton's Senate colleagues were essentially calling divine justice.

There were six stalls and four urinals in the men's room.

I'd expected the room to be packed with people, as Julian's office had. Here, there was only the ME with one assistant, and three FBI forensics agents.

And of course, Senator Mark Dalton on a gurney in a half-zipped body bag. At least he wasn't still sitting on the toilet. I did not need to see that.

Samuel Rees and Grandad were standing by the door, as much out of the way as they could be. Grandad was wearing an FBI consultant's ID on a lanyard around his neck that was identical to mine.

The third stall from the door was getting all the attention. The door and handle had been dusted for prints.

"Another one?" I murmured to Rees.

"That's for you to tell me. We have a witness this time. He was in the fifth stall and heard Dalton say, "Hey! Occupied!" Less than five seconds later, he heard Dalton's head and body hit the side of the stall. The witness…completed his business, and when he opened the door, no one was in the room, and he could see Dalton's hands hanging limply under the door to the third stall."

"No other sounds?" I asked. "No struggle, muffled voice? Spritz of an aerosol spray?"

"None. The witness called to Senator Dalton and didn't get a response, and in doing so, potentially exposed himself to whatever substance—if there was one—was used on Dalton. He pushed on the door, but it was still locked from the inside."

I would not have wanted to be the Capitol Police officer or FBI agent who'd had to crawl under that stall door to unlock it.

"The witness has shown no symptoms of any airborne toxin," Rees was saying, "but he was taken to the hospital for preemptive treatment and observation. No substances were found on either side of the gap in the door. He also didn't hear the intruder. Just Dalton expressing displeasure of someone either pushing on the door or looking through the gap between the door and stall frame."

"Security cameras in the hall get anything?"

"A man exited at the time the witness gave for the incident. He was wearing a suit, overcoat, and a hat. The brim was pulled down and he knew where the camera was. He turned his head just enough that his face was completely hidden, and his hands were in his coat pockets."

"Of course they were. Can I see the footage?"

"It'll be emailed to me, and I'll immediately forward it to you."

Rees knew what I wanted to do. Compare the way the man in the security footage on Tuesday moved compared with this new suspect.

"Any chance of me being in here alone for a few minutes?"

Rees nodded. "The ME is finishing up, and I can clear the room."

"Thank you."

I wanted to stand in front of the third stall where Dalton's intruder had stood and compare it to the sensation I had gotten in Julian's office.

"The ME will be doing the autopsy immediately," Rees was saying. "We should have the initial results before this evening. We've interviewed his aides. The only thing Senator Dalton had complained about was having to stay in town this weekend. There was no severe headache, nausea, trouble speaking, blurred vision—"

"Those aren't cardiac arrest symptoms."

"We don't believe it was a cardiac arrest."

"You weren't here, so I got this one," Grandad said from just behind me.

"Did you. . .?" I tilted my head in the direction of stall number three.

"I should think not. If it had been Julian, I would have 'taken one for the team,' as you would say. I touched the deceased. Considering how I felt about him as a senator and a poor excuse for a human being, that contact was nearly as distasteful as sitting where his. . ." Grandad shuddered. "A man looked through the gap and no sooner had Senator Dalton admonished the intruder than he was stricken with an excruciating headache."

"We're thinking aneurysm," Rees said.

"Then it wasn't the same—"

"Only you can tell us for certain. You know what his presence feels like."

"How much longer until you can clear everyone out?"

"They're ready to take the body. I can get you a few minutes after that."

If Julian Pierce and Alan Coe's killer had been here, I wouldn't need that long.

CHAPTER 22

As I waited for Mark Dalton's body to be removed and Rees to clear the room for me, I thought that there had to be easier and less risky ways to get to a US senator.

Julian and Alan had been killed in the early hours of the morning, but Dalton had been stricken in the middle of the afternoon. This killer was going to a lot of trouble, but for what? Why here and why now? I hadn't asked Rees what Julian and Senator Dalton had in common. Was it the pharma bill? Or another connection? Did that connection, even from their positions on opposite sides of the aisle, get them both killed? Did the killer want to make a statement, not just about the two dead senators, but about the Senate itself, perhaps even the entire government? Aside from the White House, Capitol Hill was seen as the ultimate symbol of the United States. They were two of the safest places in the world, symbols of power and control. The killer was doing a fine job of destroying that sense of safety.

And the elephant-in-the-room question—how were they killed?

Rees would remain inside the restroom while Berta stood guard on the other side of the door.

As the last agent and forensic tech left, the emotional white noise left behind by the Capitol Police, first responders, FBI agents and investigators, and the medical examiner and her team began to fade.

Rising in the stillness was a sense of the presence I'd felt in Julian's office, with the same intense, single-minded focus.

I went to stand in front of the stall door, which Rees had pulled closed before retreating to the area near the hand dryers. I didn't touch the door, because the killer hadn't touched the door.

His hands had never left his sides.

I closed my eyes, emptying myself of the sound of voices outside in the hall, the smell of recently used cleaning chemicals, the thoughts and theories jostling in my mind for attention. I centered my focus on the one presence, opening myself to it and letting it flow over and around me.

As my breathing slowed, my body shivered at the contact, but I remained perfectly still, letting the presence speak to me, telling me what had transpired here. It had been hours old by the time I'd gotten to Julian's office. It was much newer here, its potency making it seem more recent still.

How simple it is to kill in the so-called halls of power. I can take any of them at any time…My power flows now, amplified beyond what I'd ever dreamed…It is effortless to summon and aim. Like a weapon, a flawlessly lethal weapon…It is mine to wield, no one else's, at my command and mine alone…No one can find me. I can't be captured, because I cannot be disarmed. I cannot be stopped.

Normally, all I got from contact with a killer were brief flashes of images or impressions. This was so far from my normal, I didn't even know where to begin trying to explain it. I was there with him, inside his head, an eyewitness to his thoughts. My contact in Julian's office was what I was used to experiencing. I'd never been at the scene of a crime this quickly, but even that didn't explain…Something was wrong here, different from anything I'd experienced before.

I felt the urge to wipe my hands on my jeans, even though I'd been careful to touch nothing. It wouldn't help, but that didn't lessen the strength of the compulsion. When you made contact with what I could now only describe as evil incarnate, the first instinct was to wipe it off.

Mark Dalton's killer wasn't Gabriel Marshall.

My breathing was ragged as I backed away from the stall, scrubbing my hands on my jeans. I had to do something, anything to be rid of it. A wave of dizziness swept over me, and I staggered backward to where I hoped the sinks were. I turned and heaved, bracing my elbows on the porcelain as my knees gave way along with the contents of my stomach.

Rees's strong arm was around my shoulders, keeping me from crumpling to the floor. I dimly heard him turn on the faucet, the water hopefully washing out the sink.

I'd had bad contacts before and been told I'd looked like I was about to throw up. I'd never hurled at a crime scene, until now.

Berta would never let me hear the end of it.

I got my legs back under me and stood on my own, bracing

my hands against the next sink. I hung my head and fixed my eyes on the drain until the world stopped spinning.

He had merely looked at Mark Dalton, and within seconds, the senator had died a quick, albeit painful, death.

If looks could kill…

Could they?

A cardiac arrest and an aneurysm. Both natural, even common, causes of death. No alarms raised; no suspicions aroused.

It made for the perfect murder.

The killer was the perfect assassin.

My mouth was dry, my voice raspy. "Sam, we've got a problem."

CHAPTER 23

Outside the men's room, Grandad and Berta were waiting down the hall, but still inside the section that had been cordoned off. I'd told Rees what I'd seen, cleaned up, and splashed cold water on my face in an attempt to at least look human again. Feeling that way was going to take some time.

Grandad needed only one look at me. "Let's go home."

"I saw—"

He held up a hand. "I know. Not here. Let's wait until we're in the car."

Rees guided us out the opposite way from where Berta and I had come in and we managed to avoid the media. He'd parked in the underground garage used by senators and their staffers. I wasn't big on patience, but I managed to wait until Berta had pulled out onto Constitution Avenue.

All the questions running around in my head narrowed themselves down to two words.

"You *knew*?"

"Not until I touched Dalton and stood for a moment in front of that stall door," Grandad told me. "There was no aerosol. He did it himself, with psychokinesis at a level that shouldn't be possible."

"With emphasis on psycho. This guy's not going around bending spoons or staring at goats. This isn't a nightclub act or movie. He actually stopped two hearts and…whatever happens to cause an aneurysm. Miss Eleanor and Gabriel Marshall can toss people, but this guy—"

"Who is Gabr—" Grandad began.

"What?!" Rees blurted, something I'd *never* heard him do.

"We had ourselves an interesting time after we left Senator Pierce's house," Berta told her partner.

I gave Rees and Grandad the quick and dirty version of what had happened in David Barrington's town house.

Rees was stunned. "I never knew Gabriel Marshall was psychokinetic—"

"And this CIA agent knows about you," Grandad said.

"More than likely, you as well," I told him.

"I'm not concerned about myself. It's you—"

"I'm a big girl, Grandad. You know I can take care of myself. Gabriel Marshall hasn't shown himself to be a problem, whereas Julian's killer stopped two hearts and caused an aneurysm. He was in the same room with all three of his victims. That could either be by necessity or preference." I explained the difference in what I'd felt in the men's room. The man had killed Senator Dalton with his mind. All my crime-scene experience had been with "normal" means of murder such as guns, knives, blunt objects, or poisons. Perhaps that explained the oddness of what I'd felt. "This man could sit a couple of tables away, and his target is having dinner and minding their own business. No one would ever suspect. People die of cardiac arrests and aneurysms all the time. Or choking. Making someone choke to death would probably be easy for him."

"I knew you would get much more than I ever could," Grandad said, "and most importantly, you had sensed the presence in Julian's office and would know if it was the same man."

"It was him all right."

"We needed confirmation that one man was responsible for all three murders," Rees said. "The ME's report will say it was natural. We now know it wasn't."

I snorted. "So, just toss Rory in the deep end with no warning."

"I'm sorry, *cara*," Grandad said. "With all those people, I couldn't speak freely. And you might not have gotten as much detail as you did if I had said anything. The presence was fresh. You were only going to get one chance at this. I wanted you to get the best reading possible."

"It didn't make it any less horrifying, but you're right. What did you get from him?"

"I sensed arrogance, pride, and pleasure. He enjoyed his work. And yes, it was his job. We're dealing with a professional assassin. He was assigned to kill Julian and Mark Dalton."

A professional assassin. Like Gabriel Marshall.

"Assigned, not hired?" I asked.

Rees said, "Ambrose and I believe the killer in all probability works for an intelligence agency."

"Ours or theirs?" I paused, recalling Berta's definition of ours or theirs. "Ours meaning US. Theirs meaning the Russians or whoev—"

"We're not eliminating any agency from suspicion," Rees said, "foreign or domestic."

"Why would a US agency kill two US senators?"

Rather than answering, Rees said, "With Senator Dalton's death, we now have a connection. Julian was the chair of the Intelligence Committee. Mark Dalton was the ranking member. That is the only working link between them."

Grandad huffed a laugh. "It would have to be work. Julian certainly wouldn't have socialized with the man. He was a warrior, a man of bravery and action. Mark Dalton was—"

"A common coward," Rees said. "In death, as in life, Senator Dalton plays second fiddle to the greater man."

I chuckled. "And here I thought the FBI was politically impartial."

"Politics has nothing to do with my opinion of the late Mark Dalton."

"His colleagues outside the men's room were of the opinion he'd been dragged to where he deserved, kicking and screaming." I paused. "Just how many agencies does the Intelligence Committee oversee?"

"The CIA, DIA, NSA, NRO," Rees said, "as well as the intelligence-related aspects of the State Department, FBI, Treasury Department, the Department of Energy, and all four branches of the military."

"People you really don't want to piss off," I noted.

"The committee essentially controls their budgets," Berta said. "They also investigate, audit, and inspect their programs and activities when needed."

"I wonder if someone needed one of those inspections, audits, or investigations stopped. Someone with access to a psychic assassin. Jeez, I can't believe I just put those two words together in a sentence."

Rees said, "Which is why I've requested a briefing on all items on the committee's agenda—recent past, present, and pending."

"Best of luck with that, Samuel," Grandad said.

"I've made the request to SAC Hudson, who will bump it up to Director Montgomery, who will apply the needed pressure in the right places. We won't get the information as quickly as I'd like, which would be now, but we will get it soon." I saw Rees actually smile in the rearview mirror. "As added incentive to cooperate, Hudson will also recommend that the remaining committee members increase their personal security in case our killer has other names on his list."

"The quicker they tell the FBI what they're working on," I said, "the quicker the FBI can find and stop this guy, and none of them will suddenly find themselves dead of natural causes."

"Exactly."

"With both the chair and ranking member dead, will that put a temporary stop to any committee meetings or findings they were about to issue?" I asked.

"Any ongoing investigations will continue," Rees said. "Those aren't being done by the committee members themselves. I imagine any agenda items requiring committee debate or a vote will be postponed until after both funerals. I would say at least a week out of propriety. It won't stop anything, merely delay. As to replacements, I'm sure the maneuvering for Senator Pierce's position began before his body was cold."

"Someone might be buying themselves some time," Grandad said. "Maybe a week is all they need—but for what?"

I sat back in my seat. "In front of that stall door, the killer thought how easy it was to kill in the so-called halls of power, and how he could take any of them at any time. He enjoyed what he could do, its *amplification,* the ease with which it now worked, how effortless it was to summon and aim. He thinks he's a flawlessly lethal weapon. I get the feeling he enjoys the risk. He's not afraid of being found or caught, because he can't be disarmed or stopped. What I got from Julian's watch, Julian couldn't believe what was happening, either, that it shouldn't be possible. The killer's PK had been amplified from what it was."

"And Julian referred to a project," Grandad said. "When I touched the burner phone, I got that Julian knew it was successful months ago."

I sat back in my seat. "A project to create a PK assassin. Who the hell would work on something like this?"

Grandad raised his hand.

CHAPTER 24

I couldn't believe it. *"What?"*

"Not developing psychokinetic assassins," Grandad hurried to add, "but I did assist our government in keeping our Cold War opponent from gaining any kind of upper hand in this area. The American people knew about the nuclear arms race, but few had any knowledge of the psychic arms race happening at the same time. Thankfully, what has surfaced has been quickly relegated to the realm of crackpots, conspiracy theories, and entertainment franchises—which is where it needs to remain, for everyone's safety."

"The truth is out there and all that."

"Precisely. The truth *is* out there, and the vast majority of the world's population couldn't handle it. Our family has limited the knowledge of what we can do to a handful of people, and our lives are infinitely safer and saner for it." He gave an exasperated sigh. "This is all the Nazis' fault."

"Excuse me?" Berta said.

"*Das Ahnenerbe,* the Nazis' science and research academy. Himmler founded and ran it himself. He sent his SS officers with German scientists and archeologists all over the world to look for traces of the lost Aryan race. The Nazis wanted to prove to their people that Germans and the Nazi ideals descended from ancient Aryans, thus making them—in their minds—the superior race. I won't go down that twisted rabbit hole. Himmler had his minions searching for anything to do with the occult, legends, and magic. They wanted esoteric writings and any artifacts said to give those who possessed them ultimate power, such as the Holy Grail, the Spear of Destiny, the Ark of the Covenant, and the like. Anything they found and wanted, they stole. Even before the end of the war, the race was on between the US and the then-Soviet Union to find and secure any Nazi technology and weapons programs. That technology, and the Nazi scientists who developed it, have always gotten the most attention in history books and those war documentaries, but those weapons programs included research into psychic skills that could be adapted for wartime use, such as ESP, remote viewing, mind reading and control, and psychokinesis.

"After the war, the CIA and KGB began building on what they'd taken from the Nazis," he continued. "They worked to develop drugs to control minds and to enhance psychic abilities in those who had them, and to produce those abilities in those who weren't born with them. Ultimately, they wanted to create their own elite soldiers and assassins."

"That sounds entirely too close to what we have here," I said.

"None of those programs bore fruit, but no one was ready to admit defeat, especially after a Soviet psychic named Ninel Kulagina was filmed in a military laboratory stopping a frog's heart and then starting it again. Reaction here was split. A few factions in the military and intelligence agencies thought it was just Soviet propaganda to make us think they could do it. Others were convinced the film was real and pushed for expanding our own research. If there was even the remotest possibility the KGB could do this, the CIA wanted in on it. They were determined to not only catch up, but to be the front-runner in weaponizing psychics. In 1972, a report called 'Controlled Offensive Behavior—USSR' was written and published for the Department of Defense. It wasn't declassified by the CIA until 2004. It estimated the Soviets' psychic research budget in the early seventies at over twenty million dollars. That's a drop in the bucket now, but nearly fifty years ago, that was a substantial financial commitment."

Berta glanced in the rearview mirror at Grandad. "Other than what we may have here, how do you weaponize other kinds of psychics?"

"A remote viewer is said to be able to see classified documents, to discern troop movements, submarine locations, or classified activities at military or government installations."

"No offense, but that sounds like a load of crap."

"In my opinion, it is, and no offense taken. This report went on to warn that military equipment including aircraft, weapons systems, or satellites could be disarmed remotely by psychokinesis. Or that the thoughts or behavior of military or government leaders could be modified without their knowledge through mind control—or that they could be killed by a psychokinetic assassin. Yes, Yuri Geller can bend spoons. So what? A spoon is an inanimate object, and it certainly isn't a human heart or brain. Even if a PK assassin were possible, and that is an exceptionally large 'if,' there's difference between a frog heart and a human one. Not to mention, she stared at that frog heart in a jar for seven minutes before it allegedly stopped."

I blinked. "It was in a jar?"

"In Ringer's solution to keep it beating for a while and hooked up to an EKG to monitor it. The point is, there are a few—very few—people who can move objects. In the case of our murders, we're talking about affecting a living human being—moving, breathing, autonomous. A heart is an incredibly complex organ, a powerful muscle, and it's at the center of a human chest, protected by skin, bone, muscle, and, most importantly, a human's indominable will to live. You cannot simply overcome that in mere seconds with a glance and turn it off just like that." He snapped his fingers. "That doesn't even take into account what was done to Mark Dalton." Grandad settled back in his seat. "Most psychic experiments failed, some embarrassingly so." He smiled. "An acquaintance of mine was leading a study involving a particularly potent Mexican psychedelic mushroom said to enhance psychic abilities." He cleared his throat. "What can I say? It was the seventies in southern California. Psychic programs were more…adventurous in those days."

"This acquaintance's name wouldn't happen to be David, would it?" I asked.

"No."

"Did anything come of it?"

"Nothing. Other than some embarrassing photos and compromising videos of a few notable scientists of the day."

We'd arrived at the town house. Berta let us out, then drove around back to the alley where she could parallel park in front of the carriage house's double doors.

I unsnapped my keys from the holder in my messenger bag. Gerald usually did grocery shopping on Friday afternoons, so he might not be home. Grandad preferred to be let into the house, and I preferred to open my own doors, thank you very much.

There was no ice on the stairs, but there were still patches of slush where the trees shaded the sidewalk and stairs. Grandad was wearing his usual suit and dress shoes. Only in the most dire circumstances did he allow fashion to fall victim to practicality. I took his arm to walk with him up the stairs. He used to make a fuss about it, but I think he secretly liked it.

"We haven't even had lunch," Grandad said. "If he's home, I'll ask Gerald to make sandwiches." He turned his head toward Rees who was right behind us. "Would you and Berta like…"

He slipped. I grabbed his arm with both hands, and Rees caught him from behind.

I slid an arm around his waist. "Careful, I've got you—"

Grandad's knees gave way, his face twisting in pain, his eyes fixed and staring.

No. *No, no, no…*

Everything went into slow motion as my arms went around him, dragging him up the last two stairs to the safety of the recessed doorway. I dimly heard Rees shouting something into his phone, then he was with us on the landing, putting his body between us and who I knew was out there, close by, at our home. He'd followed us here or was already here when we arrived.

He had to see his victims to kill them.

Where were Simmons's guards?

I got the key in the lock, shoved it open, and we dragged him the rest of the way inside.

"Gerald!"

No answer.

I rolled Grandad on his back. His eyes were fixed and staring, his mouth open.

He wasn't breathing.

No. Please, dear God, no.

He wasn't going to die. I wouldn't let him.

I loosened his tie and fumbled with his shirt buttons.

Rees and I didn't need words, we just went to work. Rees on chest compressions, me on mouth-to-mouth.

"Ambulance is on the way," he said as his hands kept up a sharp rhythm on Grandad's breastbone. "Berta's looking for him. Agents and police are coming."

I kept going, tilting Grandad's head back, giving him the air he couldn't take in for himself.

"Miss Aurora!" Gerald came running from the back of the house.

I came up for more air. "Get a blanket!"

He was back in moments with the wool tartan throw Grandad had bought on his most recent trip to Scotland. He'd said it was for when he finally decided to start acting his age.

He still wasn't breathing.

"Anything?" I was grabbing all the air I could get to give to him.

In response, Rees grimly kept going.

We continued working in silence. My tears flowed from my eyes down Grandad's face as I kept breathing for him. Gerald knelt by his side, fingers on his wrist, waiting for the pulse I prayed would restart.

Pablo began rubbing up against both Grandad and me as I did mouth-to-mouth, his loud purrs vibrating against our faces. In his own way, Pablo was trying to help.

Then Berta was there with the EMTs and they took over.

Rees pulled me back out of the way as they worked on him, getting an oxygen mask in place and sticking two electrode pads to his too-pale chest. The first shock came a second later.

Nothing.

And another shock.

"I've got a pulse," an EMT said.

The most beautiful words I'd ever heard followed by the most beautiful sound.

The steady beep of Grandad's heart on the monitor.

I sent up a prayer of thankfulness.

"I'm going with him," I said, daring anyone to tell me otherwise.

"I'll be right behind you," Rees promised.

Outside, the street was filled with blue and red flashing lights. FBI and police were everywhere. My throat tightened in gratitude. If they hadn't caught him by now, though, their chance was gone, along with the assassin who had made the mistake of coming after my granddaddy.

During the ambulance trip to the hospital, I listened to the heart monitor beeping loud and strong while I held one of Grandad's hands in both of mine, feeling it get warmer, and talked to him nonstop.

As we pulled into the hospital emergency entrance, my heart skipped a beat of its own as his hand squeezed mine.

CHAPTER 25

I'd never been good at waiting, and my impatience and fear were magnified times a thousand at the thought of emergency room doctors working on someone I loved.

I was beyond grateful that Georgetown University Hospital was less than two miles away from the town house.

I went to a corner of the waiting room where I could see through the little window near the top of the swinging double doors that gave me a view down the hall where the trauma bays were. They'd taken Grandad through the doors, halfway down the hall and to the left. I'd watched entirely too many scrubs-clad people run into that bay.

"Rory."

It was Rees, but I refused to take my eyes off that window. It was the only way for me to know what was happening, my only connection to Grandad.

"You need to sit down and rest." Rees's voice was soft but firm. "You won't do him any good if—"

"I'm not moving from this spot. Not until I know."

"We were there when it happened and immediately started resuscitation. You did all you—"

"Yes, we were there when it happened, and we couldn't do a damned thing to stop it. That's what was in his mind when he killed Dalton. He can kill anyone at any time and there's nothing anyone can do to stop him."

"A bullet through his head would do it."

Samuel Rees was always perfectly in control, an island of calm professionalism regardless of any chaos erupting around him. He was a champion of the law. He wasn't talking about the rule of law or process of justice now, just putting down a predator that needed it.

Rees felt responsible, too.

"It's not your fault, either," I told him. "I don't want to think what would have happened if you hadn't been there to help us. Thank you." I clenched my teeth against the tears that tried to start. I was through crying. I knew what I wanted to do, and it had nothing to do with the law. "Grandad wanted to help. He came in with his eyes open."

And briefly died the same way.

"He feels threatened by Ambrose and you," Rees said. "Until this is over, both of you are in danger. He could be anywhere, and we have no idea what he looks like. You and Ambrose have done enough, more than enough. We have leads now. I've arranged for guards to be here with both of you. Stay here with him. You'll be safe."

Then I remembered. Guards. Simmons's guards.

"Our security company left two guards at the house." Fear for Grandad turned to rage. "Where the hell were they?"

"Dead."

I blinked. "What?"

"They're dead. They were found in the backyard, their bodies hidden behind the garden shed."

"How?" I asked, but as a chill spread through me, I knew.

"There were no wounds or outward signs of violence," Rees said.

I sank onto the chair behind me. "He lured them back there and killed them both," I whispered, "then simply waited for us to come home. He could've just as easily killed Gerald the same way." I put a hand to my forehead, trying to think. "I need to call my parents. They need to know, but I don't want them here, and if I tell them, they'll come. I can't put them in danger."

"If you decide to call them, I'll send agents to the airport to bring them here."

I turned and looked back through the window. I needed to be here. For now. As soon as I knew Grandad was going to live and that he would be safe, I was going to do everything in my power and beyond to find the thing that had done this to him.

A doctor emerged from the trauma bay, walking down the hall toward the waiting room doors, her expression grim.

I froze.

She pushed the door open and saw me. "Ms. Donati? Aurora Donati?"

I quickly stood. "Yes. I'm his granddaughter."

"I'm Dr. Deborah Beck, a cardiologist on staff here." She put out her hand to shake. It was warm and strong. She was confident in her abilities. No arrogance, just hard work, determination, and compassion in spades. "Your grandfather is in critical condition. His vital signs are stable. I understand you were there when the cardiac arrest occurred."

"Yes." I indicated Rees. "Along with FBI Special Agent Samuel Rees. He's a friend of the family."

Dr. Beck shook his hand. "How long until you started CPR?"

"Almost immediately," I told her. "Within twenty seconds." I glanced at Rees for confirmation. He nodded once. I indicated Rees. "Chest." Then myself. "Mouth."

Grim gave way to a slight smile. "You two make a good team. If you had not acted so quickly, he would no longer be with us."

I knew that only too well. The killer had caught his other victims alone. Grandad hadn't been alone. He wasn't going to be alone again.

"Is he going to be all right?"

"We're going to move Mr. Donati to our ICCU, that's Intensive Coronary Care Unit. There are no guarantees, especially considering his age, but his heart is in excellent condition and he did regain consciousness briefly and asked for you by name. I told him you were here. For some reason, he mistook that to mean you were being treated here as well. I assured him that you were fine and in the waiting room. This calmed him."

He was worried about *me*.

I couldn't tell her that I could easily have ended up in the trauma bay next to his, and that was what Grandad had been afraid of. But if we'd both been attacked like Julian and Alan, caught alone and unaware, we would have been downstairs or wherever the hospital morgue was.

"Does he have a history of heart problems or disease?" Dr. Beck asked.

"No, and there's none in our family."

"That will help. The next twenty-four hours will be critical. But if he remains stable, he has a good chance of survival."

She hadn't said recovery, merely survival. For now, I'd take what I could get.

"When can I see him?"

"He's being taken up to ICCU now. Let us get him settled and I'll send one of the nurses down to get you. I believe it will help him to see you. I'm sorry, Special Agent Rees, but for now, visits need to be kept short and limited to immediate family."

"I understand, Dr. Beck. However, Mr. Donati is presently under FBI protection, and I will need to not only post guards, but will also require the names and hospital photo IDs of everyone who will be authorized to enter his room."

She only hesitated a moment before saying, "Agreed."

In Washington, Rees's conditions probably weren't anything new.

"Until that can be done," Rees added, "we need to be with him. Now. The Donatis are private investigators consulting with the FBI on a case."

I pulled out my FBI consultant ID to show her.

"As a result of his involvement," he continued, "Mr. Donati's life is in danger. He is presently unable to protect himself. For now, Ms. Donati and I are that protection."

Dr. Beck looked from my ID to Rees's unwavering stare.

"Follow me."

CHAPTER 26

Rees and I waited outside Grandad's ICCU room while he was transferred to the bed and connected to the machines that would keep the staff apprised of his every breath and heartbeat and the status of everything in between.

Grandad was tall and lean, but it was all muscle and it always had been. He was eighty-two, but he could give men twenty and even thirty years younger a run for their money.

Now, in that hospital bed, with all the wires and tubes hooked up to him…

I swallowed. "He looks so small and pale."

"He's going to make it," Rees told me.

"You sound certain."

"I am, and you should be. Ambrose Donati won't allow himself to go like this."

Samuel Rees's shoulder was touching mine. That was as close as he was going to get to a comforting hug. I was glad.

As much as I needed it, if he put even one arm around me, I would completely lose it. I couldn't do that. Not now. I had to focus. Dr. Beck said that Grandad had regained consciousness long enough to ask about me. If I allowed myself to cry, Grandad might not see it, but he would feel it and know it. He needed strength, and I was going to be there for him, strong and steady, projecting the confidence that he was going to be just fine, and so was I. All he needed to do was rest and get better. I would take care of everything else.

I took a steadying breath. "I need to call Gerald. Is there a place where I—"

"There's a waiting room and chapel at the end of the hall," Rees said. "Take your time." He paused. "I'll be right here."

I gave a tight nod. That was almost as bad as a hug. I knew he was here, that he wasn't going anywhere, and if the assassin somehow came to the room, Samuel Rees would block his line of sight and take that cardiac arrest or aneurysm for my grandad—or for me.

I saw the sign for the chapel. Next to it was a small waiting room with a TV. Both were empty. I stepped into the waiting room. The TV was turned down and the closed captioning was on.

Julian and Alan's murders had momentarily given way to Mark Dalton's aneurysm.

The talking heads weren't buying that there was anything natural about his death.

They knew Julian Pierce was the chair of the intelligence committee with Mark Dalton in the secondary ranking member position. Entirely too much had happened over the past few years for the deaths, within days of each other, of the top senators on the committee to be accepted as anything but covered-up murders.

At least that's what the networks were going with. If there was the remotest possibility that it could be true and would send the ratings through the roof, that was what they'd go with morning, noon, and night. That is, until the truth surfaced, or a bigger story pushed it to the curb.

The FBI had a reserved spot in the proverbial hot seat. Any high-profile federal crime handled with less than perfect efficiency earned them immediate condemnation. With Julian, Alan, and now Mark Dalton's death, the temperature would be cranked up all the way on this one. There could be no mistakes. The media and the public expected nothing less than the killer's head on a silver platter.

I wanted that, too. I wanted it more than I'd ever wanted anything in my life.

Brandon Trevor and Ripton Pharmaceuticals were still being raked over the coals. The angle du jour was that the heart drug that saved American lives had possibly been modified and used to take the lives of Julian Pierce and Alan Coe, men now being touted as defenders of the people against the evil pharmaceutical companies. The conspiracy theorists still hadn't figured out how to connect Mark Dalton's aneurysm, but they were clearly working on it and I had no doubt they'd come up with something to keep the TV-watching public glued to their screens.

If only they knew.

Talk about TV worth watching. The truth was stranger than any of the fiction being concocted in any network staff meeting.

I called Gerald. I kept it positive for him. He'd known me since the day I was born and believed what I was telling him about as much as I did. We both knew it was an act, but until

Grandad woke up, got better, and walked out of this hospital, that was going to be our truth. It was what we needed, and we were gonna hold on to it for dear life with both hands. I told him I'd be spending the night at the hospital. Gerald didn't offer to come and bring food, he told me that was what he was going to do. I didn't argue with him. Gerald was family and like a brother to Grandad. I had no right to ask him to stay away, but I did tell him to wait for an FBI agent to pick him up. I knew Rees would agree and send someone.

Dr. Beck had said the next few hours would be critical.

I would be by Grandad's side for all of them.

CHAPTER 27

The night was uneventful. Thank God.

I'd kept watch even though there'd been nothing to see. No change, though that was what I desperately wanted. Grandad was breathing on his own, and he did it all night. At some point, I'd even managed to doze for an hour in a reclining chair they'd brought in.

When I woke up, I found the nearest ladies' room and did what I could to make myself feel human. I still had a toothbrush and toothpaste in my messenger bag from my flight home from Vegas, along with a travel pack of face wipes. I brushed my hair and wrestled it into a French braid and declared myself done. I looked in on Grandad before taking a walk down the hall to work the kinks out of my muscles. Next to the waiting room was a chapel. I paused outside the open door. It was empty.

I went in.

Grandad needed all the help he could get, and so did I. We all did.

A few minutes later, I felt rather than heard someone come into the room.

I knew him.

I didn't know what I expected to see when I turned around, but what I saw wasn't it.

Gabriel Marshall was dressed as a priest, complete with collar.

I stood. "You are *so* going to Hell."

"I've been told that many times." Gone was the smile, the flippant attitude of yesterday. Berta had said Marshall was the consummate showman. I didn't think this was an act. "To avoid being questioned or suspected, blend in with your surroundings. No one suspects a priest."

"They should," I told him.

Other than the clothes, Marshall hadn't bothered with any kind of disguise.

He wanted me to know it was him.

I took a step back.

"I'm no threat to you," he said.

"I know." Maybe. "You might get struck by lightning, and I don't want to share your fate. You're also blocking my way out."

Marshall moved to the opposite side of the chapel, giving me a clear path to the door.

I didn't move. "How did you know I was here?"

"I heard about Dalton's murder. I knew Rees would be there, and so would you." He paused. "And I know what happened to your grandfather. I'm so sorry."

I didn't know what to say. "Thank you" seemed intrinsically wrong. I went with a nod.

"So, you know Dalton was murdered," I said.

"Yes."

"And you know the killer."

"You need to leave this alone. We'll take care of it."

"Because you're doing such a great job so far? Three men are dead—no, make that five, he killed two of our security company's guards—and my grandfather was nearly..." I stopped in realization. "You followed Rees to the Hart Building, then followed us home."

"I did."

"You were there. You saw when he attacked my—"

"And I didn't arrive in time to stop him. I'm sorry." Marshall paused, the smooth muscles in his jaw clenching. "He got away. Again."

I saw the assassin Berta said he was in his gunmetal gray eyes. A thwarted assassin. Gabriel Marshall had failed. Twice. He had targeted his prey, and that prey had escaped. It was unacceptable to him. But there was more. This was personal. He knew the killer.

"Who is he?" My voice was a clipped whisper. "I want a name, and I want it now."

"So you can be his next victim? You don't know what you're dealing with."

"A psychokinetic assassin. The thing my grandfather said should be impossible exists, and it was lying in wait for him. At. Our. Home."

Silence.

"You weren't the first Donati to go into that men's room today," Marshall said. "Your grandfather was. And on Thursday morning, the FBI agent downstairs at the Russell Building had a list of people to allow into the building. "A. Donati" appears on your consultant's ID—and your grandfather's. Elements in the intelligence community know about his ability. They didn't know about you until very recently."

"And now you're one of them."

"Yes."

"Then it's me he wanted to kill. That should be me in that bed, hooked up to those machines."

"He'll know soon if he doesn't already that you are the most dangerous to him. Your skill goes deeper than your grandfather's. He'll be coming after you now. You need to stop. Stay here. Be with your grandfather. He won't come after you if you stay here."

"How do you know that?"

"You're not his mission."

"Then who is?"

"That's classified."

"Bullshit," I spat.

"What?"

"You heard me. You have no clue who's next. You're no closer to knowing than you were before Julian was killed, and it's eating you up. Dammit, that was supposed to be me in there. *I* was the A. Donati on the list the night Pierce was killed. *I* was the one he saw coming out of that restroom after throwing up after what I'd seen him do. He was there. Watching. The witness said he was wearing a long coat and hat. No one saw what he looked like, and he could have been wearing anything under that coat. Probably a Capitol Police uniform. They were everywhere yesterday. The bastard was probably standing there in plain sight. He could have taken me, but for some reason, he thought Grandad was the bigger threat."

"He was mistaken."

"Damn right, he was." I was shaking with rage. "And I'm not going to let him get away with it."

"Are you carrying?"

I didn't answer.

"I'll take that as a no." Marshall put his foot on the chair and removed his gun, holster and all, from his ankle. "This will do until you can get home and get your own gun. You do have one, don't you?"

"Yes, but I rarely need it."

"You need it now. If you see him before he sees you, put a bullet through his head. It's the only way to stop him."

Rees had said the same thing.

"I don't know what he looks like."

"Neither do I. He's had surgery. But you'll know him. You'll sense him if he gets close, and he'll want to be close now. When he comes after you—and if you leave this hospital and keep coming after him, he *will* come after you—when he finds you, he'll want it to be up close and personal."

He put the gun on the altar, and it slid, seemingly by itself, across the wood to me and stopped.

There it was, out in the open. He wanted me to know his power if I didn't already.

"I knew," I told him.

"I suspected. I also want you to know you can trust me. I know your secret, you know mine."

"It's going to take more than that. You're a killer." I left "just like the man we're both after" unsaid.

"I'm nothing like him. I don't know what Berta told you, but—"

"The truth. Unlike you, she's never lied to me or kept things from me."

"It's for your own good."

"Let me decide that."

"I can't."

"Then I can't trust you."

Marshall hesitated, then held out a flash drive with an OTG cable. "This will show you what you're up against."

I cautiously took it from him.

"It's just a video," he assured me. "I'm not trying to do anything to your phone. You need to see it before you even think about leaving this hospital."

I kept my eyes on him as I felt in my bag for my phone, only glancing down long enough to unlock my phone and plug it in.

The video's resolution was grainy and green. A night vision camera. The height and unsteadiness of the video told me it was helmet mounted. Whoever was wearing the helmet appeared to be in a cave.

From somewhere ahead came men speaking Arabic. I couldn't understand it, but I could recognize it when I heard it. The cave narrowed into a tunnel, and I could just make out what appeared to be a sentry up ahead. The man wearing the camera paused, and seconds later, the sentry gasped and started to fall. The man caught him, silently easing him to the floor.

A second, then a third sentry met the same fate.

Exactly what he had done to Simmons's guards yesterday at the town house.

Through it all, I heard the man's breathing. Regular and steady as he brought death on silent feet, the Grim Reaper out for stroll.

This was the man I had sensed in Julian's office, and yesterday in the Hart Building's men's room.

This was what we were hunting.

This was what would be hunting me—if Gabriel Marshall was to be believed.

The tunnel emptied into a cave with five men that I could see, two manning computer stations, two cleaning weapons, and one asleep in a corner.

He took the sleeper first.

Then the two cleaning weapons. One of the men managed to cry out before he died, alerting the remaining two. They leapt to their feet, turned toward their killer, and went for their guns. They were dead before they could draw.

Three sentries and five insurgents dead within two minutes.

Not one shot was fired.

All he did was look at them and kill.

I looked up from my phone. I had so many questions that—

Gabriel Marshall was gone.

CHAPTER 28

I put my phone down and pulled up the leg of my jeans. My combat boots had a tactical accessory strap that would accommodate a holster, sheath, or cuffs. I started to thread the strap through the holster, then stopped.

Always be suspicious of CIA assassins disguised as priests bearing gifts.

Gabriel Marshall had only said he wasn't doing anything to my phone.

I believed him when he'd said he was sorry about what had happened to Grandad. I even believed that he wanted me to be careful. But I wasn't buying for a second that he gave me his gun only to protect myself with.

I needed to examine my present.

The magazine of the little Beretta was fully loaded, and it didn't appear that anything had been modified to conceal a tracking chip.

That left the holster.

It looked like all the seams were intact, but I tugged and pulled my way around the holster anyway. If I hadn't been so thorough, I'd have missed it.

Wedged tightly between the leather layers of the holster was a tiny chip.

Nice try, Marshall. I'm not going to be your bait for a psychic psycho.

"An unusual room in which to arm yourself," Rees said from the doorway. "Though considering the circumstances, I can't say I disapprove."

I pulled down the leg of my jeans. "It's not mine, and I don't believe I'll be carrying it." I told him about my visitor, then showed him the video. While he watched it, I watched him, and saw something I'd never seen on Samuel Rees. Fear. Not for himself, but for us all.

"Marshall's not just trying to clean up a CIA embarrassment," Rees said. "This is a black ops project gone rogue—or worse, exactly according to plan. This is a national security emergency. I'll call Hudson. He needs to escalate this. With Gabriel Marshall, what's important is what he *doesn't* say. He wanted you to see this, and he didn't stay to take it back. He knew you'd show it to me. He advised you to stay away. He knows it's my job not to."

"What does that make Gabriel Marshall? Friend or foe?"

"I wouldn't call him a friend, but he has yet to cross the line into foe. We'll keep our eyes and options open. Pete found another piece of the puzzle—a call to Julian Pierce's burner from a place called MRT in Triment Industrial Park, Bethesda. MRT stands for Medical Research Technology."

Jackpot.

"We have response and forensics teams on the way there now," Rees added.

"Are you going?"

"Of course."

"Then I'm going. Berta can—"

"Keep both you and Ambrose safe."

I just looked at him. "Listen to yourself. Who better to tell you what's really been going on in this place than me? Medical Research Technology. Even the name screams 'we're hiding something.'"

Rees was looking at Marshall's Beretta in my hand. "If you insist on going, keep that and wear it."

"You're kidding?"

"I need to talk to Gabriel Marshall. Now. If you leave here, he'll be following you. I want him to."

We took the same SUV we had taken to Julian's house yesterday morning, only now I was sitting in the backseat alone, the early morning sun in my eyes. Granddad was in the ICCU fighting for his life. Rees had enough agents guarding him now that even I felt he would be safe.

On the way to MRT, I added my sunglasses to the FBI ballcap and windbreaker Berta had given me to complete my excuse for a disguise.

Like Gabriel Marshall had said, blend in with your surroundings. I was about to be surrounded by FBI response and forensics teams. If the assassin was following us, we were going to make him work to find his target.

Every metropolitan area was peppered with industrial parks bearing generic names. Some were built in areas along interstates for easy access, others made use of warehouse space or buildings that had fallen into disuse in sketchy parts of a city with desirable (aka cheap) rent. Businesses used the money they saved in rent to buy themselves enough security to persuade the local criminal elements to go elsewhere.

Medical Research Technology was a suitably generic company in an unassuming industrial park. MRT's purpose was as unknown as its history, which apparently did not exist. Rees had people digging to find every scrap of information, from who owned it down to the blood type and favorite color of the guy who'd come up with the name.

MRT was near the back of the industrial park in the last cluster of buildings.

When we arrived, there were two black SUVs and a black sedan waiting.

They were the only vehicles in the parking lot.

"Your people?" I asked.

"Yes." Rees didn't like the looks of this either.

It was Saturday morning. There'd been a light snow overnight, and the only tire tracks in the parking lot belonged to the three FBI vehicles.

Walking up to one of the agents was a man whose khaki uniform shouted private security guard. The agent showed the guard his badge.

Rees got out and went over to them. I scooted across the seat to follow.

"Stay," Berta told me in no uncertain terms. "When it's clear, we'll drive you right up to the front door. Until this is over, you're going to be seeing as little open sky as possible."

Then Berta stayed to make sure I stayed. She had her

window partially rolled down so we could hear most of what was being said.

"They moved out Tuesday night," the guard was saying. "One of those corporate moving companies brought a semi to the loading dock around back and started loading it up."

"Did you receive a notification about the move?" an agent asked.

"My supervisor said he did and assured us everything was on the up-and-up."

Rees stepped forward. "Do you have the name of the moving company and the tag number of the truck?"

"No, sir." The guard smiled. "But I think I can do you one better. I can get you the video from the camera that's aimed at MRT's loading dock. You can watch 'em drive in, load it, and leave."

Rees returned the smile. "That would be most helpful. Thank you."

The response team had a warrant, but there was no one at MRT to show it to. No one was home, and we didn't have a key, but one of the agents was gifted in all the right ways for a little breaking and entering. Or since they had a warrant, maybe it was just entering.

Rees pulled the SUV as close to MRT's door as he could get it, Berta held the door open, and I darted inside.

Inside Medical Research Technology was a whole lot of nothing.

The place had been stripped to the walls. All that was left was a nearly overpowering smell of bleach. No pleasant pine scent here, this was industrial-grade cleaner, and it'd been used recently.

After a search by the muscle contingency of the team to

ensure it was safe, the forensics half got to work. It didn't take them too long to report that there wasn't a single fingerprint to be found on any doorknob, drawer pull, faucet, or toilet handle. Every surface had been wiped clean.

The agents Hudson had dispatched had their jobs to do and they were doing them.

I went from room to room, doing mine.

I got an overall sense of controlled chaos. This hadn't been planned. This location had been compromised, and they'd evacuated. Yes, that was exactly the word to describe it. An evacuation. Whether the catalyst had been Barrington's text to Julian, or something else, I didn't know. I didn't get an indication as to the reason, just the need to get out as fast as possible.

There were no phones, no reception area, just four cubicles near the front, and two offices and a small conference room with doors.

The back half of the space Medical Research Technology had occupied lived up to its name. There had been a laboratory here. All the equipment had been removed, but the tables, cabinets, and lab sinks that had been attached to the floor or wall had been left behind. Toward the rear of the lab was what looked like an animal pen, about ten by ten, with a smaller separate pen with a gate nearby.

There was an underlying smell that the bleach couldn't hide.

"Pigs," Rees said with certainty.

Berta and I did a double take.

"Seriously?" I asked.

The agent shrugged. "My uncle raised pigs. That's a stink you don't forget."

"A noble occupation," I said. "Anyone who raises bacon has my undying gratitude. I wouldn't want to live in a world without it."

Pigs in a lab in Bethesda.

"What kind of lab would need pigs?" I continued. "Better yet, what kind of lab would wipe all their prints?"

"A lab that didn't want the people who worked here identified," Berta said. "I'm thinking this was a government lab."

"Here?"

"Anonymity," Rees said. "Government employees who need security clearances get fingerprinted. All those fingerprints are on file with their respective agencies. Whoever was here wouldn't have done such a thorough housekeeping job unless those prints were on file, and they didn't want anyone to know who they were—including the people in their own agency."

One of the other agents called for Rees. I continued exploring, and Berta gave me the space I needed without letting me out of her sight.

Off the lab was another room accessed through swinging doors with small windows at eye height that looked like hospital doors. I pushed the right door open with my elbow even though the techs were already inside and had dusted it for prints.

Inside was an airlock, and beyond was an operating room, complete with a high-intensity, adjustable light mounted to the ceiling directly above an operating table.

A table outfitted with thick, leather straps where the wrists, ankles, chest, thighs, and head on a human would be. A tech was dusting the straps for prints.

I went absolutely still as my vision narrowed to the head of the table.

They were awake. The people who had been strapped to that table had been awake while they'd undergone whatever surgery they'd endured.

No, worse than that, they had *needed* to be awake. The leather straps weren't because these people were being held against their will. It was to keep them still during the operation.

They had volunteered.

They'd *wanted* this.

The medical team surrounding the patient appeared to me as pale blurs, but I could tell that the surgery centered on the patient's head.

"Are you getting something?" Berta asked quietly from beside me.

I nearly jumped out of my boots.

"I'm sorry, I thought you were finished."

"I was, but next time make some noise."

"I'll try to breathe louder. What did you get?"

I told her what I'd seen—and my conclusion.

She spat a single word.

"I couldn't agree more," I told her.

Rees met us outside the operating room. "Your visitor is back."

CHAPTER 29

Rees had his phone in his hand. "Gabriel Marshall just called and wants to meet."

"Where?"

"The loading dock. Now."

Just before we reached the loading dock door, Berta stepped in front of me.

"I'm going first," she said.

"So you can punch him first?"

"Something like that." She shrugged out of her jacket and tossed it over the pig pen gate.

Berta wore a holster and gun under each arm. She was a deadly shot with either hand.

Rees stopped at the door. "Berta?"

"Yes?"

"Stay alert to any movement *behind* Marshall in the unlikely event he was followed. He's not the danger, not this time."

"If you say so."

Berta didn't like it, but she'd do it. We all knew she could undo it in an instant. Just because Rees didn't think it'd be necessary, didn't mean he wasn't in favor of her being overprotective. I agreed.

"You know that man's deep water," she added.

"I know." Rees caught my confused look. "In the ocean, light can only reach down to two hundred meters. From there, it gets darker and colder until it reaches a depth where humans can't survive."

"You're losing me."

"We're saying Gabriel Marshall has a lot of layers, each one darker than the last. He can set his humanity aside when the need calls for it. Have you touched him yet—other than grabbing his ankle the other night?"

"No."

"I think you might need to." Rees reached for the door handle. "Ready?"

He stood on one side of the door, Berta and I on the other.

When he opened it, the small loading dock was empty.

Berta's left gun was in her hand. "Son of a bitch."

"That's not fair, Agent Pike," a familiar voice called out. "You've never met my mother."

Gabriel Marshall stood on the edge of the woods beyond the parking lot. He had taken off the priest's collar, put on a black leather jacket, and secret agent man was back.

"May I come in?" he asked. "I'm rather exposed here."

"Is inviting a CIA assassin inside the same as giving a vampire permission to cross your threshold?" I wondered.

"This isn't our threshold," Berta replied.

"Good point."

Rees gestured Marshall to the loading dock, and Berta lowered her gun, which was about as much as we could expect from her at this point.

Berta planted herself in front of me—and Rees.

Marshall sighed. "We can have a staring contest or wrestle, or we can go inside and I'll tell you what you're looking for. We're on the same side, Berta. You can keep your gun on me if you like."

She didn't budge. "I'd definitely like."

"I'm here alone. As Sam can attest, I don't work and play well with others—except in dire emergencies, which is what we have now."

"Let's go inside," Rees said.

He led us to the small conference room, with Gabriel Marshall getting his fair share of interested glances and a few openly hostile stares along the way. Apparently, Berta wasn't alone in the "I hate Gabriel Marshall" club.

As Rees closed the door, Marshall gave the room a visual once-over. "Has it been swept?"

"Twice," Rees told him.

"Thorough. Good. Then you won't mind a third."

"Not at all. Be my guest."

Marshall took out a device the size of a lighter and quickly moved around the room. The gadget didn't make any screechy noises, so I assumed it was satisfied with our techs' work.

He took a seat at the table. "I take it I can I count on your discretion?"

"Can we count on you to tell us the truth?" Berta shot back.

"Yes. I'll even keep both hands on the table."

I took the chair next to him. "One will do." I extended my hand, palm up. "I want the other one."

Marshall smiled. "But we just met."

"And now it's time to get intimate. I don't have time or patience for anything else."

Gabriel Marshall met my eyes and put his hand in mine. I closed my fingers around it.

His skin was cool, his hand strong. The heel of my hand rested against the pulse in his wrist.

When I touch someone, I get a glimpse of the kind of person they are. Children are exceptional at it. They instinctively know bad or untrustworthy people when they meet them, no touching necessary. Since they haven't been conditioned to "be nice," they tell it like they see it. Don't get me started on parents who make their kids hug or, even worse, kiss people. When neither children nor dogs like or trust someone, pay attention. That's a big, red flag. Unfortunately, as we get older, we're less honest with ourselves, trying to convince ourselves that any unease is just our imagination, or we feel compelled by our upbringing to be polite.

Gabriel Marshall was a complicated man, but not an evil one. Yes, he'd killed, and he would kill again. It was his job. Much like a soldier, he derived no pleasure from either the act or the result. He killed those whose deaths he felt would make the world a safer place. I couldn't condemn him for that. There was an honesty to it, a forthrightness. I didn't think he would lie. He might not tell us everything, and I'd be surprised if he did, but he wouldn't lie to us.

That didn't mean I wasn't going to ask for it.

"Now tell us everything you know," I told him.

"David Barrington developed an implant to boost PK. That's psychokinesis," he said as an aside to Berta.

"I know what it is."

"They tried to recruit me," he continued. "I told them no. I like my brain the way it is."

"Who tried to recruit you?" Rees asked.

"Barton Renwick was brought in to run the program."

At the mention of the name, Rees's mouth twisted in distaste. "By whom?"

"I've asked and not been given an answer. Barrington might know, but he's not here to ask."

"That's probably the only reason he's alive."

"Who's Barton Renwick?" I asked.

"He went to medical school with David Barrington," Marshall told us. "He's built his entire career from riding on Barrington's lab coattails. After school, they joined the CIA together. Barrington went into R and D, and Renwick managed the department Barrington was in." He huffed a humorless laugh. "If you're not talented enough to develop new tech, manage those who are. Renwick was the one who got the CIA to pay attention to Barrington's implant. Barrington is the only one who can perform the operation. The two senators who could blow the whistle or pull the plug on the project are dead, Barrington is in hiding, and Barton Renwick is in the wind along with their psychotic lab rat."

I was stunned. "He went from helping paralyzed people walk again to creating a psychic assassin?"

"He thinks he's still helping people. He believes psychic enhancement is the next step in evolution for the human species. It's called the Entity Project."

"Entity?"

"A thing with a distinct and independent existence. In this case, an assassin who can work independent of any external weapons, including his own fists and feet. His mind is the weapon. The Entity was created to kill dictators, warlords, oligarchs, any individual deemed to be a danger to world peace." He barked a laugh. "Like there's ever been such a thing as world peace. The deaths would look natural, so no country could be blamed, thereby lessening or eliminating any retaliation. In theory, it could help end wars before they started. Instead, we have multiple people dead, and a man in ICCU because he got too close to the truth. No one besides Barrington and Renwick thought it would even work. They convinced higher-ups in the CIA and Julian Pierce that it was worth the investment. Mark Dalton weaseled his way into the information and set himself up to work both sides. He wanted to blame Pierce and destroy him politically if the project failed or went off the rails, or take credit and be the hero for saving the US from its enemies if it succeeded as planned."

"Instead he was deemed a loose end and died on the toilet with his pants around his ankles," I said.

The corner of Marshall's mouth twitched in a quick smile. "I wondered if the location of the hit was chosen or was simply an exploited opportunity too good to pass up." He looked to Rees. "You need my help and I need yours. I've been asked to clean up this mess, but I'm starting to feel like I've been dropped in the middle of Chernobyl. I don't know who to trust among my own people. They're not telling me everything, and what they have told me is more than enough to get me killed."

I realized something. "The pigs."

Marshall grinned. "I agree with the sentiment. My colleagues—"

I shot him a look. "I mean they kept pigs in pens out there next to the loading dock. A pig heart is similar enough to a human heart that parts, like valves, can be used in replacement surgeries. The Entity practiced here by killing pigs."

"What is this Entity's name?" Rees asked Marshall.

"Elias Halverson. And before you ask, no, I'd never seen or heard of him until a week ago. I thought I was black-ops, but this guy's subterranean. You can look, but there's no record of him that I could find. If it's there, it's buried deep. If you hit pay dirt, great. I'd love to see it."

Rees steepled his hands in front of his face. "And the CIA wants you to find Barrington."

"And I will." Marshall gave us a grim smile. "I'll find him, but I'm not telling anyone in Langley where he is. Not until I untangle this mess and know where everyone's loyalties lie." He glanced at Berta. "I'm going to reach in my pocket for a photo. Don't go Han Solo on me."

Berta's smile almost reached her eyes. "Greedo shot first."

"You keep believing that." He gave the photo to me.

I took it. "So, this is him."

Marshall nodded. "The man who tried to kill your grandfather."

"He's as generic-looking as this building."

"The best assassins don't attract attention."

I passed the photo to Rees. "Is that why you got out of the program?" I asked Marshall.

"I didn't agree with some of the targets I was being given."

"What's your mission?" Rees asked him.

"Find and protect Barrington. Find and kill Halverson. That's a target I can agree with. He's had two surgeries. Three, if you count implanting that chip in his head. He might not look too much like that photo, but it's the best I have." He paused. "I want to know why two of the top people in the CIA want

Elias Halverson dead, and the other two want him kept alive at all costs."

Rees leaned forward in his chair. "Two want him alive, but you're hunting him."

"I don't take my orders from them."

"Have they sent people to stop you?"

Gabriel Marshall's smile was chilling. "If they have, they're going to lose those people."

"How about the two that want Halverson dead?" Berta asked. "They're embarrassed their shiny new assassin went rogue?"

"No," Marshall said quietly. "They're terrified that he didn't."

Rees went utterly still. "And that he's following orders."

Marshall lightly tapped his nose twice. "And what are those orders? And who is his target?"

"If we want answers, we need to go to the source," I said. "The man who made the monster. David Barrington."

CHAPTER 30

Rees got a phone call and stepped out in the hall to take it, leaving me and Berta in the conference room with Gabriel Marshall. None of us were in the mood for small talk, and Marshall was intent on his phone's screen, reading an incoming text. I'd dropped his hand when he'd gotten it, but I was still sitting next to him.

I sat back and crossed my arms. "You drugged our cat."

Marshall didn't so much as glance up from his phone. "I wasn't attacked, and he enjoyed himself. A win-win."

"How did you know he'd attack you?"

"Your grandfather has worked with the FBI Art Crime team as well as others in the intelligence community. He's occasionally hosted those meetings in his office. Word gets around."

I wasn't finished. "You threw me across the yard."

"I *detached* you from my leg, and you were lighter than I anticipated. My apologies."

A compliment and an apology. Nice try, Mr. Secret Agent Man. I wasn't buying it. "And you—"

Rees opened the door and stuck his head inside. "Agent Pike, Ms. Donati, we need to leave. Marshall, this meeting is over."

The CIA officer dropped his phone in his front jacket pocket. "I'm going with you. Barrington will talk to me. He doesn't know you."

Silence.

Marshall tapped his breast pocket. "I couldn't depend on you to share information, so I took steps. I apologize, but it's necessary. I got the text version of your phone call with Elaine Pierce as you were speaking to her. She knows where Barrington is. Shall I continue?"

Berta was instantly on her feet. "You bastard!"

"That's your opinion. I call it doing my job." Marshall swiveled his chair to face Rees. I thought he was crazy to turn his back on Berta. "You need me."

"That's your opinion," Rees said mildly.

"David Barrington knows and trusts me," Marshall said. "I was his first choice for the project. He had no other candidates. I don't know how Elias Halverson was ultimately chosen, but Barton Renwick would've had everything to do with it." He smiled. "Barrington is career CIA. You're FBI. With me there, you at least have a chance he'll tell you what went wrong and who was behind it."

I hated it when jerks were right—especially when those jerks were assassins who might be looking to put a bullet between the eyes of the man we absolutely had to find.

"How do we know you won't kill him?" Berta asked.

Sounded like I wasn't the only one who doubted Marshall's motives.

"I'm equally adept at protecting," he replied. "David Barrington is a brilliant scientist and a good man. The world needs more like him, not less. Any more questions? If not, we're wasting time, unless you want Renwick or Halverson to get to him first."

Go fish.

Julian Pierce's last text to David Barrington was telling him to run.

It also told him where to run.

Not merely to one of the lakes or rivers where they used to vacation together with friends, but to a specific place, the exact cabin.

A cabin named Go Fish.

The owner had built it as a place for his family to spend summers together. A grandson, now grown, had insisted they play Go Fish on the front porch every night before bed in lieu of a bedtime story. Thus, the cabin had been named Go Fish, complete with a woodcut sign of a cartoon fish that looked like one of those Goldfish crackers.

Elaine Pierce had found a photo of her grandfather and his friends posing in front of the cabin with their catches of the day. After seeing the photo, she remembered the story of how the cabin had gotten its name.

We had a destination.

Go Fish in the Pharaoh Lake Wilderness in the Adirondacks, about a hundred miles north of Albany, NY.

"Another hundred miles north would put him in Canada," I noted.

"He wouldn't be safe there, either," Marshall said.

SAC Roger Hudson had arranged a jet to take us to Albany, and a helicopter to get us within two miles of the cabin's coordinates. That was the closest landing site. Rees told us we'd have to hike in from there. Normally, it'd be impassible this time of year, but the winter so far had been too warm for the snow to be measured in feet.

I hadn't been dressed for a winter hike, but Rees had taken care of gear for the three of us. Naturally, Gabriel Marshall had his own gear in his car's trunk, including winter camo and more weapons than most men would need in ten lifetimes.

Hudson had also arranged to have a few heavily armed friends accompany us to Pharaoh Lake. We were in two helicopters, one of which was as heavily armed as its occupants. Berta carried a bag similar to Marshall's that I was sure didn't contain mittens and a thermos of hot chocolate, though the latter would've been nice right about now.

"Does the cabin have a phone?" I asked anyone who might know.

"It doesn't even have electricity," Rees said. "Though Elaine thinks it has a generator."

"I've heard of the owner," Marshall said. "Carter Perry is retired CIA. A legend. The closest comparison would be James Bond's Q. His specialty was surveillance equipment. Barrington will probably know we're there before we land. No wonder Pierce told him to go there."

We landed and began our hike in. Snow concealed the ground, and ground tended to be uneven, especially in the mountains. I quickly learned that at least in this instance, it was better to follow in the footsteps of others than to lead. Two of Hudson's commandos led the way, with the other two bringing up the rear. If being surrounded by that much FBI firepower made Gabriel Marshall uneasy, he didn't show it, and I couldn't sense it.

We crested a rise and saw the cabin in a shallow valley below.

Go Fish was an actual, honest-to-God log cabin. It was one story with a front porch running its length. There were windows on the two sides that we could see, but they were shuttered tight for the winter. There were no lights, and no sign of Barrington's rented white Land Rover, though with all the snow and underbrush, it wouldn't have been difficult to hide.

It looked like no one was there, and no one had been there since fall.

Which was exactly how it was supposed to look.

David Barrington was here—or someone was. I could feel it.

"We're being watched," I murmured.

"And probably scanned," Marshall said.

"So, we just wait?"

Rees was calmly watching the cabin's two doors. "We're the guests. We wait."

Berta snorted. "To be shot?"

"It won't be long."

"That's good. I'd hate to have to wait to—"

"You are trespassing on private property. Identify yourselves immediately."

The computerized voice came from every direction.

"Sounds like HAL 9000 on steroids," I said.

Rees stepped forward. "Special Agent Samuel Rees and Alberta Pike, FBI."

Silence.

"Is HAL going to open fire?" I wondered.

"We're probably being scanned for facial recognition," Marshall said. He was grinning. "Gabriel Marshall, CIA."

"*Now* we're gonna get shot," Berta muttered.

A few seconds later the cabin's front door opened, and a smiling Dr. David Barrington eagerly waved us in.

Marshall flashed a smile of his own. "See? He's glad to see me."

Berta shook her head. "This just keeps getting stranger."

CHAPTER 31

The cabin was rustic inside and out.

Except for the bank of computer screens showing what I assumed was every approach to the cabin.

David Barrington had lost weight since the photo on Julian's study wall had been taken last fall. Though if I was hiding from a psychokinetic assassin in a log cabin fortress a hundred miles from the Canadian border in the middle of winter, I'd probably be a shadow of my former self, too.

Rees was looking around. "Impressive."

"The owner likes his privacy," Barrington said.

Dr. David Barrington had had an unexpected reaction when he saw Marshall.

He'd relaxed. Not just a slight easing of tension. We're talking total relief, as if Gabriel Marshall was an angel sent by God himself. For a moment there, I thought Barrington was going to hug him.

I wasn't the only one who noticed.

"I don't think I've ever had anyone this glad to see me," Marshall said.

"You don't know how good it is to see someone I can trust."

Marshall didn't need to say, "I told you so." The smug grin he tossed Berta said it for him.

She snorted. "All that means is Hell's in the process of freezing over." ·

The only sources of light were two oil lamps—and the wall nearly full of surveillance monitors.

Marshall made the introductions, and you bet I shook David Barrington's hand.

For all his relief, Barrington was terrified, giving off waves of adrenaline like a cornered animal. Despite being nearly giddy to see Gabriel Marshall, he felt utterly alone, had no idea what he was going to do or where to go next. Would he be killed, or arrested and taken back to Washington as a traitor? He knew his career was in tatters; his life, for all intents and purposes, was over.

I felt sorry for him and wanted to deck him at the same time. What he had to say for himself in the next few minutes would determine which impulse I gave in to.

Marshall was checking out what I could only describe as the security command center. "Carter really values his family's privacy. He's got cameras, motion sensors, and body heat detectors in a hundred-yard perimeter around the cabin."

"It's powered from a solar array at the top of the ridge behind us," Barrington told him. "Carter can monitor it from home back in Alexandria. When he installed all this, he borrowed a tiny piece of real estate on a CIA satellite."

Holy crap.

"Is he monitoring it now?" Marshall asked.

"Yes. Thank God. It's the only thing that's kept me sane."

"How much do you know about what's happened?"

Barrington took a ragged breath. "Julian and Alan are dead. Mark Dalton, too."

I wanted to throw the blame for Grandad at his feet, but I held my tongue. Barrington might trust Marshall, but I sure as hell didn't trust Barrington. We didn't know how much of this was his fault, and until we did, I'd ask questions, but I wasn't going to answer any from him.

"When you turned me down," Barrington continued, "I should have refused to go further with the project right then. I knew you were the only possible choice."

"Except I don't want an implant in my head and to be ordered around the world killing every dictator who pisses off the US—or just Langley. That's not what I do."

"You know about Elias?"

"Just that he's who you went with instead of me."

"His PK was off the charts, like yours, and his CIA service record was impeccable."

"That's when you should've gotten suspicious. No one's record is that clean."

"Barton recommended him, and I trusted Barton." His expression darkened. "At least I did. It was either accept Elias into the project or shut it down. The human mind is the greatest unexplored and undeveloped frontier. I believe the next step in human evolution is the expansion of the brain's capabilities, and now is the time to take that step. The Entity Project isn't the direction I would have chosen, but it fills a critical need. There are too many madmen with their fingers on nuclear buttons. I couldn't afford to wait. The world couldn't wait. We'd come too far with the project. We were so close."

"To creating a psychic assassin," Rees said.

"There is so much evil in this world, Special Agent Rees. Wouldn't you agree?"

"We do seem to have had more than our fair share lately."

"Throughout history, every country has used assassins. I'm not an advocate of murder, but consider the multiple assassination attempts against Adolph Hitler. Think of the millions of lives that could have been saved by the elimination of just one man. More than seventy years after his death, the evil he spawned is still spreading. With the Entity Project wars could be prevented before they started. No country would be blamed for what would be believed to be a natural death. No nuclear retaliation. No terrorist attacks. Wars averted. Peace, Agent Rees. I just wanted to give the world peace."

"Except your avenging angel turned out to be the fallen variety," Marshall said, his voice clipped and hard.

"He was the only candidate with the level of existing skill to allow it to work. Except for you."

Skill. David Barrington believed it was a skill to murder and have no one trace it back to you. I could see where his passion was coming from. In an ideal world, Elias Halverson wouldn't have gone rogue. But thinking about Grandad lying in that hospital bed…It was all I could do not to go after Barrington with my bare hands. I went to the monitors and kept watch for any movement. HAL would know before I would. Still, it gave me something to do besides pound the crap out of David Barrington.

Marshall wasn't doing much better in the self-control

department. I could feel it coming off him in waves. Professionalism prevailed. For now.

"And you thought you could control him," Marshall said. "You're playing God, but all you've done is create a monster, and now it's turned on you. What can he do besides cardiac arrests and aneurysms?"

"That's it for now."

"For now?"

"For older subjects he would use cardiac arrest, younger would be aneurysms. If a subject had a particular health problem, Elias could work on customizing his method."

Subject? Customize his method?

That did it.

"Your monster killed my grandfather." I felt myself losing the last bit of control I had. I hadn't given in to my grief in the hospital. I'd kept it inside. Listening to David Barrington had twisted it into rage, and that rage was coming out. I had the man responsible right in front of me. "If Rees and I hadn't been there with him when Elias used his 'skill' to stop Grandad's heart, he would have stayed dead. He's in ICCU, hooked up to machines, and we don't know if he's going to live or die." My voice dropped to a hissing whisper. "If he dies, you had better hope whoever is hunting you gets to you before I do." I quickly turned and went to the other side of the small room. I couldn't trust myself not to go after Barrington now.

"Her grandfather is Ambrose Donati," I heard Rees saying as I tried to get myself back under control. "The two of them are consulting detectives for the FBI. Julian Pierce was a very good friend of Ambrose, and he and Aurora are helping us find his killer. Elias Halverson felt threatened and induced a cardiac arrest in Mr. Donati on the doorstep of his home." Rees's voice went dangerously quiet. "He is eighty-two years old."

Barrington collapsed into the computer chair, like a puppet whose strings had been cut. "Oh God. God, I'm so sorry."

His horror and regret were sincere, but I didn't want either one. Neither would heal Grandad.

"I don't want your apology," I spat. "I want to know where this thing you've created has gone to ground."

Rees pulled up a chair close to Barrington. "Where is Elias, Dr. Barrington? I assume he killed Pierce, Coe, and Dalton out of self-preservation, to protect the project and its mission. He attacked Ambrose Donati for the same reason. What is that mission?"

"I don't know. I warned Julian about him," Barrington said. "I don't know how Mark Dalton found out there was a problem."

"What problem?"

"There's a stability problem with the implant."

"The implant is defective?" Marshall asked. "Or is Elias Halverson unstable?"

"Or did the implant make him that way?" I added.

"The implant is a booster," Barrington said. "A battery, if you will, to enhance Elias's psychokinetic ability. It should have had no effect on his mental stability."

Marshall crouched on the floor in front of Barrington, putting them eye to eye. "But it did, didn't it?"

Barrington took a breath and shook his head. "I don't know for sure. Before the operation, he was level-headed, sociable, all his psychological testing came back normal, well within acceptable parameters. He was a perfect candidate for the project. After the surgery, he learned to work with the implant, trained with it. We had anatomic models for him to use. They were made of materials of the same density and texture of a human body. The hearts were wired to beat. He was proud of his progress, but not in a way that raised concern. It was only after he began working with the pigs that…"

"He liked it," I said. "He enjoyed the killing, didn't he?"

"Yes."

Rees leaned forward. "What is his mission?"

"He's supposed to be deployed overseas; that's all I know."

"What made you contact Julian Pierce?"

"Last week, Barton told me my part was over. I said it was too soon. Elias needed more observation. Barton told me not to worry about Elias, and that he would take it from there."

Berta huffed a laugh. "That's when you knew you *really* needed to worry."

"Barton also wanted to expand the project beyond Elias. I told him I disagreed. We didn't know the implant's long-term effects. Barton seemed to accept it, but on Tuesday morning, the three backup implants and batteries I had made were missing from the safe in the lab's clean room."

I stared at him in disbelief. "*Three* implants? Renwick can make three more assassins?"

"No. Not without me. I'm the only one who can do the surgery." He paused. "Though Barton did assist me with Elias's implant."

Wonderful.

Barrington took a deep breath and it all came out. "Soon after the project began, Barton assured me we were fully funded. I asked Julian how much the committee had allocated for the project." He paused. "It wasn't anywhere near as much as we needed. But Barton had provided everything I'd asked for, without question."

"So, Barton had gone shopping for investors." Marshall's eyes were hard, relentless.

"That's what Julian and I thought. Last year, Barton took his family to Europe on their annual vacation. I remembered his wife telling me about their trip to Prague, Vienna, and Budapest. She said Barton only had only a few business meetings this time, so it hadn't ruined the family's fun."

This time.

"Let me guess," Marshall said, "when he came back, not only was the project suddenly flush with cash, but he had a recommendation for a replacement for me."

"Yes. Barton called the lab late Tuesday morning and told me he wanted my notes on the Entity Project. I didn't tell him I knew he'd taken the implants. I told him it'd take a couple days to get the notes together. I tried calling Julian, but couldn't reach him until Wednesday. He told me to come here."

And several hours after that, Senator Julian Pierce and Alan Coe were dead.

Barrington put his face in his hands. "I've known Barton my entire medical career. He was like a brother to me."

Said Abel about Cain.

"Where are your notes?" Marshall asked.

"I destroyed them."

"I don't believe you."

"I don't expect you to."

"Why didn't you call the CIA?"

"I didn't know who I could trust."

"There's a lot of that going around," Marshall said smoothly. "Sam, we need to find Barton Renwick. Now."

CHAPTER 32

"*Perimeter breach in multiple sectors—*"

The front window shattered, and a bullet slammed into the server cabinet, silencing HAL mid warning.

Rees dragged Barrington off the chair and onto the floor.

Shots continued and sparks flew as Carter Perry's home security network was destroyed.

"Where are your men?" Marshall shouted to Rees over the gunfire.

Berta returned fire out the shattered window. "They're out there."

She was right. It sounded like a small war outside. With HAL permanently out of commission, we had no clue how many were out there, or where. Our team of four was up against an unknown number.

"Comms are out," Rees said. "We're being jammed."

A tear gas canister flew past Berta and landed in front of the fireplace.

Rees jerked Barrington's collar. "Is there another way out?"

The doctor lifted the rug next to the computer chair, revealing a trap door. "This goes to the basement. There's a door on the north wall." He started to cough. "Mining tunnel. . . goes up to the ridge."

Marshall made a grabbing and throwing motion with his hand, and the canister that was nearly ten feet away went flying out the way it came. Berta and Marshall grabbed their duffels as we scrambled down the stairs, but there was no way to put the rug back over the trapdoor. If they had to look for our escape hatch, we might gain a few critical seconds.

I grabbed Marshall's arm. "Can you put—"

"PK the rug back and tidy up a bit?"

"Yeah, that."

"I'm insulted you had to ask."

Berta looked up at the now closed trapdoor. "Is there anything to block this with?"

Barrington quickly ran a hand around the doorframe. "There's supposed to be a deadbolt—"

"Found it." Berta pulled the bolt and locked the door from our side.

I heard the computer chair rolling as Marshall used his PK to not only replace the rug, but put the chair on top of it, hopefully hiding our exit, or at least buying us more time to escape.

Barrington was at the back wall, lifting the bar hooked across a low door. Rees pulled him back as Berta opened it, shining her gun-mounted light into the tunnel beyond, then plunging inside. "If it's not clear I'll make it clear."

Rees and Barrington followed, with me and Marshall bringing up the rear.

Barrington stopped. "There's a bar on this side, too." He found the bar behind the door and fitted it into hooks mounted on either side of the doorframe.

"What kind of family does Carter Perry have?" I asked.

Marshall flashed a grin. "Typical multigenerational CIA family."

We moved quickly as we could, considering the rocks underfoot and the unlevel tunnel floor. The tunnel was definitely manmade. Barrington had said it was a mine tunnel, yet there were no intersecting tunnels, just the one we were in that continued to go up and hopefully out.

I dropped back to where Marshall was bringing up the rear. "What if we have company waiting for us up top?"

"Between me and Berta, we've got enough ammo to start our own war."

"I just want to finish the one we've got."

"I aim to please, ma'am. Hopefully Rees's people called for backup when they got ambushed."

"Unless their comms are jammed, too."

"I'll bet you're a ton of fun at parties."

"I don't like parties."

"Why am I not surprised?"

"Too many people with too many emotions isn't my idea of a good time." Talking was helping to calm my nerves, so I kept doing it. "So, what can you do with *your* PK?"

"I can't stop human organs from working, if that's what you're wondering."

"I wasn't, but thanks for getting that out of the way."

"You believe me?"

"Yeah. I've been around you enough to get a good read. I know when you're lying."

"Have I been?"

"No, but you haven't told us the whole truth, either."

"I'll bet you're a ton of fun in relationships, too," he said, deftly shifting the topic from him to me.

"They're not fun for me, either." I turned away and picked up the pace, leaving Marshall behind.

When I had prolonged contact with someone, I found out way too much. Sex increased that knowledge a hundredfold. We all have fantasies, and some of them we'd rather not share with anyone, regardless of how close the relationship. Sex released more than inhibitions; it released the fantasies. When the body lost its inhibitions, so did the subconscious.

Normally, a couple was together for a while before they started sharing that which possibly should not be shared. I got it all during the first kiss with the surge of hormones, or if the guy had exceptional self-control, during foreplay. I saw what he wanted to see, what he imagined himself doing—and with, or to, whom.

It was distracting to say the least; and at worst, I couldn't turn it off, which made it next to impossible to get turned on. For me, TMI took on a whole new meaning.

"I can get a beer out of the fridge and never leave the couch," Marshall said quietly.

I glanced back at him. Marshall's gaze was searching my face, not intently, but trying to assess my mood. He knew he'd crossed a line and he sincerely wanted to make up for it.

Sincerity.

Not something I would've associated with Gabriel Marshall.

He'd made an effort; so could I.

"Can you make a plate of nachos from the couch?" I asked.

"That'd be pushing it, but I could work on it."

I gave him the slightest of smiles. "Well, when you're good enough, let me know."

It felt like it took forever to get to the end of the tunnel. We stopped a few times to listen for sounds of pursuit. There were none. Either Rees's people had won, or there'd be an unfriendly welcoming committee waiting for us at the other end. A glance at my watch told me it'd only been twenty minutes.

Berta stopped in front of another door.

It was time to see what was out there.

Gabriel moved up beside her. "You want to go play in the snow with me?"

Berta shrugged, never taking her eyes from the door. "I can think of worse things to do." She glanced at her partner. "Rees?"

Rees had his gun out. He stepped in front of Barrington. "Have fun, children. And don't play nice."

Marshall's smile was more like a baring of teeth. "I never do."

Berta and Marshall stocked up from their duffel bags. He turned to me. "You got my Beretta?"

The CIA officer was bristling with weapons and knives. "You need it back?" I asked in disbelief.

"No." He dug into his duffel. "Here's two extra mags. Just in case."

If Marshall and Berta couldn't handle what was out there, I seriously doubted two extra mags would do the rest of us a whole lot of good.

Rees held up his hand for quiet. "Say again."

Comms were back up. Thank God. Being at the top of the ridge must have put us out of the jammer's range.

Rees told whoever he was talking to where we were, and that we had Barrington. From the back and forth, I gathered that the team had one wounded, though not badly. "We'll be there."

"It was a team of six," Rees told us. "Four dead, one captured, one unaccounted for. There's a clearing on this ridge to the west. Our pilot should be able to land there."

"It's about a hundred yards," Barrington said.

Rees nodded. "Let's get there and go home."

The door opened into a shallow cave. Just as Barrington said, we were at the top of a ridge, home to Carter Perry's solar array. The view across the mountain range was gorgeous in the midday sun, but we had a chopper to meet, and an unaccounted-for hired killer to avoid.

That last one was easier said than done.

Halfway to the clearing, we found ourselves pinned down by a lone and increasingly desperate sniper. To make matters worse, he was a really good shot.

But there was only one of him against five of us—and two of us were Alberta Pike and Gabriel Marshall.

"Any trip over four hundred miles from home, I *will* bring back a souvenir," Berta declared.

Marshall and Rees kept the sniper busy exchanging fire, and Berta circled around behind and bagged herself that souvenir.

Four dead. *Two* captured. One CIA doctor recovered.

Our day was looking up.

While the sniper was still unconscious, Rees emailed a photo of him back to Washington to see who Berta's souvenir was.

Pyotr Kharkov. Enforcer for Russian oligarch Grigori Dementiev.

"Dementiev conducts a lot of his Western business from Prague," Marshall said. "I'm betting Barton Renwick paid him a visit while on vacation. Dementiev prides himself on his US investments."

David Barrington was looking a little queasy, and I didn't think it was from the helicopter ride.

"Do you know if he speaks English?" Rees asked, indicating our trussed passenger.

Marshall bared his teeth again. "Let's find out."

Berta was good. She'd hit Pyotr Kharkov hard enough to knock him out, but not enough to keep him that way for long.

She'd knocked him out. Marshall woke him up.

It turned out the air above upstate New York was seriously cold in January.

Marshall opened a small window and shoved Kharkov's face through it. Consciousness and the screaming that came with it only took a few seconds.

Marshall indicated the back of Kharkov's neck, which was bare. "Find out if he speaks English."

I put a hand to the Russian's neck. There were plenty of words going through his mind, but none of them were in English.

I drew back and shook my head.

"Too bad. We'll have to do this the hard way."

Marshall pulled him back in and asked him a question in Russian. I didn't understand Russian, but to me, Kharkov's smarmy reply sounded like an insult to Marshall's parents and the manner in which he'd been conceived.

Rees asked a question of his own, in Russian. I didn't know he spoke Russian.

Kharkov's mouth moved, but it wasn't to talk.

Before he could spit, Marshall shoved his face back out the window.

"I need to make him more afraid of us than he is of Dementiev," Marshall told Rees, "or whoever's paying him for this job. You said the pilot's name is Mike?"

"Yes."

"Mike?" Marshall call out.

"Sir?"

"I'm going to open the back door to let in a little fresh air." He winked, then jerked his head at the Russian.

"Go right ahead, sir. Fresh air is healthy."

Not for our Russian passenger.

He was already bound hand and foot, but it was amazing how much fight he had when Marshall and Berta tied the Russian's legs to the rope ladder. When Marshall opened the door, the man's words came in a torrent of rapid-fire Russian.

Marshall was unimpressed, or at least not impressed enough not to do what he did next.

He kicked the Russian out of the helicopter.

Beautiful.

I couldn't help but think that Grandad would approve. I'd have to tell him all about it.

Berta's smile lit her entire face. "I hope your knots hold."

Marshall grinned back. "Me, too."

I'd been wondering what it'd take to get those two on friendly terms. Now I knew.

Berta leaned out and looked down. "Mike, can you get a little closer to the treetops?"

"Yes, ma'am."

For the next few minutes, Russian was yelled back and

forth. A shouted question from Marshall, then increasingly desperate words punctuated by screams from the Russian dangling from the ladder over the tall pines of upper New York State.

Marshall leaned back in. "Fat, pasty American. Sound like anyone you know, Doc?"

At the description, Barrington went a little pasty himself. "Barton."

"Somebody find a photo," Marshall said. He and Berta got a good grip on the ladder. "We'll haul him up for confirmation."

Rees got out his phone and found a photo of Barton Renwick. "Is this recent enough, Dr. Barrington?"

"Yes." He looked like he wanted to strangle the man on the screen.

Rees handed Marshall his phone, who in turn showed the photo to the nearly frostbitten Russian.

"*Da.*"

We all understood that.

CHAPTER 33

I had to admit, the Russian was an inventive storyteller.

Once in a comparatively hospitable interrogation room in the FBI's Washington Field Office, Pyotr Kharkov was downright eager to sell out the pasty American who was the source of his present troubles. As to what a team of Russian commandos was doing in upstate New York, Kharkov insisted they were there to protect Barrington from CIA assassins as he fled into Canada and from there to Russia. He said Barrington had chosen the cabin for its proximity to the border. When told that two of his comrades had a drug that would have rendered Barrington unconscious for hours, Kharkov claimed to know nothing about it.

Concerning his employer, oligarch Grigori Dementiev, he said nothing.

An international APB had been issued for Dr. Barton Renwick and Elias Halverson, who had either wormed their way even deeper underground here or had already fled the country.

David Barrington was safely ensconced upstairs in what I could only describe as an in-house safehouse. The FBI actually had a set of rooms that looked like a hotel suite. Nothing that'd earn many stars, but it was friendlier than a cell or interrogation room. I imagined it came in handy for people you wanted in custody, but didn't want to feel like prisoners.

The doctor had been talking nonstop for the past three hours, that is, once he'd been assured that he wasn't going to be charged with treason or kicked to the curb for the Russians to find. Right now, he was working with an FBI artist to make any needed adjustments to the photo Marshall had of Elias Halverson. A doctor was sworn to protect life, but right now, all David Barrington wanted was Halverson dead, and probably Renwick, too.

We were in a small conference room adjacent to SAC Roger Hudson's office. Rees, Berta, Marshall, and I were seated around the table. Roger Hudson came in and closed the door behind him. He was in his late fifties, with short salt-and-pepper hair, and brown eyes that could either warm you to your soul or pierce a hole straight through you, depending on what you'd done to be on the receiving end. He was a kind man and a straight shooter, but God help you if you messed with his people.

"Ms. Donati, I am so sorry about your grandfather. Rest assured we are doing all we can to apprehend everyone involved. I consider both you and Ambrose part of our family here."

"Thank you for authorizing the guards at the hospital," I said. "I want to be there, but your people protecting him puts my mind at ease."

"I wish I could do more."

"You're doing all you can. We all are."

He extended his hand to Gabriel Marshall, who stood and shook it. "Officer Marshall, on behalf of myself and ADC Williams, thank you for your help and cooperation. Rees has briefed me on today's events. You all have had a busy day."

"Yes, we have," Marshall replied, completely at ease in the FBI's WFO.

I was pretty comfortable myself.

I was also warm and full of fried chicken and doughnuts Rees had thoughtfully ordered sent over from Astro, and the only danger I was in was from dozing off. Even better than the icing on the maple bacon doughnut I'd just finished off had been a call from Gerald at the hospital. Grandad's condition had improved a little, and he was showing signs of regaining consciousness. I desperately wanted to be there with him, but I needed to be here. I couldn't do anything to help Grandad get better, but I could help catch and stop Elias Halverson. I knew exactly where Grandad would want me to be, and what he'd want me to be doing.

"Dementiev is a mid-level oligarch who's been angling for a way to move up the ranks," Marshall was saying.

"So, he bought his very own CIA research project," Hudson said.

Marshall nodded. "Dementiev isn't a member of Putin's inner circle, so he's been able to avoid attracting too much attention and isn't under sanctions. He won't be satisfied with getting Elias Halverson in his personal arsenal. He'll want more. If Halverson and Renwick escape and reach him, Dementiev will have bought himself the assassin of his dreams and the means to make more with the implants Renwick stole.

No more novichok on a doorknob or polonium in a cup of tea. Halverson doesn't need to carry a weapon, so he can pass through any security checkpoint. He only needs to see his target to kill them. Any world or religious leader could be assassinated anywhere at any time, and no one would be the wiser."

Except us.

"We don't know what Halverson's connection is to Dementiev or whether his loyalty is to Renwick," Marshall continued. "As far as Dementiev is concerned, he's paid for Halverson and he wants what he paid for. Dementiev does his western business out of Prague. We have the city covered. When Renwick or Halverson show themselves, we'll have them."

"And if they don't show themselves?"

Marshall's smile was slow and dangerous. "Then I'll go and find them." He took his phone out of his pocket. "With your permission, I'd like to bring Theodore Chisholm in on this."

That was a name I hadn't heard before. "Who is—"

"The man I report to."

I turned to Rees. "Should we feel sorry for this guy?"

"Very."

Marshall made the call and put his phone in the middle of the table.

"Chisholm. About damned time you—"

"I was busy finding Barrington," Marshall told his boss.

"You have him?"

"He's safe, though he came close to being drugged and on his way to Russia right now."

"Where are you?"

Marshall grinned. "FBI Washington Field Office. The

coffee's not as good, but their hospitality more than makes up for it. As you can probably guess, I'm not alone."

Silence.

"Call me back later," Chisholm said.

"I can't do that."

Chisholm didn't say anything, but I detected the faintest hint of a growl.

"Hello, Theo," Hudson said.

More silence. "Roger."

Normally, I needed to at least see a person to get a read on what they were thinking. It wasn't necessary with Theodore Chisholm. He felt ambushed and understandably unhappy about it. Also, he and Hudson were on a first-name basis. Interesting.

"What are you up to, Marshall?"

"My job, sir. You told me to find David Barrington and neutralize Elias Halverson. I've found Barrington. Locating Halverson is proving to be a challenge."

"If you're not up to it—"

"Nice try. You know I've never failed a mission and finding that human guinea pig isn't going to be the first time."

"ADC Williams is on the Hill today or you'd be talking to her right now instead of later," Roger Hudson told Chisholm. "So your people will have time to work on their story as to why they didn't come to us sooner. I'll be giving her a full report on what is said here."

Marshall leaned back in his chair with a wicked grin.

He was enjoying this.

So was I.

I pulled a notepad out of my messenger bag. *Going to be looking for a new job soon?* I wrote.

Marshall used his own pen to reply. *Nah. I've done much worse.*

"I think it's time for some of that agency cooperation we're supposed to have been doing since 9/11," Hudson said. "Two US senators and an aide dead in two days, murdered in their offices."

Hudson left Grandad out of it. I was grateful.

"I know you don't want to be the one who didn't bring every resource to bear to take down their killer," he continued. "Especially when creating that killer was the result of a CIA project? Don't worry, Theo. Your people can still do the right thing *and* cover the company's ass. Dr. Barrington told us Elias Halverson was to be deployed overseas for his first mission."

"He wasn't supposed to have been activated yet," Chisholm said. "Renwick reported a week ago that the project was proceeding to plan, but that Halverson wasn't ready for deployment and was still in training. Those deaths prove Halverson is way past the need for training. The team overseeing the project called Renwick and told him they wanted to see Halverson's progress for themselves."

"After that call was when Renwick cleared out the Bethesda lab," Marshall told us.

Silence again from Chisholm.

"Yes, they know about MRT. The FBI was there this morning. I made myself available to assist." Marshall flashed a smile. "Intra-agency cooperation at its finest. It'll play well in the congressional hearings if this gets even worse than it already is. Barrington told us he'd made three more chips, and that Renwick stole them from the lab safe."

"Dammit."

"When Renwick asked for Barrington's notes, that's when

the good doctor called Senator Pierce, who told him to run for the hills." Marshall then proceeded to tell his boss about Go Fish and our Adirondack adventure with a Russian oligarch's goons.

"Barton Renwick sold the Entity Project to Grigori Dementiev," Chisholm said. "That son of a bitch."

No one here was going to disagree with his assessment.

"We have an international APB out on Renwick and Halverson," Hudson told him.

"Dementiev does business out of Prague," Marshall said, "and according to Barrington, that's where Barton Renwick and his family spent some of their most recent vacation. When he came back, suddenly Barrington got everything he needed."

"We've got Pyotr Kharkov on ice," Hudson said. "He gladly threw Renwick under the bus, but refuses to as much as say his boss's name."

"Where are Barrington's notes?" Chisholm asked.

"He said he destroyed them," Marshall replied. "I don't believe he has, but I think he should have. When he got suspicious, he went to Senator Pierce to ask how much money the Senate Intelligence Committee had released for the Entity Project. It wasn't nearly as much as Barrington had been given to spend. Barrington told Senator Pierce about the discrepancy. As Pierce's senior aide, Alan Coe would've known that figure, as would Senator Dalton as the ranking member. Barrington told Pierce there was a problem with the project—either with the chip or Halverson. I don't know how Dalton found out, but whether or not he knew a Russian oligarch had funded the project, Halverson was still ordered to kill him. I think we can safely assume Barton Renwick either gave that order himself or was directed to by Dementiev. Either way, Renwick is in this up to his neck."

"We're keeping Dr. Barrington in protective custody for now," Hudson said.

"You may have to prove to some people here that you're not holding him against his will," Chisholm said.

"Considering he doesn't know who he can trust among those people, I don't think that will be a problem."

"I'm so glad I have nothing to do with R and D," Chisholm muttered.

Marshall blew out a breath. "You and me both, sir."

Chisholm hesitated. "I'm being pressured to have you bring Elias Halverson in alive."

Now the silence was on our end.

"By whom?" The anger rolling off Marshall made the hairs on my arm closest to him stand straight up.

"I can't say."

"Sloane and Kinney."

"I didn't tell you."

"You didn't need to," Marshall shot back. "Andrew Sloane and Richard Kinney are two toads in the same swamp with Barton Renwick. I'm not bringing that thing in alive."

"I'm not asking you to," Chisholm said. "You already have your orders. Carry them out." He hung up.

CHAPTER 34

Berta stood. "Come on, Rory. I'm taking you home."

"What?"

"You heard me. There's nothing more you can do here, at least not now. Last night, you dozed for an hour in a chair at the foot of Ambrose's bed, and the night before that, you didn't get any sleep at all. And *I* spent last night standing guard and not sleeping so *you* would sleep."

"You said you slept."

"I lied. But we're not doing any of that again. You're going home, and I'm going home with you. Think of it as a sleepover where everyone actually sleeps."

"You're right."

Berta blinked. "What?"

"You heard me." I smiled. "You just want me to say it again. You're right."

Berta nodded in satisfaction. "And I have witnesses. It's

been a good day. Let's make it a restful night. I have a feeling we're all gonna need it." She gave Gabriel Marshall a look. "Except for the Caped Crusader here. Sounds like you got a job to do."

Marshall shrugged. "I do need to make a few stops before going back to the Bat Cave, but I agree with you about getting some sleep." He stood. "I've learned to get it when I can." He inclined his head to me and Berta, then Rees and Hudson. "Ladies. Gentlemen. I'll be in touch."

I waited until he'd left and closed the door behind him. "So, how does the CIA do this? Does Marshall leave the body on Langley's doorstep like a cat leaving a dead rat?"

Rees scowled. "Unfortunately, I don't think Elias Halverson is going to make this easy for any of us."

I agreed to go home, on one condition. I wanted to stop by the hospital and see Grandad first.

Berta relented. I knew she wanted to check on him, too.

It'd been a little over twenty-four hours since Grandad had been brought to Georgetown University Hospital. I was sitting next to his bed, holding his hand. It was warm and his color was better.

I was a true believer in the benefits of talking to the deeply unconscious. Dr. Beck said Grandad wasn't in a coma, but he was close to it. I knew he could hear me. I squeezed his hand tighter. I knew he could feel me. I sat there, holding and talking, willing him to fight his way up through the darkness and come back to me.

"I know you're tired," I told him. "We all are. But I have good news. Great news. We found David Barrington. He's safe and he's talking. We know who did this to you and how he did it. The same man killed Julian and Alan, and Mark Dalton. There are people tracking him down right now—and no, one of them isn't me." I gave him a little smile. He couldn't see it, but he could feel the emotion. "And you were wrong about who's behind it. It wasn't the Nazis. It's the Russians. Go figure, right?" I gave his hand another squeeze. "But I'm not going to tell you how he did it. You have to wake up and ask me. Believe me, it's quite a story. You definitely want to hear this one."

I searched his face for any sign of movement. Nothing. Yet, I told myself. There *would* be a reaction. Tomorrow. He needed rest, and so did I.

I rubbed his hand. "I know you want me to go home and get some sleep, so that's exactly what I'm going to do, but don't get used to winning any arguments. I'll be back tomorrow, and the only way you'll get rid of me then is to open your eyes and tell me to go home. *Ti voglio bene,*" I whispered, tears blurring my vision. I raised his hand to my lips, kissed it, then put it back by his side.

Dr. Beck had said Grandad had been worried about me when he'd been brought in. I debated telling him that Berta was going home with me and that we had FBI agents at the house to further put his mind at ease. But he'd know all those precautions would only be in place if I was in danger, so I didn't mention any of it. If I said anything, he might pick up images from me of what had happened with Simmons's guards and why Berta had assigned herself as my second shadow. I could hide my emotions from everyone else, but I'd never been able to fool Grandad.

Berta and I had passed through the gauntlet of FBI agents to get to Grandad's room, and again to leave. There was an agent at the stairs and another by the elevator, one in the hallway, and two flanking the entrance to his room. Grandad was as safe as he could possibly be. I remembered the grainy, green video of Elias Halverson in that cave. If he really wanted to get to Grandad, he probably could, but Gabriel Marshall was right. As far as Halverson and his game was concerned, Grandad was a piece that had been taken off the board. It was me Halverson wanted now.

I had news for Elias Halverson, Grandad wasn't a threat to him any longer.

I was.

I was going to be careful, but I wasn't about to let caution stop me from tracking him down.

"I don't like that look," Berta said as she pushed the elevator button.

"What look?"

"You look pissed and way too determined."

"Really?"

"I'm taking you home, and you will sleep."

"I'm not arguing with you. I need the rest. Tomorrow's going to be a big day."

Grandad was going to recover. I no longer needed to tell myself that. I believed it.

I slept.

When I woke up, I had drool on my pillow and sheet prints on my face.

I immediately checked my messages, and when there wasn't one from the hospital, I called for an update.

There hadn't been any change.

I told myself that wasn't bad news. He was already better; further improvement would take time.

I'd let Berta talk me into spending the night in the town house rather than my carriage house apartment. I could see her point. My apartment consisted of three rooms—the living area/kitchen, a bedroom, and the bathroom. Once an intruder was in, there was only one door between them and me. The town house consisted of multiple levels, multiple rooms, and was more easily defensible. Roger Hudson had augmented Simmons's guards with two FBI agents. Simmons's people were outside, Hudson's inside. The security system was fully operational and being closely monitored.

Like Grandad in the hospital, I was as safe as I was going to be.

I was surprised I'd slept as well as I had. There was a reason I lived in the carriage house. The place was huge, so space wasn't a problem. I liked my privacy, though it wasn't like I had much need for it. Unlike the earthquake we'd just had, my love life wouldn't even register on the Richter scale.

I lived in the carriage house because I couldn't get a decent night's sleep in a house filled with antiques. To my heightened psychometric senses, the furniture and art seemed to give off a continual buzzing, like fluorescent lights times a hundred. Grandad slept just fine. He said it was because he was an antique, too. I preferred my furniture new and my art minimal. Though last night, I think a marching band could've come through my room and I wouldn't have budged.

I took a shower and got dressed to go downstairs for breakfast. With Gerald home, I was guaranteed a pre-hunt feast. He'd promised to make his incomparable cinnamon rolls.

I was hunting Elias Halverson, but I hadn't lied to Grandad.

I wouldn't be hunting Halverson himself. I'd be looking for his psychic spoor.

It had been about thirty-six hours since Halverson's attack on Grandad. When he'd killed Julian and Alan, he had stood only a few feet away from them. Mark Dalton had been attacked from even closer. I'd been at the Russell and Hart buildings within a few hours of those murders. I didn't know if distance affected the strength of Halverson's PK. I would think that the closer Halverson was to a victim, the less psychic energy he would need to use. Depending on where his perch had been outside the town house, there was a chance he might have had to work harder to do the same damage. Regardless of the psychic physics involved, I would find that perch.

Halverson had plenty of time after he murdered Mark Dalton to kill Simmons's guards here and get in place.

He would've had to wait for us to get home. While he waited, he would have thought and possibly planned. Elias Halverson had a strong personality and psychic imprint. I'd sensed him twice. If I could find where he had waited to kill Grandad, perhaps even after a day and a half there would be enough left for me to determine where he was now and what he was going to do next.

My phone beeped with an incoming message.

Berta.

Guess who's here? Marshall. Brought cinnamon rolls. Gerald insulted.

So much for peace in the house.

I walked into a silent kitchen.

There was a bag from Dog Tag Bakery on the table. I loved

anything from there, and their cinnamon rolls were to die for, but Gerald's had a special place in my heart and stomach. He had set an extra place in front of Gabriel Marshall and had graciously plated the Dog Tag cinnamon rolls next to his. It looked like I'd have to eat one of each; after all, Marshall was going to kill the man who'd briefly killed Grandad.

The sacrifices I had to make.

It sounded like there was a small outboard motor under the table. I lifted the cloth. Pablo was rubbing and winding himself around Marshall's legs.

"Pablo doesn't like strangers," I told him.

"Marshall's his drug dealer," Berta said. "He wants another hit."

"Actually, I did bring something for him." Marshall reached in his jacket pocket and pulled out what looked like a small whiffle ball. It was filled with tiny jingle bells. Marshall gave it a single shake and instantly had Pablo's undivided and absolute attention.

"Sorry, Pablo. My last present didn't go over too well. No catnip this time." Marshall tossed it toward Pablo's bed, and the big tom scrambled after it.

Gerald set a smoothie in front of me that I knew from its unappetizing greenness had all the fruits, veggies, vitamins, and minerals necessary for the kind of big day I had planned. He gave me a knowing look.

I'd never been able to fool Grandad—or Gerald. He knew I was up to something, and he wholeheartedly approved.

Once I'd downed the smoothie, I was free to enjoy two cinnamon rolls. While I did, I told Berta and Marshall my theory.

Berta was the first to weigh in. "You're going to step

outside where this psycho attacked Ambrose and sniff around until you find the direction it came from, and then go there."

I saluted her with my coffee mug. "Exactly."

"Oh, hell no."

"As soon as I go outside, I'll know if he's still in the neighborhood or not. And if, for whatever reason, he's still in the country, I seriously doubt he's hanging around here waiting to knock me off."

"But there's no way you can be sure."

"No, there's not, until I go out there. But there's a good chance that if he had to wait for us to get home, he was there long enough that I can pick up an impression, maybe even some images. It's more than we've got now." I looked to Marshall. "Unless you got lucky last night on your way home to the Bat Cave."

He grinned. "No, I most definitely did not get lucky last night."

"No rat on Langley's doorstep, huh?"

"What?"

"Never mind."

Marshall took a sip of coffee. "I agree with Berta."

"You're batting a thousand," I told her. "Me last night, now Marshall."

Berta leaned back in her chair and crossed her arms. "If he agrees, that just means there's something in it for him. What is it?"

"Nothing. I simply agree that Rory shouldn't go outside."

I put down my fork. "I don't seem to recall asking either one of—"

Marshall held up a hand. "Hear me out. You shouldn't go outside until you know Halverson's not lurking in a parked car on the street. Can you determine that from the bay windows next to the front door? We can open the window closest to the front steps and leave the sheers pulled. He can't see you, but you can still work your mojo. Would that do?"

I had to think about that. "Maybe. If it'll make the two of you feel better, I'll try it. But if it doesn't work, I'm gonna go play outside."

CHAPTER 35

I never considered that setting foot outside my own front door could get me killed.

A lot can change in a day and a half.

While the weather was mild for this time of year, most people would consider it too cold to open a window. I wasn't interested in fresh air. I wanted to catch the psychic scent of a killer.

At the base of the bay windows was a curved padded bench that had been one of my favorite places when I was a little girl and we'd come from California to visit Grandad. I would get a book from the library, and Gerald would fix me a pot of tea and let me choose my own cup and saucer. With book, tea, and whatever cookies Gerald had just baked, I'd happily spend hours curled up here.

Today, Gerald had fortified me with a power smoothie and a cinnamon roll, but it wasn't for hours of reading. I'd asked

Berta and Marshall to stand back to give me space to work. I could see down the street in both directions from the three windows, but I'd already determined that the attack had come from down the street to the right. To the left were more town homes on both sides. While it would've been possible for Elias Halverson to have hidden in one of our neighbors' bushes, it was highly unlikely. To the right of the front door were more town homes, but near the end of the street on the opposite side were a coffee shop, a tavern, and a cigar bar—all with a direct line of sight to our front walkway.

Just before Halverson's attack, Grandad had turned his head to ask Rees and Berta if they'd had lunch, and at the instant of the attack, his eyes had become fixed and staring in that same direction. Was it a coincidence, or had Grandad sensed on some level what was happening and had looked toward where he felt the attack coming from? Once I'd realized what was happening, I'd been completely focused on getting him inside. The FBI and police hadn't found anyone, but how could they have known who they were even looking for?

Elias Halverson was a professional. He wouldn't have run. Immediately after the attack, he could have simply gotten up and walked out of wherever he was. By the time the police arrived, he would've been long gone. On the other hand, I'd sensed extreme arrogance from him in the Hart Building men's room. He'd just made his third kill. He was high on his new power. He wasn't killing pigs any longer; he was hunting and killing humans with his mind, and he liked it. I wouldn't be surprised if he'd stayed right where he was after he'd attacked Grandad. He might have even volunteered to answer questions from the FBI or police when they'd canvassed the neighborhood.

I sat back. "He's not out there now. His perch was either the coffee shop or tavern. My money is on the coffee shop. Berta, would you call Rees and see if he has that updated sketch of Elias Halverson? It's time to show it around."

I was having a hard time thinking of our neighborhood coffee shop as a psychic assassin's grassy knoll.

I went back to my apartment to change into something other than sweats. Berta and Marshall went with me. Despite my assurance that Elias Halverson wasn't in the neighborhood, let alone lurking in our backyard, they didn't insist on accompanying me so much as not give me a choice. I was a believer in picking my battles. This one wasn't worth the effort.

We went through the garage to get to my apartment stairs. Marshall stopped to admire my restored 1957 Harley Sportster.

"*Very* nice," he said.

"I agree. This Wednesday, a '41 Indian Sport Scout will be in the next stall. Your BMW isn't half bad, if you go in for that sort of thing."

Marshall shrugged. "Sometimes a man has a need for speed."

"When fleeing the scene of a crime," Berta shot back.

Marshall's gray eyes met mine. "So it was you who found her."

I spread my hands. "Guilty as charged. You did a good job of muting yourself and hiding your trail." I grinned. "But not good enough. How did you get here this morning?"

"The BMW. Again."

"I hope you didn't park her in the alley this time."

He tilted his head toward the garage door. "No, she's right outside."

I pushed the button to raise the door. "I've got a spare stall. Bring her in out of the cold."

That earned me identical surprised looks from Marshall and Berta.

Marshall recovered first. "Thank you."

"You're welcome."

I went upstairs to change. Berta ensured my bedroom and bathroom were Elias-free before returning to my small living room to wait with Marshall.

Once back in the town house, Berta used the printer in the office to print out the FBI's new sketch of Elias Halverson while Marshall admired the da Vinci drawing hanging on the wall to the left of Grandad's desk.

"I stayed longer than I should have the other night," he confessed, never taking his eyes from what the master had probably considered a mere doodle. "This is like being in a museum. I'd heard this drawing existed, but I've never seen it."

"A gift from a grateful Florentine businessman from his private collection," I said. "Grandad recovered Caravaggio's 'Portrait of Maffeo Barberini' for him." I gave him a quizzical glance. "You're into art?"

His eyes continued to drink in every detail. "Oh yes."

Berta came up behind us, copies tucked in a folder. "Ready when you are."

She was the first one out the front door. She gestured for me to stay put while she scanned the immediate area for anyone who could have remotely been Elias Halverson. I waited patiently until she gestured me forward. Berta was one of my best friends, and she needed to protect me right now, so I let her do it. Besides, I was protecting her, too. I knew Halverson wasn't out there. We were all safe.

The three of us walked down the street to the coffee shop. It was almost eleven o'clock on a Sunday morning and the place was packed. Berta went to the counter to talk to the baristas while I scanned the bar that ran the length of the front window.

Every stool was occupied—except for the one closest to the wall.

Elias Halverson's killing perch.

No one wanted to sit there.

Just like the area of carpet where Halverson had stood in Julian's office. People sensed an alpha predator, and even though that predator was long gone, his psychic scent remained, and people unconsciously steered clear.

"That it?" I heard Marshall ask.

I gave a single nod.

"I'll get us some coffee."

"I'll take that seat."

I took a slow breath and let it out—and sat where Elias Halverson had waited to kill my grandfather.

Not surprisingly, only a few people had occupied the stool since Halverson had, and then only briefly. Fortunately, they were as psychically inert as rocks, so nothing was between me and Elias Halverson.

I placed my hands on the counter and looked out the window toward the town house. An unobstructed view.

Halverson had sat, drank coffee, and waited for us to come home.

I got even more than I had in the Hart Building, and it came in a dizzying rush.

He'd brought a laptop with him. He'd turned the stool at an angle so that the back of the screen faced the town house.

He'd typed gibberish, pausing as if thinking, and then typing again. All the while, he would glance over the top of the screen, watching for our arrival. He blended in perfectly; no one thought anything about the man working in the corner.

He'd been out of breath, not from running or any type of exertion, but from excitement. It was almost too easy.

Greed had killed Dalton…He had merely made the delivery. The two senators went easily; the aide was only in the way. He'd had plenty of practice on DC's homeless…Now his skill in killing from a distance would be tested. The old man psychometric and his granddaughter would be his first official distance kills…

Me. He was supposed to have killed me along with Grandad.

When the SUV had pulled up in front of the town house, Halverson had removed his glasses and briefly squeezed his eyes shut, pinching the bridge of his nose as if tired. Then he looked out the window as if resting his eyes, watching our every move.

He didn't know if it would work. It was the farthest he'd ever been from a target.

The old man was between him and the granddaughter. He couldn't see her. So he focused first on the old man, pictured his heart inside his chest, imagined it clutched in his fist, quivering as it struggled to beat. He squeezed harder and the old man's legs gave way. Satisfaction surged through him. He squeezed harder still. This would be his most important kill. Renwick had said it was a dress rehearsal. Then the FBI agent blocked his view of both targets as he and the granddaughter quickly carried the old man out of his sight, and the granddaughter out of his range.

He pushed down his rage. He should have taken the FBI agent first, leaving the old man and granddaughter in his sights.

He calmly powered down and closed his computer, gathered his coat, and tossed his empty coffee cup in the trash as he left.

I set my elbows on the bar and rested my forehead on my raised hands, my breathing ragged. I sensed rather than saw the man seated next to me quickly get up and leave. I must have looked pretty bad. I didn't blame him. No one wanted to be thrown up on.

Marshall slid onto the now empty stool. "Do you need anything?" he asked quietly.

I swallowed on a dry throat and gave the barest shake of my head as nausea threatened to overwhelm me. After a few moments, I forced it down and slowly raised my head, focusing my eyes on the countertop, then Marshall's arm in its leather jacket, and finally his concerned face. Berta was standing close behind me, blocking me from view.

Suddenly, it was way too warm in here. "I need to go home."

CHAPTER 36

"I got it all."

We were back at the town house, in the office. Gerald had brought a ginger ale and saltine crackers to where I sat on the room's small sofa. Berta was next to me, and Marshall had pulled over one of Grandad's guest armchairs.

The only thing that came close to describing how I felt was drunk—and not the fun kind. Instead of overindulging in alcohol, my brain had been overloaded with a psychic download of Elias Halverson's murderous thoughts.

I washed down a bite of cracker with more ginger ale. "It feels like I jammed a fork in a light socket. Too much, too fast. Direct current."

"Any theories as to why—" Berta began.

"It has to be the chip," I said. "It magnifies Halverson's PK, maybe it does the same to his thoughts. I've been picking up impressions since I was two—or so Mom and Dad tell me—

and I've never experienced anything close to this. The only difference between those people and Halverson—besides every kind of rampaging psychosis—is that chip. I've gotten impressions of killers from weapons, objects they touched, even from the bodies of their victims if they did their killing hands-on, but I've never felt like I had a direct link to what they were thinking. In the Hart Building's men's room, Halverson said that his power had been amplified when he was killing Mark Dalton."

"Like a guitar with an amplifier versus unplugged," Marshall said.

I nodded. "Good analogy. I don't know if that's the reason for the loudness or clarity of Halverson's thoughts, but it's the only explanation I've got."

"How you can do it isn't as important as what you got from him," Berta said.

"What I sensed from the spot in Julian's office was the closest to normal," I said. "The impressions were hours old, and he stood there for only a few seconds. Dalton's murder was fresher and much more intense, like I was inside his head as he killed. But again, he was only there for less than a minute." I took a long drink. "He had to have sat on that stool for at least an hour, probably longer." I turned to Berta. "What did the baristas say?"

"They remember the guy in the corner, but he didn't look anything like the sketch."

"Great. Though I'm not surprised. He's a young, white guy who successfully impersonated an elderly black man. I wouldn't put any disguise beyond him."

"I asked the one who remembered him best if she'd be willing to sit down with one of our artists. She said she'd be glad to. I can't see Halverson using a different disguise every time. She said he came in, ordered a large coffee and sat on that stool without budging for just under two hours, focused on that laptop. It stands to reason that to be there that long, he would've used the disguise he felt the most comfortable with."

Marshall's voice was soft. "You're stalling."

"You bet I am," I snapped.

"What did you see?"

I focused my eyes on a small Cezanne on the wall by the sofa in an attempt to organize my thoughts. "His first target was Julian. Poor Alan was simply in the wrong place at the wrong time. Halverson killed Alan because he had to get past him to reach Julian." I paused. "And because simultaneous kills were good practice. Mark Dalton suspected where Renwick had gotten the extra money for the Entity Project. Rather than report him, Dalton had the bright idea to blackmail him to get some of that Russian money for himself and his reelection campaign. Halverson said greed killed Mark Dalton, and that he merely made the delivery. Halverson was also wearing glasses. Probably fakes, but have the artist ask the barista about them."

"Will do, Berta said.

I took a deep breath. "He said Renwick told him that killing Grandad and me—"

Berta went dangerously still. "He was supposed to kill you, too?"

I nodded. "Renwick told him we'd be his dress rehearsal. He said, 'The old man and his granddaughter know too much and could soon discover even more.' Halverson referred to us as his first official distance kills."

Berta swore, and Marshall made his own contribution.

Marshall leaned forward. "He specifically said *first* official?"

"Yeah." I took another sip to settle my stomach. "He practiced distance killing on the homeless in Franklin Square, and when he found three clustered together, killing them all at once. The son of a bitch smiled while he remembered 'those nights in Franklin Square, strolling through the park like the Grim Reaper himself, looking for clusters of two or three huddled together.' He said he hadn't needed confirmation of those kills because he'd felt them die."

Berta's dark eyes were on Marshall. "I can't tell you how to do your job because I'm not an assassin, but you damned well need to do it quick."

"Count on it."

"I am. We all are."

"I don't know how many he killed or when," I continued, "but you could find out how many homeless supposedly died of heart attacks or aneurysms in the past month or so." I took a steadying breath. "Then I saw him killing Grandad and how he pictured his heart inside his chest, imagined it clutched in his fist, struggling to beat. He squeezed harder as Grandad fell. He enjoyed it. The bastard got off on it. He kept squeezing until his view was blocked by me and Rees. He didn't get a shot at me because we moved too quickly getting Grandad into the house. He wanted to take me and Grandad together, but Rees was in the way. After we got Grandad in the house, he said he should have taken Rees first. That would have left me and Grandad in his sights."

"Jesus," Berta breathed. "Rory, I am your shadow. No, cancel that, I am your *conjoined twin*. Do you hear me?"

"I thought you already were."

"That was unofficial. Now it's official. At least it will be once I call Rees and tell him what you just told us."

My phone rang from inside my purse. I scrambled to get to it.

Georgetown Hospital.

I didn't need Elias Halverson to stop my heart, it was doing a fine job by itself.

"Aurora Donati."

"Ms. Donati, it's Dr. Beck. I wanted to let you know that your grandfather is awake and talking." I could hear the smile in her voice. "And he would like very much to see you."

I still felt light-headed, but now it was from profound relief. "Thank you so much, Dr. Beck. Tell him I'll be right there." I ended the call, grinning from ear to ear. "Grandad's awake and talking. We're going to the hospital."

I ran into the kitchen to tell Gerald. He wasn't there, so I ran up the back stairs to his room. I knew Grandad would want to see him, too. When I came back, Berta was alone in the office.

"Where's Marshall?"

Berta gave me a fierce smile. "He's gone to do his job. He got a call, too. Elias Halverson has just been spotted near the UN."

Gerald brought cinnamon rolls and a thermos of coffee in case Grandad could have them, and we made a party of it. A low-key party because we were still in the ICCU, but Dr. Beck told me that if Grandad continued to improve, he would probably be moved to a private room in the cardiac unit tomorrow.

I'd never been happier to see those blue eyes open and

looking at me. His left hand had an IV attached to it, so I was holding his right hand with both of mine.

I'd just finished telling him—quietly, of course—that his cardiac arrest had nothing to do with his health, and everything to do with a microchip-enhanced psychokinetic assassin, the same man who killed Julian, Alan, and Mark Dalton. Those were all Grandad had known about before his attack. That a PK assassin existed was more than enough for Grandad to process in his condition. I did tell him that said assassin had been seen in New York, and that the FBI and New York's finest were coming down on him like a ton of bricks as we spoke.

I didn't tell him what he was likely doing there.

Berta had filled me in on the drive to the hospital. Tomorrow morning was a UN Special Session. The newly inaugurated US president would be there in her first meeting with international leaders including the French president, Canadian prime minister, the German chancellor, and the British prime minister—any of whom could be the target of a PK assassin presumably doing the bidding of a Russian oligarch looking to impress his boss. After the special session would be a reception where world leaders would be mingling and standing together, talking and laughing, getting to know the new US president.

Elias Halverson would see them as clusters of targets ripe for the killing as he drifted through the room disguised as a waiter, a guest, or anyone.

I kept telling myself that the FBI knew this and that my part was over, and that the FBI and a certain CIA assassin were more than qualified to take it from here.

"What about Barrington?" Grandad's voice was rough from the breathing tube. "Did you find him?"

"Yes, we did. Turned out he's one of the good guys. Kind of. The FBI has him in a safe house, in quasi custody."

Grandad nodded and swallowed painfully. I helped him drink from a cup of water with a bendy straw. Dr. Beck had nixed the coffee and cinnamon rolls, but Grandad was just happy to have the scent wafting around him.

I gave my seat to Gerald for a while. Berta had darted in and given Grandad a peck on the cheek soon after we arrived, then had stepped out to take a call. She was back now and gestured me out into the hall.

"I thought you might like to have an update," she said.

"You thought right. They got him?"

"Not yet."

"What do you mean 'not yet'?"

Berta looked like she wanted to hit someone. "Too many head chefs in too small a kitchen, and one of them has a big mouth. Rees doesn't know how it got out, but the *Washington Post* has a 'highly placed source' saying that Mark Dalton's death was a murder and the person of interest is…" She reached in her jacket pocket and pulled out the sketch of Elias Halverson she'd showed the barista just hours ago.

"You're kidding?"

"Wish I was. This picture is online and trending."

"How?"

"I don't know, but heads are going to roll when Hudson finds out. And now the tin-foil-hat crowd are connecting Senator Pierce and Alan Coe to him as well."

"The method sucks, but since it's true, isn't it a good thing?"

"Not if it's driven Halverson to ground."

"Didn't the ME release Dalton's cause of death as an aneurysm?"

"Official cause of death doesn't matter if the story's juicy and starts trending. The UN is locked down, and Rees says that place is just one clown short of being a circus."

"He didn't actually say—"

"No, but that's what it is."

"Has anyone heard from Marshall?"

Berta gave me a flat look. "He's not a 'phone home' kind of guy."

I glanced through the door at Grandad. His eyes were closed and his chest gently rising and falling. He was asleep. Gerald was fussing with his covers.

I went in the room, got my phone, and came back out in the hall to Berta. "Marshall said you had his number. Give it to me."

Berta shrugged and scrolled to her contacts. "Can't hurt to try," she muttered. "He likes you more than me."

I entered his number. "That might change."

CHAPTER 37

Gabriel Marshall didn't answer either call or text. I left a voice mail and left him alone. Hopefully our CIA assassin was a busy man.

If he'd been a normal person, I might have been worried that something bad had happened to him, but he wasn't normal, and I didn't have time to worry.

At least not about him.

I needed to go back to the coffee shop.

I'd been so hyperfocused on Halverson describing his kills that I might have missed a lot. Berta told me I'd sat there for about four minutes, though it'd felt like an eternity to me. According to the barista, Elias Halverson had been there nearly two hours. There had to be more information that I could access, a lot more.

Gerald was going to stay at the hospital with Grandad a bit

longer, and one of the FBI agents said he'd arrange to see him safely home when he was ready.

Berta and I went to my apartment to get my laptop, but rather than leave her car there, we went around the block to see if there was parking close to the coffee shop. I hoped there wouldn't be a repeat of this morning's link-induced nausea; but if so, I'd only have to stagger to Berta's car.

It was late Sunday afternoon, not a busy time for a coffee shop, so she found an open spot one space down from the door. The area directly in front had a fire hydrant.

There were a few people inside. A couple was at one of the small corner tables, and a group of friends were relaxing on two small sofas facing each other.

No one was sitting at the bar in front of the window.

I went with Berta to the counter and ordered a ginger tea. In case I had a repeat, I wanted a medicinal beverage on hand.

I sat on the stool next to Halverson's. I wanted to better prepare myself this time. Berta took the stool next to mine.

My phone chimed with an incoming text. I took it out of my purse and looked at it.

Gabriel Marshall.

I'd texted from the hospital: *Have you found him?*

His response just now: *NO*

I showed it to Berta. "Well, at least he's alive. And maybe too busy to chat. Or too pissed—either at me or Halverson."

"Or yes to all of the above. Like I said, he's not the phone home type. Now explain to me what we're doing here again?"

I glanced back at the counter. The barista Berta had spoken with earlier wasn't there. The customers weren't paying any attention to us, but I still kept my voice way down. "Your barista said that Halverson sat on that stool for nearly two hours. I got from Halverson's thoughts that he was typing gibberish to look busy. Absolutely no one can stare at a screen and type nothing for that long. He had to have surfed or read. But what?"

"You said you didn't get anything like that from him."

"Because I wasn't looking for it. My four minutes versus his two hours tells me that I only saw a small slice. I got the deaths and the attack on Grandad because that was what I knew about, so it stands to reason that was what I picked up."

"Does it work that way?"

"It never has before, but I've never linked with a microchip-enhanced psycho who's sat in one spot for two hours. I'm breaking new ground here. That's why I wanted to come back, to see how much is really here. It'd be like walking out of an interrogation room only five minutes into a confession."

Berta thought for a moment. "You wouldn't think he'd look up or do anything sensitive here. The Wi-Fi in places like this isn't what you'd call secure. But then again, this is a man who murdered two US senators—one in his office, the other on the toilet in his office building. I imagine he wouldn't be too concerned with some kid scooping up a password off his laptop. Though if anyone hacked Halverson, it'd probably be the last hack they'd ever do."

"Precisely," I said. "My questions are: What was he doing when he wasn't watching for us to come home? Checking email? Confirming his flight reservation to New York? Or was he just typing 'All work and no play makes Elias a dull boy' for two hours? And when he left here, which way did he go? Did he have a car parked nearby? Or had he taken the Metro? There's a station on the next block. Where had he been that day, besides the Hart Building?" I glanced at the corner stool next to me. "I won't find answers to any of those until I try. I don't want to watch what he did to Grandad again, but if I can pick up anything worthwhile, it'll be worth it." I gave Berta a small smile. "And if I get sick, your car's right outside."

"Don't you throw up on my upholstery."

I raised my right hand. "I swear."

"Scoot on over then," she said. "I'm here if you need me. If I get a call, I'll step outside. Rees said he'd call before six."

I nodded. I'd already begun my preparation for what I was about to do. I opened my laptop in front of the last stool and tilted the screen in the same direction Halverson had. Then I scooted over, putting my messenger bag on the stool I'd just vacated.

The impulses were still strong, but I blocked them until I was ready. I hadn't done that this morning, and that'd been stupid. Holding off images this powerful wasn't easy, like pushing a door closed against gale-force winds, but I wouldn't let Halverson's thoughts overwhelm me again.

Everything he had thought was still here. This time, *I* would control what I saw, and it wasn't going to be a replay of Halverson's twisted murder highlights reel.

I kept my breathing deep and even as I pretended to push my laptop's power button. I didn't want it on. I wanted to let the darkened screen be a mental canvas for what I hoped to see.

My eyes were drawn toward the town house.

It was the same time of day as when Grandad had been attacked exactly two days ago.

I slowly allowed Elias Halverson's mind inside.

I concentrated on his screen, not his surveillance. I didn't want his thoughts this time as much as what he was looking at while he waited.

He did have a Word document open and was typing gibberish, but he minimized it occasionally to do other things. He Googled the names of his three kills, reading the coverage of his crimes, amused to see how little the media knew and even more amused at some of the theories the fringe was spreading on social media.

I sensed Berta get up and go outside.

I let my focus soften until the screen and laptop in front of me blurred into a haze.

I thought back to what I'd learned and knew, reasoning my way through it, piecing it together.

Barton Renwick had told Halverson that killing Grandad and me was his dress rehearsal. He needed to practice distance kills…He killed two and three homeless at a time…A dress rehearsal was a practice for opening night or for a gala performance. What did an actor do to prepare? He would study his lines, immerse himself in his character, memorize his marks, his position, on the stage.

His stage.

Where was Elias Halverson's gala performance?

His desktop screen was crowded with icons. I couldn't get a sharp focus on any of the icons or make out any of the names underneath. He touched his mousepad, taking the cursor to a shortcut in the lower left corner and clicked on it.

A list of three files. The names were abbreviations and numbers that didn't mean anything to me.

He clicked on the third one.

A floor plan.

These weren't the floor plans you could get online showing meeting rooms and offices, or where the bathroom and elevators were. These were detailed, blueprint-level plans, showing every nook and cranny, including maintenance access points in ceilings and behind walls for lighting and sound, fire and structural inspections.

Where a PK assassin could see out, but no one could see in.

As Halverson scrolled across it, I recognized it as the US Capitol building. He made his way across, then zoomed in on one room.

I recognized it instantly, even in all its confusing detail. Nearly any American would.

The Hall of the House of Representatives, or more commonly known as the House Chamber.

The location of the president's annual State of the Union address.

This year there wouldn't be a State of the Union address; President Catherine Archer had just been sworn in ten days ago. But she would still speak to a joint session of Congress. Seated behind her would be the vice president and the Speaker of the House.

Two or three clustered together.

It was tomorrow night.

No wonder the FBI and Gabriel Marshall couldn't find him. The UN attack was probably a decoy.

I suddenly shivered. No one had opened the door. It wasn't cold in here.

I froze. I was being watched.

The sensation wasn't coming from behind me. It was outside, through the window.

He was outside, watching my every move. It was his eyes I felt on me.

He was cleaning up loose ends. Me.

Berta was on the phone, walking up and down the sidewalk.

He was watching her, seeing me watch her. The bastard was enjoying this.

If I called Berta, and she switched over to answer, he could kill her before she could take cover.

If he killed her or me, someone had to know what I'd seen.

I looked back at my screen. He wouldn't kill Berta unless I was watching. I had to take that chance. Without looking down or moving my torso, I reached over and pulled my phone out of my bag. I'd have to take the chance that Halverson couldn't see my hands. I shifted my eyes down just enough to see my phone screen. My texting app opened to the last text I'd sent.

Gabriel Marshall.

I typed.

Elias here. Now. Coffee shop. Saw house chamber floor plan. Sotu tomorrow night. Stop him.

I silently thanked the programmers of Messenger for word shortcuts, so I didn't have to fully type everything. It was an address to Congress and not the official State of the Union, but Marshall would know what I meant.

I added Rees as a recipient and sent it.

I'd done all I could do.

Time to get Berta.

CHAPTER 38

If he could see me, it meant I could see him.

Across the intersecting street was a small park, little more than a few trees and benches. There he was, near the back, in the shadows, on a Kawasaki Ninja. The bike's silhouette was unmistakable. The visor was down on his helmet, so I couldn't see his eyes, but I didn't need to see them to know that Elias Halverson was staring straight at me. If his PK was a laser-sighted sniper rifle, I'd be sporting a red dot between my eyes or over my heart.

I stared back, and the connection was immediate.

He wondered if I heard his thoughts. He hoped that I did. He wanted me to know that he could kill me in seconds, but he didn't want to do it while I was in the coffee shop. I'd just drop to the floor, and then he wouldn't be able to watch me die.

Perhaps he would kill Berta. That would flush me out of hiding.

He wanted me to come outside. Then he'd strike, watching me collapse on the sidewalk in front of Berta, passersby either helping or ignoring me, or standing frozen and staring in shock or indecision. Self-preservation would win. It always did. They always ran. When he'd worked with a sniper's rifle, his work had always been made easier by the inaction or shock of the herd. The horror as the head of someone close to them exploded. He wished he had his rifle now, that way he could take me where I sat. The window would explode along with my skull. It would be more satisfying.

He slowly raised his visor, and we locked eyes.

He wanted me, not Berta.

This was a game for him, and he was enjoying it. He liked that I saw him, that I knew what he was, what he could do to me. Yet I still stared at him, not in terror, but in challenge. If he killed me now, his fun would end along with me.

I took the chance that he wanted the game to continue a little longer.

I closed my laptop and slid it into my messenger bag, putting the strap over my head and across my chest. Then I slowly walked to the door, my eyes never leaving his.

Halverson shifted on his bike, sitting a little straighter. He hadn't decided what he wanted to do, but he liked that I was coming outside to him. He liked it a lot. If he had any idea what I'd just seen on my blank screen, I'd be a dead woman walking.

Berta still had her back to me, but had nearly reached the end of the section of sidewalk she'd taken as her pacing path. The car was close, but was it close enough?

The timing would be critical.

He raised his gloved hand and pointed two fingers at his own eyes and then at mine.

I wasn't feeling smart. It was probably suicidal, but I did it right back. Then I extended my arm, those two fingers still raised. Smiling, I slowly lowered my index finger—thus flipping off quite possibly the most powerful psychic in the world.

It felt good.

Berta saw, comprehended, and reacted.

Next thing I knew, we were on the sidewalk with Berta's car between us and the Grim Reaper on a crotch rocket.

I heard the Ninja screaming away.

Berta swore and reached for the door handle.

"Zero to sixty, three seconds," I told her.

She pounded her fist on the car door. "Piece of shit!"

"Agreed." I slouched against the rear tire. The adrenaline spike had come and gone, leaving me exhausted and shaky. "We can call it in…I know the make and model…He and that bike are long gone, but he'll be back. I know where he'll be tomorrow night."

They wouldn't find him, but he'd already made his biggest mistake by coming back.

If he had ever gone to New York in the first place.

Next time, I promised myself. Next time he wasn't going to get away.

He was probably thinking the same about me.

One of us would be right. The other would be dead.

"He was watching us," I told Rees and Roger Hudson. "He wanted me to know how easy it would be for him to kill us both, but he was enjoying himself too much to actually do it."

Within minutes after texting Rees and Marshall about Halverson, black sedans with sirens wailing had descended on the little coffee shop. A few minutes after that, I got not a text, but an actual phone call from Gabriel Marshall. Judging from the amount of profanity directed at Halverson, I think he might have been worried about me.

I was back at the Washington Field Office. I really didn't want this to become a habit. Only this time, we were in SAC Hudson's office and not a conference room.

Marshall was right. FBI coffee left much to be desired. I set the cup aside. I didn't see myself sleeping tonight as it was. I didn't need caffeinated jitters on top of the jitters I already had.

I'd already told them what I'd seen on Halverson's laptop screen.

That'd kicked the hornet's nest.

"I've spoken with ADC Williams," Hudson told me. "She's meeting with Director Montgomery right now. Don't worry, your name will never come up. Our information came from a trusted source."

"She knows what kind of killer Halverson is?"

"She does."

"How's she going to work *that* into the conversation?"

"Quite openly, I'd expect."

"You're kidding?"

"I never kid or joke, Ms. Donati. Ask Special Agent Rees."

I glanced at Rees.

"I have not witnessed it."

"What are you going to tell the president?" I asked. "If she gets a sudden headache, dive behind the podium?"

"We're hoping it won't get that far," Hudson replied. "I've called Theodore Chisholm."

"Warning him that he and the CIA are about to get thrown under the bus?"

"He would do the same for me."

"Thrown under the bus or warned?" I asked.

"Both," said a familiar voice from the now open doorway. Gabriel Marshall came in, closing the door behind him. "That was careless," he told me.

"Stop with the nice. You say 'careless,' but you mean 'stupid.' You would've done the same, and probably more, if you'd been there."

"I'm qualified. You're—"

"I was *in his head.* Barrington was wrong. The chip didn't change him. Elias Halverson has always been a sadistic psycho. He was enjoying himself too much to kill me or Berta. He killed two people I cared about and one I loved. Thank God, he was brought back. So yes, when I had a chance to look him in the eye and flip him off, I did it. I do not cower, and don't you *dare* tell me I should." Normally, this was when I'd be up and in someone's face, but right now, it was just too much work.

I think Marshall sensed as much and moved on.

"He was relaxed," I told them as I tried to do the same. "As if he was exactly where he needed to be. Maybe he's killing time until tomorrow night—no pun intended."

"We're canvassing hotels and short-term rental apartments in the area," Rees told Hudson. "To see if he's been staying anywhere close by, though I can't see him remaining in the area now."

"Unless he's confident he's well hidden," Marshall said.

"That Ninja's certainly memorable," I noted. "Though easy enough to tuck away."

Marshall raised an eyebrow.

"An H2," I elaborated. "Not sure of the year, probably no more than two years old."

"We're checking registrations down the East Coast," Hudson said. "Chisholm shared that Elias Halverson had briefly been based in Miami and New York."

I glanced at Marshall. "But we're not holding our breath on that paying off, *Mr. Granger*."

Marshall shrugged and took a seat. "I value my privacy."

"Any sign of Barton Renwick?" Rees asked him.

"Chisholm has reason to believe he's left the country under an alias, Malcolm Preswick."

"With the chips."

Marshall scowled. "Yes, with the chips. Halverson works alone. Having Renwick underfoot would just slow him down and increase his risk of capture. How's the president going to be told?" he asked Hudson.

"Chisholm is taking this to your director. Director Montgomery is awaiting his call to coordinate a briefing with the Secret Service and President Archer. The recommendation is that the address be either postponed or given from the Oval Office."

"I don't see her going for that," I said. "She's the first woman president. If she doesn't show up, she'll be politically eviscerated. They'll say, 'See? We told you. Women aren't brave enough, or strong enough, or tough enough to be president.' Or what would probably become a trending hashtag—NotManEnough."

"Officially, Elias Halverson is a rogue CIA officer," Marshall reminded us. "Dementiev, or whomever he's trying to impress, wants to make it look like the CIA assassinated the top three people in the US government. With Elias Halverson in his arsenal, he can deliver death around any corner, in front of a few or millions, with no danger of detection, no concern of capture. Halverson can get through any security checkpoint because he doesn't need weapons. He *is* a weapon. Dementiev—or whoever pays him enough for Halverson's services—can bring chaos to any country, any government, any administration—*at a glance.*"

"And if Halverson got ambitious tomorrow night, he'd have his pick of more than the three on the podium," I told them. "All broadcast live. No one knows what he looks like." I paused. "*I* don't need a description to find him." I met the eyes of each man in turn. "I can find him in a crowd. He'll have his PK going at full power to kill three people in as many seconds. His psychic spoor should be like a strobe light in a dark room. I'm the best chance you've got to stop this." I had an unwanted flashback to Grandad's attack. "All he needs to do is get in the House Chamber. Line of sight. That's all he needs."

Hudson blew out his breath. "What do you want me to do?"

Marshall stepped forward. "Get us in the room. We'll take it from there."

CHAPTER 39

President Catherine Archer refused to cancel her Tuesday night address to the joint session of Congress.

She said that her time in office would be filled with danger, both political and physical. There would always be the possibility of a sniper on a roof, a killer in a crowd, or an assassin waiting on the proverbial grassy knoll. She refused to hide in the Oval Office.

While I didn't blame her, I wished she would have reconsidered just this once.

I'd always been confident in my skills, but I didn't want to be put to this level of test.

The meeting at the UN with President Archer and the European leaders on Monday had been uneventful. So was our search for Elias Halverson. Since I'd flipped him off on Sunday, he'd gone to ground. It was now Tuesday, the day of the presidential address.

"They told her what Elias Halverson is?" I asked Berta.

She nodded. "Hudson said the president and her personal detail were given all available facts."

"Did they laugh?"

"I don't know." She lowered her voice. "But they were also told that Halverson killed Senator Pierce and Alan Coe with cardiac arrests, and Senator Dalton with an aneurysm. If that didn't stop the giggles, it should have."

"And she's still speaking tonight."

"She is."

And that was why I'd asked Gerald not to let Grandad watch the address on TV.

There would be checkpoints to ensure every invited guest was who they said they were. They had all been cleared by the Secret Service ahead of time. The streets around Capitol Hill were closed. The Secret Service was in charge of security. However, they worked with the military, parks and local police, Capitol Police, and the FBI. There were committees and subcommittees, drills and training exercises to counter any type of attack.

Except a psychokinetic assassin.

I was surprised to see that some members of Congress were already there when we'd arrived in the House Chamber just before noon.

Berta noted my reaction. "It's first come, first seated."

"They camp out?"

"Pretty much. It's a free-for-all, especially this year with the first woman president."

"See and be seen. If only they knew."

Elaine Pierce would be here tonight. Normally, as a member of Congress, she'd be seated in the lower seats with her colleagues. But because she was Julian Pierce's daughter, President Archer was giving her a seat of honor in the front row of those lower seats directly in front of the rostrum. I'd wanted to warn her, but Hudson had nixed it. Elaine wasn't in danger, unless she drew attention to herself, and if she knew her father's murderer was in the same room with her, she would be scanning the crowd just as I would. I didn't like having her here, but I agreed with Hudson.

Rees had told me that security for the State of the Union address or a presidential address to a joint session of Congress was planned months in advance, and last-minute additions were frowned upon.

I was a last-minute addition.

It'd taken the insistence of ADC Williams, FBI Director Montgomery, and CIA Director Patrick to get me and Gabriel Marshall inside. We were credentialed as FBI security consultants.

Part of that agreement had been to let the FBI disguise my appearance to protect me from Halverson. I didn't have a problem with that. Yes, he knew what I looked like, and I'd rather he didn't. But mainly, I didn't want the FBI, Secret Service, Capitol Police, and every security consultant and expert to know what I looked like. My job was to point out an assassin and I planned on doing it quietly, but crap happened.

I was wearing a short blond wig and glasses, and the FBI makeup artist had lightened my skin to porcelain doll levels. To blend in further, I was wearing a dark suit like most of the other FBI agents. When I'd looked in the mirror after she'd finished, I didn't even recognize myself. If different hair and glasses worked for Clark Kent, why not me? The irony of Elias

Halverson disguising himself to kill Julian and Alan wasn't lost on me. I hoped payback would indeed be hell.

Marshall, Berta, and I were standing in the back of the room for the noon security briefing.

Every photo, sketch, and security video still of Elias Halverson had already been distributed to those who would be stationed inside the Capitol during the address. That included his Nate Baxter disguise. I couldn't help but notice that some of the Secret Service agents were impressed.

"Elias Halverson is five ten," said the agent giving the briefing. "He has a lean build, meaning he could be disguised as either a man or woman of any race, age, or physical condition."

Halverson wouldn't need to move quickly to escape. In fact, it would be in his best interest if he didn't. He would attract less attention by staying right where he was and acting as stunned and horrified as everyone else. Then he could simply leave inside the protection of the herd like a wolf among the sheep.

"His most likely location will be in the gallery," the agent was saying, "but we can't afford to ignore any location or group, even President Archer's personal guests, or lesser known members of Congress. We believe this attack has been planned for at least a year, so no one person can be eliminated with any confidence."

After the briefing, Berta led us to our perch for the evening. I needed to be able to see the entire House Chamber while not being in the room itself. I knew Elias Halverson's presence better than I would've liked, but I was grateful that I did. I hoped to be able to pick him out from the hundreds of people in the room with him.

Not all the people in the gallery would be guests, and

those seated on the main floor were members of Congress. The Secret Service and FBI had agents seated in every section.

The doors to the gallery would remain closed for the duration of the address, but there was an attic-type space that began above the gallery doors and extended through the ceiling. It was mainly used for ceiling light maintenance. What appeared to be large wallpaper-covered panels concealed screens that allowed for a great view down into the room. I was behind and above the rostrum where President Archer would be standing, with the vice president, and Speaker of the House seated behind her.

I would be able to see everyone in the room watching her. Everyone's eyes would be on Catherine Archer, but not with Elias Halverson's intensity.

I'd never had to locate a killer in a room full of people, but I'd had several contacts with Elias Halverson and knew what I was looking for. Rees had seen to it that I had some serious binoculars. I'd also been equipped with comms that let me speak directly to Rees and the four takedown team leaders. My job was to point out Halverson. The Secret Service and FBI would take it from there.

Rees had set me up with a tablet and I was flipping through the photo IDs of all the guests and media who would be there. This wouldn't help me identify Halverson, but it did give me a way to distract myself from the nearly overwhelming pressure.

I wasn't eliminating anyone, including the FBI and Secret Service agents. Grigori Dementiev wanted it to look like the CIA had created a psychic assassin to kill the three most important people in the US government. How much better would that be for Dementiev—and more humiliating for the

US—if the assassin had infiltrated the FBI or Secret Service guarding the president?

Rees had taken me on the rounds so I could scan each and every Secret Service agent who hadn't been in the noon briefing. Every man and woman had been professional, dedicated, and hyper-focused. It wasn't possible for a human to be more alert than they were.

None of them were Elias Halverson.

The closer we got to the time of the address, the more likely it appeared that Halverson would use the cover of a guest.

There was one guest who was not in my photo lineup.

Director Montgomery had arranged for Dr. David Barrington to be in attendance.

Barrington insisted that since he had worked with Elias Halverson for nearly a year, he knew him better than anyone. I knew he felt responsible for every one of Halverson's kills, especially Julian, and while there was nothing he could do to make it right, he desperately wanted to help bring Halverson down. Director Montgomery relented, but insisted that Barrington be seated with an FBI agent on the gallery's top row close to a door.

With less than an hour until the address started, I saw Barrington and his FBI escort taking their seats. Barrington's only disguise was a wig.

"I don't like him being here," I said.

"Neither do I," Berta said, "but if he can help. . ."

"That's not what I mean. I'll take all the help we can get, but if Halverson realizes he's here—"

"Halverson won't touch him," Marshall said. "He's pro. He has his mission. He won't let a personal vendetta get in the way, either Barrington or you. This is a performance for him, a show. He won't risk anything that might stop the president's speech. He'll need all his strength and focus. If his practice sessions in Franklin Square are any indication, he's going for a hat trick."

I just stared at him, mildly horrified. "Assassins use that term, too?"

"No, I'm a hockey fan." He raised his own binoculars back to his eyes. "Go Caps."

"This is a game to you, too."

"I'm a hunter. This is what I do. Anyone I hunt deserves to have me after them—especially Elias Halverson."

This may have been partially a game for Marshall, but he wasn't enjoying himself.

David Barrington had said that a taser would be an extremely effective countermeasure against Halverson's chip. Concentration was critical. Hit him fast enough or hard enough and his focus was shot. A high-charge shock would literally scramble his circuits, albeit temporarily. The decision had been made. I would locate Elias Halverson, and he would be immobilized by taser, removed, and blindfolded. Select medically trained agents were standing by to render Halverson unconscious until he could be locked behind steel doors. Hopefully, all this could be done without disrupting the speech. But if necessary, Secret Service agents would be ready to immediately get the president, vice president, and Speaker down and out of Halverson's line of sight.

Rees told me there had been talk of Barrington operating on Elias Halverson one last time—to remove the chip.

Gabriel Marshall favored a more direct solution.

I agreed with him.

CHAPTER 40

The emotional waves flowing back and forth through the House Chamber were overwhelming and sharply divided along party lines. Relief. Derision. Pride. Scorn. Satisfaction and happiness. Resentment.

The FBI and Secret Service agents nearby weren't any better. These men and women were Type-A alphas. They'd trained for this, and now that they knew POTUS was about to enter a room with an unknown assassin waiting and ready, their aggressive and protective instincts had kicked into overdrive.

To me, the emotional volume was like a stadium full of screaming fans.

I held out my right hand. It was shaking.

Dammit.

I couldn't get the agents to take it down a couple dozen notches, but I could do something about a certain CIA agent beside me. Maybe if I could get at least a bubble of calm around me, I could concentrate.

"Marshall, I need you to dial it back."

"Excuse me?"

I decided to be polite. "You have a strong presence. You either need to dial it back or leave."

"A strong presence," he mused. "I think I like that."

"Told you so," Berta said.

"You're a perceptive woman, Agent Pike. However, I have two jobs tonight. Protect Rory from Halverson and kill Halverson."

"Killing isn't part of the plan," I reminded him.

"That's the FBI's plan. Besides, I didn't say I would be doing it tonight. I'm a patient man."

I let it go. That wasn't a battle I was going to win, or even one I was interested in fighting. "Fine. About your first job. You don't need to worry about me. Yes, he wants me dead, but he wants to be up close when he does it." I pulled a taser out of my jacket pocket. "Berta gave me a present, and I really want to use it."

Five minutes later, President Catherine Archer entered the Hall of the House of Representatives.

There were cheers from some and applause from all—though it was more enthusiastic or restrained depending on the party affiliation. When I was in the room with a killer, I instinctively wanted all my senses on full alert, but this was more than I could take.

This was precisely why I avoided crowds. It was overwhelming.

I was here to find Elias Halverson—and now I had serious doubts that I could do it. If I failed, three people died. I couldn't even let myself think that they were the three most important people in the US government. World wars had started over less.

Find Halverson. That's it. That's all you have to do.

I was surrounded by FBI and Secret Service agents who were all too eager to take it from there.

It sounded simple, but nothing could be further from the truth.

I stepped up to the screen and scanned the gallery, then the floor seats. David Barrington was seated in the left section of the gallery with his FBI escort.

I couldn't pick out any one person. It was one huge emotional roar to my senses.

Panic was building in my gut.

What if I was wrong? What if he wasn't even here?

You're not wrong. He is here.

"Barrington's scared to death," I told Berta. "He shouldn't be here."

Neither should I.

I shook my head. "There's too much going on. I can't—"

"Stretch out with your feelings, Luke."

I shot Berta a dirty look, though it probably looked more like raw terror.

"Humor always helps," she said.

"Except when it doesn't."

Berta slipped her arm around my shoulders. "If he's not here, it's a good thing. But you're right and you know it."

"Thanks, Obi-Wan."

She gave my shoulder a squeeze. "It's what I do."

I tried again then shook my head. "This isn't working for me. I need to get closer to the people in the gallery." I took a deep breath. "I need to go in."

"That's my girl."

I looked around. Our little trio was down to a duo. "Where did Marshall go?"

Berta muttered a curse. She hadn't seen him leave, either. "We probably don't want to know."

Berta walked with me to the back of the gallery. I selected the door that would put me behind the center section of seats directly in front of President Archer. If Halverson had his preference, he would want to look straight at her, eye to eye.

Don't fight the crowd, Rory. Use it. Look for the one who doesn't belong. The quiet one. The hunter.

I opened the door and slipped into the gallery. All eyes were on Catherine Archer.

I leaned against the wall and bowed my head so I was looking at the carpet. The only sound was the president's voice.

Take a breath. Let it out. Relax.

I wasn't going to find Halverson with my eyes. I let my vision soften until the carpet and everything around it was a blur.

I acknowledged my fear of failing, embraced it, then gently pushed it aside. I stood absolutely still and waited.

There. To my right.

Breathe in…and out.

Two sections over.

In…out.

In the exact middle. A wolf hiding among the sheep.

I opened my eyes and slowly raised my head. The gallery was steep, and even though I was two sections away, I could see him.

Dark suit, thinning brown hair, and probably wearing a pad around his waist to give him a middle-age spread. The perfect average of nearly every man here.

And he had an earpiece in his left ear. An accomplice?

Like me, Elias Halverson was holding himself utterly still. Instead of the strobe light I'd hoped for, he was a laser pointer.

Because of me.

He knew he was surrounded. He knew I was here and what I was capable of, so he wouldn't allow himself to think of what he was about to do until the instant he did it.

Everyone else was focused on Catherine Archer and her words, her message.

Elias Halverson didn't hate the president. He wasn't listening to her speech. He couldn't. He was like a serpent under a rock shelf, coiled and waiting. Even if he wanted to listen, to choose the most significant moment in her speech to strike her down, he couldn't.

The timing of his attack had been decided long before now. His was a waiting game now.

I continued to control my breathing. Halverson couldn't pick up emotions as I could, but he was keenly attuned to prey or another hunter, whether in front of him or behind.

Don't be hunter or prey.

My earpiece was silent. They were watching me, and I was watching Halverson.

During the next round of applause, I slipped out through the nearest door. Rees, Berta, and a Secret Service agent were waiting, the one who had given the briefing. I couldn't remember his name. There was still no sign of Gabriel Marshall.

I went to the door for Halverson's section. I cracked it just enough to peer through. "This section. Fifth row down. Sixth seat from the left. Dark suit, receding brown hair, and wearing an earpiece in his left ear."

The briefing agent smiled. "We have a man at the end

of that row." He spoke into his mic, and things moved very quickly. These people trained every day for the worse-case scenario. They hoped it never happened, but they were in their element now. They lived for this.

I just hoped none of them died.

The lights flickered. President Archer said something I couldn't make out and nervous laughter went up from the chamber.

The lights flickered again and went out.

No.

At least with the lights out, Halverson couldn't see to kill.

But the Secret Service couldn't see to capture.

There was a sharp report from inside. It could have been a microphone hitting the podium, or any number of things striking wood, but it only took one person to panic.

"Gun!" someone screamed from the gallery.

"Shooter!"

Emergency lights came on, flickered, and died.

Terrified people poured out of the gallery doors, cutting me off from Berta. Unless he had already been taken down, Elias Halverson could have been allowing himself to be swept along with them.

Their fear was like an emotional riptide, dragging me under. I was bumped and pushed, each persons' terror piling on top of the one before, adding to my disorientation.

Find a wall, Rory.

As the crowd surged toward the National Statuary Hall. I pushed my way across the current of bodies to the closest wall, pressing myself against it, getting my breathing and rising panic under control.

I couldn't let Halverson get away, but I couldn't find him

if I didn't clear my head. He knew I was here and would have gone silent, letting the noise of the panicked herd cover his escape. From the Statuary Hall, he would go down the stairs into the Rotunda, then outside and down the Capitol steps to freedom.

That was it. That was how he was going to do it.

He was silent. Elias Halverson would be the only person who *wasn't* panicking.

That was how I would find him.

I stepped away from the wall, steeled myself against the contact and allowed myself to be swept along. He knew I was here, and he wanted me dead. If he couldn't kill Catherine Archer, he'd make do with me. His ego wouldn't allow him to leave without a trophy.

He knew I was coming for him. He'd wait for me.

By the faltering glow of the emergency lights, I saw a man go down beside the Rotunda railing.

David Barrington. His FBI bodyguard was nowhere to be seen.

I pushed my way out of the crowd and went to my knees beside him. His face was pale and he was struggling for breath—and his hand was clutching his chest.

Oh shit.

A hand locked itself around the back of my neck, lifting me to my feet. "This is too easy. I expected more from you."

I didn't struggle. My right hand was at my jacket pocket and the taser inside. I couldn't help Barrington without first helping myself. I tried to swallow, but my mouth was too dry. "Don't you want to look me in the eye when you kill me? You've seen my face. I've never seen yours."

Chaos continued all around us. Hundreds of people

stampeded down the stairs in the near dark, no one seeing or caring about what looked like two people standing by the Rotunda railing.

As Halverson spun me around to face him, he clamped his other hand around my throat.

And I shoved the taser into his side and pulled the trigger. Nothing.

Halverson merely smiled and squeezed harder. My vision began to darken.

"You really expected me not to be wearing a vest? I'm disappointed in you."

Then Halverson grunted in pain and I was jerked forward as his hand convulsed around my throat. Then it was gone, torn away, and I dropped to my knees, desperately pulling air into my burning throat. From nearby came the sounds of struggle, grunts and curses, punches thrown, and kicks landed.

I recognized one of those curses.

Gabriel Marshall.

I crawled over to David Barrington. He was barely conscious, his breath coming in pained rasps. I took his hand in mine. He was trying to speak.

"Don't talk," I told him. "We'll get help."

A wet gurgle rose in his throat. He squeezed my hand. "I trusted Julian…to do…the right thing." Then his grip loosened and fell away, as his eyes became fixed and staring.

Someone slammed into me from behind.

Halverson.

I snarled and jammed the taser I still held straight up.

Elias Halverson was wearing a vest. He wasn't wearing a cup.

That, combined with the meaty impact of Marshall's fist

to Halverson's side, sent him over the Rotunda railing to the floor below.

Then Marshall was beside me, lifting me back to my feet.

"Not bad for in the dark." I couldn't take my eyes from Elias Halverson's broken body sprawled on the marble floor below, illuminated in the red glow of the now-working emergency lights. I half expected him to get up and walk away.

"It wasn't perfect," Marshall said.

"It was good enough. Thank you."

"You okay?"

I pulled my eyes away from the dead assassin and focused on the living one. No, not an assassin. A soldier perhaps or a righter of wrongs, but not an assassin. "Couldn't be better."

He gently straightened my crooked wig. "Liar." He looked down at David Barrington. "Halverson's dead, so David got what he wanted."

"Not yet," I said, remembering his last words. "But he will."

CHAPTER 41

An unexplained power failure during President Catherine Archer's first address to the joint session of Congress was in the news for only half a day before it was bumped from the top spot. The media said that it was remarkable there had only been two deaths. Renowned neurosurgeon Dr. David Barrington had died of a heart attack during the chaos of hundreds of people fleeing the House Chamber and Capitol Building in the darkness, and a guest had fallen to his death from the lower Rotunda balcony.

That was what the public was told.

The person responsible for the power failure was now the target of a massive FBI, Secret Service, and CIA manhunt—or woman hunt. The earpiece Elias Halverson had been wearing hadn't yielded any clue as to who was on the other end. The theory was that when Halverson knew he'd been identified, he'd signaled his accomplice, who took out the lights so he could escape.

The morning after the presidential address, I was at the hospital to visit Grandad. I paused just outside the door to his room.

"I'm sorry, Mr. Donati," a nurse was telling him. "You're not allowed to have coffee yet."

"Then why did you wake me up?"

"It's time to—"

"To talk to me," I said from the doorway.

Grandad's eyes lit up.

My eyes filled up. I couldn't help it, and I didn't even try to stop it. In the next instant, I'd crossed the room, wrapped my arms around my *nonno,* and had myself a good cry.

"I'm sorry," I said, when I could finally speak.

"You keep your emotions inside, Aurora. That's not healthy. Crying is good." To show me just how good it was, his own eyes were filled with unshed tears.

"I called Mom and Dad this morning," I told him.

Grandad winced, but not in pain. "I'll bet that wasn't pleasant."

"No, it wasn't. I stuck to the bare facts—Grandad and cardiac arrest. Naturally, I got raked across the coals for not calling sooner."

"But, of course."

"They're catching the next flight from LAX. When I pick them up, I'll tell them all the unbelievable details." I lowered my voice. "Being psychic themselves, they'll believe me. Probably. Anyway, they'll be staying at the town house," I continued, returning to normal volume, "so when you get home in a few days, you'll have a houseful. I'll even move over from the carriage house for a while."

Grandad positively beamed.

I thought that'd cheer him up. There wasn't an Italian grandfather who didn't love having his entire *famiglia* around him. I knew Gerald would be just as happy. He lived for a houseful of guests to cook for.

Later, Berta and Rees came by. The past few days had been beyond intense, so they kept the conversation light. Grandad still tired easily.

"SAC Hudson wanted me to ask you again if you're ready to officially work with us," Rees said.

I laughed. "Oh, hell no."

Rees smiled. "I told him as much, with a different choice of words."

"The FBI doesn't want me. I have authority issues."

"I believe he realizes that."

"And I'm allergic to cubicles and paperwork."

"Then you definitely don't want the FBI."

"Told you."

Grandad pulled himself up in bed and waved me off when I tried to help. "It was nearly impossible to get details from Aurora, but am I correct in concluding that she found this man among hundreds of people?"

Berta answered that one. "You bet she did."

He smiled. "I *would* bet on that—and on her."

"We bet on that, too," Rees said. "Safest bet we ever made."

"Though I couldn't have finished the job without a certain secret agent man," I told them all.

"Aurora shared just enough with me to make him intriguing." Grandad gave me a sly wink. "I want to meet this young man."

"We'll see," I told him.

A few minutes later, Grandad's nurse politely shooed us all

out, saying that Mr. Donati needed his rest. I walked Berta and Rees to the elevator. The nurse said Dr. Beck would be making rounds soon, and I wanted to stay and speak with her. As the elevator doors closed, I got a text from Gabriel Marshall.

Come to the chapel?

I walked down the hall to the small chapel. Marshall was waiting for me, only this time, he wasn't dressed as a priest. He'd also dialed back his intensity to a simmer, and while I could still read him, I didn't feel like I needed to. I almost felt comfortable around him.

He sat in a chair on the front row. I took the seat across from him.

"How is your grandfather?" he asked.

"Good. If he can behave himself, he'll be coming home in a few days. Dr. Beck told me yesterday that Grandad's made an amazing recovery. He's a fighter and more than a little stubborn."

Marshall smiled. "It must run in the family."

"You only met me last week."

"And I immediately knew you were stubborn."

"So, what happens to the project now? Or can you not tell me?"

"Officially, the CIA has declared it a failure and has shut it down."

"What about this Andrew Sloane and Richard Kinney you mentioned? You said they and Barton Renwick were three toads in the same swamp."

"Barton Renwick has been declared a rogue element, and any coconspirators either inside or outside of the CIA will be found and disciplined at a level commensurate with their involvement. As to Sloane and Kinney, Director Patrick took issue with two of his people pushing to keep a project alive that nearly cut the head off the entire US government." Marshall gave a grim and satisfied smile. "They are in custody now and are being questioned regarding just how close they were to Barton Renwick and Grigori Dementiev."

"And if they were involved?" I asked.

Silence.

I held up a hand. "Enough said. I don't need to know."

"There is something that you do need to know. Sloane was responsible for the bugs in your apartment and the town house."

"You knew?"

"I suspected he'd had them planted. When I needed to get into your office, I scanned the house and found them. I lucked out and was listening when your grandfather changed the security password."

I just looked at him. "How did he get someone in the house?"

"That's the part you need to know. He had someone on the inside at your security company. Their clients include a few people Sloane was interested in."

"You said 'had.' This person isn't there anymore?"

"Edward Simmons found him out. By any chance was your systems software updated two weeks ago?"

"I believe it was."

"That was when Simmons had a patch installed to disable any bugs that had been planted."

"It didn't work."

"Simmons knows that now. After my visit, I daresay that several of his high-profile clients received calls from him requesting to sweep their properties. He was persuasive in convincing Sloane's man to be forthcoming as to his recent activities." Marshall grinned. "I'm familiar with Mr. Simmons's work before he left his agency for the private sector. He was impressively thorough and effective in obtaining information."

"Ouch."

"No doubt."

"So where's Sloane's inside guy now?"

"Do you really want to know?"

"I don't need to." I thought for a moment. "What about the Senate Intelligence Committee? Won't they question the project being closed?"

"A minor CIA research project they voted to fund nearly two years ago?" Marshall shook his head. "Renwick only gave one report to the committee, back when Barrington was still developing the chip. Only Senators Pierce and Dalton ever knew how far it'd actually gone, and that it'd been bought and paid for by a Russian oligarch. They're dead. Presumably without telling anyone what they knew. That they died within days of each other will be deemed a tragic coincidence. When it comes to dispelling or diminishing any conspiracy theories, the CIA has learned that the best action is no action."

"Ignore it and it'll go away."

"Address it and it gains credibility."

"By the way, Grandad wants to meet you, though he's sleeping now."

"And I would very much like to meet him. How about after I get back?"

"You're going after Barton Renwick and those chips, aren't you?"

"I am. I'm flying out within the hour, but I wanted to see you before I left."

I didn't know how to respond to that, so I went with another question. "Do you know where he is?"

"I know where he's going. When he arrives, I'll be waiting."

"Do you think he still has them?"

"Oh yeah. With Halverson and Barrington dead, those chips are all he has left to bargain with."

"What will you do with them?"

"What Barrington should have done when he realized the project had been corrupted. Destroy them."

"What are you going to do with Renwick?"

"I have orders, and I agree with them. Though Director Patrick wants him brought back for questioning."

"What about David Barrington's notes?"

"If he didn't destroy them, they don't need to be found. People are weak, and those who aren't are fallible. There are no good hands for this technology to fall into. Anyone can be coerced, manipulated, threatened, bought, or blackmailed."

"Not everyone."

"Even if it was to save the life of someone they loved?" he asked quietly.

I didn't have an answer for that. Not now.

CHAPTER 42

Two days later, Arlington National Cemetery gleamed in the early afternoon sun for the interment of Senator Julian Pierce. The sea of white marble headstones was blanketed by just enough fresh snow to cover the ground.

The funeral had been held that morning in the National Cathedral. President Archer had attended, as had many of Julian's colleagues past and present. The pallbearers were a mix of his personal friends and Senate colleagues. Julian had left detailed instructions. His memorial service was an artful balance of his public and private lives.

Elaine Pierce had invited me to attend both the funeral and the interment, which limited to family and close friends. She told me she considered us family and promised to visit Grandad in the next day or two. Grandad had asked me to extend his regrets to Elaine and to tell her he'd be there in spirit.

Dr. David Barrington would be buried here the day after tomorrow. I wondered who would attend. He had two ex-wives on the West Coast, but there hadn't been any children from either marriage. Theodore Chisholm had invited me along with Rees, Berta, and Roger Hudson.

I had already extended my regrets.

I knew Gabriel Marshall wouldn't be there. He was doing what David Barrington would want him to be doing. Tracking down the man he'd trusted like a brother.

Elaine had moved into her grandfather's home in McLean while she looked for a smaller place closer to Capitol Hill. Her older brother and his wife had a one-year-old daughter, with another baby on the way. They would be moving into the McLean house once the transfer from his firm's Chicago office to DC was finalized. Elaine wanted the home to again be filled with family, love, and laughter. The Pierce family was gathering at the house after the internment. Their church had prepared a light dinner. Elaine asked that I join them.

After dessert and coffee, I wandered into Julian's study.

The presence of the man was as strong as it had been the day I'd found his burner phone. I closed my eyes and breathed in the scents of the freshly polished wood paneling, the leather upholstery, and the paper in the hundreds of books.

I wasn't looking for what Julian might have recently touched. The sense of him filled the room and always would. It was his center, where he had been truly himself, at home, secure, and happy.

I'd come here for David Barrington.

Going to his graveside service wouldn't do anything for

him, and it might endanger me. Elias Halverson had known about me, so did Barton Renwick. Now Andrew Sloane and probably Richard Kinney had been added to the list. Who knew who else they'd told?

Right here, in Julian's office, was where I could do the most good for David Barrington—by doing what I believed he wanted. I already had my suspicions, and David had confirmed them just before his death.

He'd been here. I knew it now, especially after holding his hand as he died. I could sense him in this room. He'd been here recently, and when he'd visited, he'd left part of himself behind. Something he'd treasured.

His greatest work.

His abject failure.

Left in the care of a friend, a brother in arms he'd unwittingly endangered, that risk ending in that friend's murder by his creation.

David Barrington had trusted Julian Pierce more than anyone in the world.

He'd told me so with his last words.

I scanned the books that had been so lovingly and meticulously arranged by subject or genre and then by author.

The book I was looking for wasn't difficult to find. It was right where it was supposed to be.

The Origin of Species by Charles Darwin.

There was no dust on the spine. It had been recently handled. Not by Julian Pierce, or I would have sensed it when I'd found the burner phone.

This book had been taken off the shelf by David Barrington. I didn't know when he had done it, but it would have been after he realized he'd been betrayed by Barton Renwick and the people in his own agency and government. He'd begun the Entity Project as a means to ensure peace by enhancing the psychokinetic ability of a man he saw as an avenging angel, and ideally the next step in human evolution.

I removed the book from the shelf and opened it.

In an envelope, taped to the inside back cover, was the disc with Barrington's notes on the Entity Project. I slowly peeled off the envelope, taking extreme care not to damage the book. It was a first edition, and no doubt Julian had treasured it, as he had his friendship with David.

I tucked the envelope and disc into my purse. I'd deal with it later.

My eyes went to the last line of Darwin's work.

There is a grandeur in this view of life, with its several powers, having been originally breathed by the Creator into a few forms or into one; and that, whilst this planet has gone cycling on according to the fixed law of gravity, from so simple a beginning endless forms most beautiful and most wonderful have been, and are being, evolved.

ABOUT THE AUTHOR

Lisa Shearin is the *New York Times* and *USA Today* bestselling author of the SPI Files novels, an urban fantasy series best described as *Men in Black* with supernaturals instead of aliens, as well as the Raine Benares novels, a comedic fantasy adventure series. *The Entity Game* is the first in her new Aurora Donati thriller series.

Lisa is a greyhound mom, avid tea drinker, vintage teapot and teacup collector, grower of orchids and bonsai, and fountain pen and crochet addict. She lives on a small farm in North Carolina with her husband, four spoiled-rotten retired racing greyhounds, and enough deer and woodland creatures to fill a Disney movie.

Website: lisashearin.com
Facebook: facebook.com/LisaShearinAuthor
Twitter: @LisaShearin

Printed in Great Britain
by Amazon

86634941R00176